Find the Body

Find the Body

Find the Body

JEREMY YORK

The Macmillan Company, New York

FIRST PRINTING

The Macmillan Company, New York
Collier-Macmillan Canada Ltd., Toronto, Ontario

Printed in the United States of America

Contents

Find the Body

· 1 ·

THE NEW PEOPLE

MILDRED CASTLE watched the moving van as it backed slowly toward the front door of Spindles. She was smiling, but her expression was thoughtful, for already she felt sorry for the new people, who had arrived several hours before the van and had been walking aimlessly about the house and grounds. They had, in fact, declined an invitation to come into the vicarage, but that was probably because Agnes had conveyed it. Agnes was too bad; she took an instant dislike to anyone who came to live at Spindles and invented the most absurd reasons for her hostility. The truth was that she wanted to live there herself, longed to go back to the house where her husband had died.

"Whoa, Tom!"

Several men bellowed in unison as the platform at the back of the van touched the pillar of the porch.

"Forward a foot, Tom!" called one of them.

The engine of the van had stopped, and the grating noise of the self-starter and the snort of the engine as it spluttered were unfamiliar, and for Agnes, probably disruptive. Mildred rather liked the excitement. It was monotonous to lie in bed month after month, to see nothing but the trees in the grounds of Spindles, and to watch the garden going to rack and ruin. Had it not been for the birds it would have been unbearable. Except for Harry, too, of course; dear, patient, harassed Harry.

The wind was blowing from Spindles, enabling Mildred to hear every word spoken in a normal voice. The new people had talked in subdued tones, although the man looked rather flamboyant, "loud," as Agnes had already said. The young woman, presumably his wife, was well dressed, tall but too thin, and gave Mildred the impression that she was subdued. That was not surprising in anyone who came to live at Spindles in its present condition; Agnes was certainly right when she asked whether any

sane people would come to live at the place before it was thoroughly cleaned and redecorated. According to Agnes it was filthy.

The only time, until now, that the new people had raised their
voices enough for Mildred to hear was when Maude had taken
them some tea and biscuits. Mildred and Agnes had battled for
an hour before Agnes had agreed, with bad grace. The struggle
had tired Mildred, but she had been rewarded by the look of
pleased surprise on the young woman's face, and her spontane-
ous:

"Oh, how kind!"

"Jolly decent of you," the man had said.

"Please thank your employer most warmly," the woman had
added, while Maude, who hated meeting strangers, had gone red,
shuffled her feet, and hurried away, promising to come back for
the tray later. The tray was now standing on a wicker garden
seat, and all the biscuits had gone. That was really rather funny,
because when Agnes had finally given way she had asked Maude
to make the tea, adding:

"And of course, send *all* the biscuits we have in the house!"

Maude always took her literally, as she took everyone, and
when Agnes saw that empty plate she would fly into another
rage. Happily Harry would be back as soon as she was, and he
would bear the brunt of her ill temper. Happily? Or unhappily?
It was not really fair to add to Harry's burden. It was time something was done to increase his stipend; how *could* the villagers
really respect a vicar whose clothes were patched and who always accepted with eagerness any little gifts of eggs or home-
made jam? Harry was a big man with an enormous appetite, and
she knew that he was often hungry.

On the bedspread, itself patched and darned, were Harry's
socks and shirts, which needed mending in half-a-dozen places.
Thank God she had the use of her arms and hands and could per-
form that service for him. Before this paralysis had gripped her
legs she had been a good and loyal wife to Harry, although not
until she had been struck down had she really appreciated his
qualities. She often thought how sharp-tongued she had been in
the days when Agnes and her husband had been wealthy and
she had envied her sister. The truth about the first fifteen years
of Mildred's married life with Harry was that it had failed be-

cause they had had no children. Harry had wanted children very
much, and so had she; the fact that she was barren had not
helped her to sympathize with Harry and try to make up for the
disappointment; troubles were no easier to bear because one was
responsible for them oneself.

"Be careful!" roared one of the men near the van.

"All right, Jack, keep yer 'air on," said another.

They had taken a number of things out of the van; Mildred
had hardly noticed what these were, which would vex Agnes,
who would be full of questions when she returned.

Now Mildred saw that four men were carrying a grand piano
out of the van and turning it on end to get it through the doorway. It was a beautiful instrument, and Mildred eased herself up
on her pillows to have a better view. The flamboyant-looking man,
who wore red corduroy trousers and a green shirt, was superin-
tending this operation, but only succeeded in getting in the way
and obstructing the removal men. He was waving his arms furiously, and Mildred could see that his face was red with anger.
Suddenly he lunged forward, grabbing one of the piano legs from
the man nearest to him—the man slipped, and the piano leg
scraped against a pillar; the strings gave a deep, clanging note,
which was drowned in a bellow from the piano's owner.

"You clumsy idiots, what are you trying to do? Ruin the only
good piece of furniture I've got?"

"If yer don't mind, mister," said the foreman with commendable
restraint, "we can't get the pianna in until you've moved aht of
the way." So saying, he backed into the red-faced man, who disappeared, and during his absence the piano was taken safely into
the house. When they reappeared a few minutes later, Mildred
saw that the moving men had been deeply antagonized by the
red-faced man's outburst. She watched them strolling slowly
toward their van and disappearing inside, heard their guffaws
of laughter as each emerged holding the tiniest item of furniture
he could find, which he then carried with exaggerated caution
into the house. The last man, very old and small, swaggered up
the steps and failed to see a piece of sacking which one of the
others had dropped. He caught his foot in it and went sprawling,
saving himself from falling heavily by thrusting a cake stand
against the pillar. The frail stand broke with a loud crack.

"*Strewth!*" gasped the little man.

The new owner—or tenant—of Spindles stared speechlessly at the broken stand and then rushed forward, picked it up, and looked as if he were going to belabor the unfortunate miscreant.

"Why, you—you clumsy lout!" he roared, words suddenly bursting forth. "You did that deliberately, you ruddy scoundrel! I'd like to break your neck! You—"

"Now 'arf a mo'," said the foreman, appearing on the scene. "That's enough 'o that, mister. Who do yer think you are, leadin' orf like that at one o' my men? You made 'im nervous, that's wot you did—made 'im nervous, starin' at 'im the way you did."

"I'll make him——"

"'Arf a mo', 'arf a mo'," repeated the foreman firmly. "I'm haccustomed to working for *gentlemen*, I don't take kindly to this kind o' treatment, that's a fact. Do yer want yer furniture left *hinside* or aht?"

"You insolent swine!" roared the red-faced man. "I——"

"Julius!" called the woman, appearing from the house. She looked distressed, and Mildred Castle, her own cheeks aflame with embarrassment, felt extremely sorry for her. "Please don't lose your temper," said the woman appealingly. "These men are doing the best they can." She turned to the foreman. "Please go on with the work," she said. "We are very tired—we were up all night packing. Julius, come and sit down in the shade for ten minutes, you look tired." She led him away and they sat on the bank of the drive, still in sight from the vicarage, the man scowling and sullen, the woman pale and distressed. The foreman had a consultation with his men, and then they began to move heavier furniture. Mildred was interested chiefly in the couple, who were talking in undertones, but she noticed that the furniture seemed oldfashioned. Some pieces took the six men all their effort.

After what seemed to Mildred like twenty minutes or so, the man and woman got up and walked back to the house. Mildred thought they looked distraught and was heartily glad that Agnes had not been there. She would have got a very bad impression of the man, and Mildred, who now took a charitable view of most people, felt uneasy and sorry for the woman. She did not think she would like the man. Agnes would almost certainly dislike both of them—and the news that a piano was installed would not please her.

"Why, there's Harry!" exclaimed Mildred.

Her husband was striding along the drive of Spindles, his head held high and his long legs carrying his big frame with easy grace. When she had married him he had been the most handsome man in her circle of acquaintances, and there had been much envy among her friends. No troubles could spoil Harry's good looks, it seemed, although he was too thin now, and at times looked positively gaunt. To the world, and most of the time to her, he showed a smiling face, and that was helped by his genial, genuinely friendly manner. If Harry had a fault, it was that he was too trusting, too ready to believe the best of everyone.

It was like him to walk into the house without knocking. Even though he was now out of sight, she could hear him.

"Is anyone about?" he called.

Mildred laughed; she could hear the noises of furniture being moved and footsteps on the uncarpeted staircase.

"Oh, hallo!" boomed Harry, obviously spotting someone. "Please don't think I have come to be a nuisance. I simply want to find out whether there is anything I can do."

The woman answered him, but Mildred could not catch the words. Harry spoke more quietly, and she had to strain her ears to hear what he said.

"Are you quite sure? I live next door, and nothing would be any trouble, Mrs.——" He broke off.

"*Miss* Stafford," said the woman, with some emphasis.

"Miss!" echoed Mildred.

"Nothing would be any trouble, Miss Stafford," Harry repeated extravagantly.

Mildred knew that he meant it; if he were asked to help them shift furniture from one room to another, lay carpets, or do any of the hundred and one jobs inseparable from settling into a new house, he would take off his coat and set to work with a will.

Anne Stafford, little though she felt like smiling, managed to do so successfully.

"You're very good," she said, "but my brother and I can manage very well, and we mustn't impose on even such friendly neighbors. The tea and biscuits were very welcome, thank you so much."

"Did they send some in?" asked Castle. "That would be my wife. She is confined to her room, unfortunately, or she would have been here in person to offer help, I know. Have you got everything you need?"

"I think so, thank you," said Anne. "I really, oh—there is one thing. If you've a small loaf of bread to spare, or could tell me where to get one, I would be grateful."

"Gladly, gladly!" declared Castle. "I'll fetch it myself!"

Anne saw him to the door, and Mildred heard him say with a laugh in his voice: "If you don't mind I'll take the shortcut over the hedge. We'll have to have that fence repaired when you get settled in. My brother-in-law used to live at Spindles, and it saved us such a lot of time. I won't be many minutes, you can rely on me."

Anne Stafford turned back into the house, negotiating a large, four-seater settee which the moving men had decided to leave in the hall, and made her way to the kitchen. Standing by the open window, she watched the Vicar disappearing into the vicarage garden.

"Who the deuce was that?" demanded Julius Stafford.

Anne started. "I didn't hear you come in. It was the Vicar, and I thought——"

"I hope you sent him off with a flea in his ear," said Stafford roughly. "We don't want meddling parsons in and out of the place."

"Julius, can't you be more sensible? It was very thoughtful of him to come, and he's going to bring some bread."

"You ought to have brought some," said Julius.

Brother and sister were of equal height, but because she was so thin, Anne looked taller. Julius, now scowling furiously, looked as if he drank too much, and yet there was a hint of boyishness about him, due chiefly to his surprisingly clear blue eyes. The only real likeness between brother and sister was in the eyes.

"I wonder how much longer these brutes are going to be," he muttered. "They're being as awkward as they can. If they'd put their backs into it we would have got rid of them a couple of hours ago." He glared toward the stairs, down which came three of the men, who returned his glare. "I'll be damned thankful when we're on our own," he added, loosening his tie. "You're sure Tony and Gillian won't come this evening?"

"They said definitely that they'd be here Friday night," said Anne. "You read the letter. We've two days to—to clear up and get everything—everything settled."

"Shut up!" hissed Julius. He stalked away as the men came back, and went to the door. The van was practically empty, and two of the men were coiling rope slowly and methodically. Julius went into the van, without speaking to them, and scanned every inch of the floor. When he left, one of the men said audibly:

"Thinks we've took something, do 'e?"

Julius turned round in exasperation, but his sister approached him and he restrained himself. "It's all right in the van," he said in a whisper, and then went upstairs, raising small clouds of dust as he walked. Two men were putting up a bedstead in one of the bedrooms, and another man was sitting on a canvas trunk in the same room, pulling at a pipe.

"If you don't get off that trunk I'll—" began Julius in a low-pitched voice, "I'll——"

"What will yer?" the man demanded truculently. "I've moved some people in my life, but I ain't never met a cove like you. Come on, you blokes, let 'im do the rest hisself. If I was Bert," he added in a loud aside, "I wouldn't take a check from 'im, I'd hinsist on cash."

Julius glared at their departing backs before going slowly toward the trunk. He stared down at it fixedly. He was sweating and seemed unable to tear his gaze away, but he swung round when the foreman came in with his bill. Anne was with him. Julius paid the bill in cash, watched the foreman receipt it, then snatched it away.

"Now get out," he snapped.

"I'm goin', *just* as soon as I can," said the foreman, "and if you want to move again, mister, don't come to my firm. They wouldn't touch it for a fortune."

He turned and went downstairs. The others were waiting for him, and presently the front door slammed. Anne and Julius stood in the bedroom, Julius trembling from head to foot, his sister's face colorless except for her bright eyes.

"Julius, you must keep your nerve," she said.

He did not speak but turned from her and stood looking into the neglected garden. It was a long time before he stopped trembling. At last he looked up at her with an apologetic smile, his voice sullenly submissive.

"I'm sorry, pet, it was that swine of a foreman; he nearly drove me mad. You should have seen the way they dropped the—" He broke off, looked at the trunk, then took her arm and led her out of the room.

· 2 ·

A VISITOR AT SPINDLES

THE REVEREND HARRY CASTLE would have returned to Spindles in time to hear Stafford's outburst had it not been for his wife. But he had been upstairs to see her, and had seen that her pillows needed shaking and her sheets smoothing. He performed these services neatly; it was difficult for her to move herself, but once someone had helped her, she could remain in a sitting position.

"You've been too interested in the new people," he said with a smile. "You're getting as bad as Agnes. My dear, I wish you could see inside, I really do."

"Why?" asked Mildred. "Thank you, darling. Sit down and talk to me."

"Well, I did promise them a loaf, but that can wait for a few minutes," said Castle, sitting on the foot of the bed. "What was I saying?"

"About the inside of Spindles."

He threw up his hands. "I've never seen such a mess! They haven't attempted to clean it out; there's dust everywhere and carpets put down on top of it. I must stop Agnes going over there until they've had a chance of putting the house shipshape, or the story will be all over the village. No, I've never seen such a mess, and the moving people seem to have made it worse. Bedroom furniture downstairs, and goodness knows what upstairs. I felt like taking my coat off and sending for a bucket of good hot water and half a dozen packages of detergent."

"What are the people like?" asked Mildred.

Castle looked at her thoughtfully.

"Well, my dear, I took to the girl at once. There's something very nice about her; she's rather like Agnes used to be." His voice was quite free from bitterness. "The man is a different type, I think. I should hate to jump to conclusions, but he gave me the impression he was rather wild. I didn't see him at close quarters, but he was looking at me from a doorway. I don't think I was very welcome," he added with a laugh, "and I don't think we're going to see him in church very often. Well, I'd better take them that loaf. But I don't think they'll ask me to stay, so I'll probably be back very soon. Are you comfortable now?"

"Perfectly," said Mildred.

When he had gone, she felt puzzled and surprised. Only a short while before she had been reflecting that Harry was too ready to believe the best of anyone. He must have formed a very poor opinion of the man next door; it was unlike him to voice such sentiments even to her.

She saw him swinging along the drive with the paper fluttering about the loaf of bread. She heard a car change gear; then there was a squeal of brakes, followed by Harry's hearty voice. He sounded a bit scared.

"Well, *that* was a close shave!"

"I'm terribly sorry," said a man's voice, "it's the hedge—you can't see past it. But it was my fault, I shouldn't have swung in like that. Are you sure you're all right, Vicar?"

"Oh, yes," said Castle, "you didn't touch me. Er—I suppose you've come to the right house, Inspector?"

"I think so," said the man, and Mildred recognized the voice and managed to get to a sitting position without help. Inspector Foster, of the Milshire Police, was a rare visitor to the village; in fact, she and her husband would probably never have met him but for the enquiries he had made after Agnes' husband's death.

What on earth was he doing at Spindles on the day the new people had moved in?

Anne Stafford was standing in the front bedroom that overlooked the drive when the car turned into it and nearly knocked the Vicar down. She heard her brother's footsteps on the stairs. He heard the engine, and demanded:

"What's that?"

"We've a visitor," said Anne.

"What does anyone want here?" snapped Julius angrily. "Why can't they leave us alone?"

"Julius, if you don't take a firmer hold on yourself we shall be in serious trouble," said Anne in a low-pitched voice. "It's probably a tradesman come to solicit orders."

"I don't believe it."

"Oh, stop being a fool!" said Anne. "You're telling everyone as plainly as you can that you are frightened out of your life! First you upset the moving men, then you're rude to the Vicar——"

"I wasn't rude!"

"Don't you think common politeness required you to ask him in and thank him for his offer of help?" demanded Anne. "Instead, you were hardly civil and you banged the door, probably in his face. Julius, do you understand what we *have* to do?" she entreated. "We've got to hide——"

There was a loud knock on the front door.

"If that were a tradesman he would go to the back," muttered Julius. "Of course I know what we've got to do, but it's a strain, a terrible strain."

"I don't need telling that," said Anne. "I've never known you as bad as this, no matter what scrape you've got yourself into." Her voice and eyes had hardened. "Stay up here and keep out of sight. I will speak to the man downstairs. And listen to me——"

The knock came again.

"Stay here," said Anne. "Julius, listen to me. I have helped you a dozen times when you were in serious difficulties. This time *I* want *your* help."

"Aren't I doing everything I can?" muttered Julius.

"You're doing it very badly," said Anne. "Keep quiet, and don't move out of the room until I've got rid of him."

She hurried out, closing the door behind her. The man knocked again. She ran down the stairs, her footsteps clattering on the bare boards, and opened the front door.

She felt quite sure that the caller was not a tradesman. He was well dressed and in different circumstances would have created an excellent impression. He was good-looking in a rather severe way, but the severity of his features was relieved by a charming smile. He took off his hat.

"Good evening," he said. "I know you have only just moved in and I'm really sorry to worry you now, but I feel sure you will forgive me. You are Miss Stafford, aren't you?"

"Yes," said Anne. "Who—?"

"Is your brother in?" asked the caller pleasantly.

"He—no, he's just gone out," said Anne.

"Oh, that's a pity, I wanted a word with him particularly," said the caller. "May I wait until he returns?"

Anne said, "I don't know how long he will be. I— But please come in."

She was angry with herself for keeping him standing there for so long, thus behaving in the way for which she had reproved Julius. The caller had unnerved her by knowing their name and that they had just moved in.

"Moving is a terrible job, isn't it?" he remarked pleasantly. "My wife says that it takes a year to get everything in proper order." He was taking a card from his waistcoat pocket. "But I must introduce myself," he said, and handed it to her.

There *was* something unnerving, almost threatening, in his manner. His eyes seemed to take in very much more than the chaotic state of the hall and the rooms that could be seen through open doorways. The fact that she had gone pale, for instance. She stared at him as she took the card, and then glanced down at it.

For some reason, it was not a shock. Why not, she didn't know, but it was not even a surprise to read INSPECTOR MARK FOSTER, MILSHIRE CONSTABULARY on the card. A policeman in the flesh, standing and smiling at her as if he knew everything; and he must have some information or he would not be here.

She stared at the card for what seemed to her a long time. At last she faced him.

"This is rather unexpected, Inspector. I didn't know that the police visited all newcomers to the county." She tried to sound flippant, but her voice sounded toneless in her own ears. "How can I help you?"

"I think your brother can do so," said Foster. "Is he likely to be very long, do you know?"

"I don't think so, but——"

"I mustn't stay *too* long," said Foster, glancing round as if looking for a chair.

Anne flushed and said, "Come this way, please." She led him into the great drawing room, where there was a miscellany of small furniture. It looked lost in that room, and the sun shining through the high window showed up the thick dust, the cobwebs, and the soot that had fallen in the hearth. Paper was peeling from the walls, hanging down in various lengths. There were three drawing-room chairs, one of which she pushed forward. "I do hope you will excuse the muddle," she said. "We haven't had a chance to get things straight yet."

"It does look rather as if you came in a hurry," said Foster.

"What do you mean?" she demanded sharply.

Foster looked startled. "Simply that, Miss Stafford. What else should I mean?"

"Oh, dear, I'm afraid I'm rather touchy about the state we're in," she said and hoped that it sounded plausible. "Please tell me why you have come. I feel sure that I can help you as much as my brother."

Then, suddenly, it occurred to her that Julius had done something on his own which had sent the police after him. The man's insistence on seeing Julius was an indication of that; she was foolish to think anyone had the remotest idea of *her* particular trouble. Julius was always in difficulties; she had bailed him out twice for motoring offenses committed when he was drunk. Then she thought: But if it were a motoring offense an Inspector wouldn't come.

Foster was looking at her steadily, giving the impression that he was watching for the slightest slip. He seemed faintly puzzled, too; in a sudden, wild moment she wondered whether his expression would remain like that if he knew that in a canvas trunk upstairs there was a dead body—of a man who had been *murdered!*

She clenched her hands, fiercely reminding herself that she must keep her composure. If she went on this way she might blurt out something incriminating and precipitate the police investigation she feared so much.

"I wonder if you can?" said Foster at last. "Do you know where your brother was yesterday afternoon between three and five o'clock?"

"No," said Anne involuntarily. A great wave of relief passed through her, and she felt weak. "That is, I believe he was at his club. Inspector, what on earth are you driving at?"

"Miss Stafford," said Foster, "Scotland Yard telephoned me this afternoon and asked me to send a man out to see your brother. When I learned that you were moving in today, I thought it might be better if I came in person—I like to know everyone in the larger houses, and it seemed a good opportunity. Did your brother say anything about seeing an accident in Whitehall Place?"

"Why, no," said Anne.

When Julius had come home, about half-past seven, she had been in no mood to listen to him, but had talked swiftly and without ceasing. Her story had shocked him and had sobered him up pretty quickly. He had behaved very well until the start of the journey, when they knew that the canvas trunk with its grisly contents was on the moving van. But the waiting here had been frightening for them both, and now Julius had begun to crack.

Foster was saying: "There was a rather nasty accident in Whitehall Place, which was seen by two or three people, including, it is thought, your brother. Scotland Yard told me that the porter of the National Club said that your brother left only a minute before the accident. There was a fatal casualty, and you know how necessary it is to get all possible evidence in such matters."

"Yes," said Anne faintly. A fatal accident, presumably to someone whom neither of them knew. What a fool she had been to work herself up into such a state. "He certainly told me nothing about it, as he probably would have had he seen anything at all serious."

"You would think so," said Foster. "I'll have to wait for him, I'm afraid. Don't let me stop you from doing anything. Look here"—he smiled again—"can I help at all?"

"How very nice of you," said Anne. "But no thank you. We'll probably just make up the beds and leave everything until the morning." She looked round desperately for something intelligent to say. "Is there a decent hotel in the village, do you know?"

"There's The Angler," said Foster, "and you can get a good meal there. It's a fishermen's haunt, mind you, and you will probably get very bored. Do you know the district well?"

"Hardly at all," said Anne.

"Unless you fish, you're finished socially," said Foster, and added with a gay laugh: "That's an exaggeration, of course, but angling is to Bray what bridge is to a cathedral town. I'm told that the man who built this house came here because he was a fanatical angler. He—" Foster paused and looked a little discomposed. "He came before my time," he added quickly. "It's mostly trout in the Mille, Miss Stafford—good-sized fish too, I'm told."

"Is the river very deep?" asked Anne.

"Deep? No, only a few feet in most places. It's a tributary of the Ord, of course, and that gets pretty deep a few miles from here."

Foster was sitting back with his legs crossed and somehow managed to look quite at home in spite of the surroundings. She thought he would be a difficult man to embarrass, and now that she was beginning to think more clearly she came to the conclusion that Foster was rather enjoying this tête-à-tête with an attractive woman. It was some time since Anne had thought of herself as attractive, and it helped her to recover her poise.

"If you like swimming, we have our lido at the other side of the town," went on Foster, "but I don't recommend it. There's rather a good pool between here and Milton—it's a private club. I will gladly recommend you for membership, if you like."

"That's very kind of you," said Anne.

She felt almost lighthearted now. Here was a police inspector flirting mildly with her, while upstairs, probably not twenty feet away from his head, there was the body of a murdered man!

Her thoughts changed. In a few minutes she would have to leave him, tiptoe upstairs, and tell Julius to come down and pretend to have entered through the back door. She would be able to prepare him for the questions, and he could wait for a few minutes to steady his nerves.

"I don't know how you will get on in Bray," Foster was saying. "There aren't many young people in the neighborhood, not of the kind likely to appeal to you, at all events. You might find the Carvers interesting, but perhaps you already have friends here."

"No," said Anne. "We bought the house because it was cheap and there was good room for all of us. My married sister and her husband are going to live here," she added, "and we shall probably entertain quite a lot. It isn't too far from London. There's the big room upstairs which will just suit my brother, too."

"The studio," said Foster. "I've heard about that. Does your brother paint?"

"Oh, no—he is a composer."

"*That* Stafford!" exclaimed Foster with lively interest. "I had no idea that the village was so favored."

Anne laughed. "He isn't as famous as all that. I——"

Then she swung round, for Foster started as the door was flung open and Julius, who had obviously been drinking, barged into the room and approached the policeman aggressively.

· 3 ·

JULIUS MAKES A FURTHER
BAD IMPRESSION

"HAVEN'T YOU the ordinary politeness to choose a better time than this to call?" demanded Julius in a thick voice. "Who are you, sir?"

Foster jumped up and eyed Julius with astonishment, which rapidly changed to mild disgust. Julius, emboldened with drink, was prepared to be unpleasant. If Foster used his title, however,

before Julius was warned, all the pomposity would ooze out of
him, and there would be no telling what he would say.

"My name is——" began Foster.

Anne made a surreptitious kick at a chair and then pretended
to fall over it. Both men turned to her in alarm, and she straightened up.

"I'm sorry," she said. "I didn't see it. Oh, Julius, did you see an
accident in Whitehall Place last night, just as you left the club?
The police want to find witnesses." She spoke lightly and prayed
that Julius had the wit to see why she had mentioned the police.

"Accident?" he repeated.

Foster grew much more formal as he explained. He did not
know that he was giving Julius time to recover, and Anne thought
Julius was putting up a very good front. He frowned throughout
the narrative and was scowling when Foster finished.

"I did hear something of it," he admitted, "but I didn't get a
clear view. I'm no good as a witness, I'm afraid."

"That's a pity," said Foster.

"It's a fact. I was behind a stream of parked cars when it happened. I didn't wait to see. I don't even know what cars were involved. You haven't come all the way from London to ask this,
have you?"

"Good heavens, no!" exclaimed Foster, and explained again
why he had preferred to make the inquiry himself. He also mentioned that he had been to inspect the village police stations
between Milton and Bray.

But it was already clear that Julius had made another bad
impression, and his subsequent remarks did not improve on it.

"Ever since we arrived we've had nothing but curious visitors,"
he declared rudely. "If it goes on like this I shall be sorry we ever
bought the place."

"I hope I don't have to trouble you again," said Foster formally.
Anne flashed a warning glance at her brother, then turned back
to their visitor. "I'm amazed that you knew so much about us,
Inspector."

"There isn't anything amazing in that," said Foster. "Scotland
Yard sent a man to see Mr. Stafford this morning and got your
new address from your ex-landlady—landladies are notoriously
garrulous." He was looking at Julius as he spoke. Thus he gave

Anne a badly needed reprieve, for they had hidden the dead man
in the attic, and she had been terrified in case the landlady
should come up while they were there and see anything to arouse
suspicion. Later, because they were moving out, there had been
every excuse to scrub the attic thoroughly and remove all traces
of blood.

"You're quite sure you saw nothing of the accident?" Foster
was asking.

"Absolutely," said Julius. He opened the door with a flourish.
"Sorry I can't be of assistance, Inspector," he added sarcastically.

Foster went out, after giving Anne a formal little bow and a
faint smile. Julius saw him off the premises and waited in the
doorway until the car had disappeared. His eyes were bloodshot,
his hands trembling, and his voice unsteady.

"I don't believe he told the truth. He suspects something.
He——"

"Don't be absurd," said Anne. "How can he suspect anything?
We're making a hell for ourselves when there's no need to. No one
even knows that Lovelace is dead, and probably no one will ever
know. If only we can get rid of—" Her voice trailed off.

"The body," said Julius roughly. "We needn't keep up the pretense between ourselves." He was making a great effort to regain
his composure and managed to smile tremulously. "I know I've
been a pretty foul companion today, but this really has unnerved
me. I don't think I realized what we'd done until I saw the
van move off and knew the body was in it. If they'd opened the
trunk—"

"It's locked and padlocked," Anne said. "They couldn't have
opened it even if they'd wanted to. Julius, we've only got to keep
our nerve and everything will be all right. No one knew that
Lovelace was back in England, and he certainly couldn't have
been recognized. I've never seen a man who'd altered so much."

"You almost make me wonder whether it was Lovelace," Julius
muttered.

"Don't talk nonsense! He'd altered as anyone would alter after
seven years in a South American jungle."

"His voice was the same," admitted Julius.

"Of course it was. So was the scar on his neck; so were
his hands, with those little short fingers." She was speaking very

quickly. "Julius, he's not been in England for so long. Everyone
thought him dead. No one dreamed he would ever turn up again,
and he told us that he had seen no one else. The body of an unknown man will be found, but there'll be no connection with us.
Even if he were recognized, no one would know that he had come
to see us."

"Except that blasted landlady!"

"Who heard him call himself Smith," said Anne.

"I suppose you're right,'" Julius conceded grudgingly.

"Of course I'm right!"

Julius said slowly, "There's one thing you forget. He was killed
at the flat—there isn't any doubt about that. If no one else knew
he was in England, what made the murderer come to the flat? He
wouldn't kill an unknown man named Smith who had only just
arrived in England. It just isn't reasonable."

"It happened!" cried Anne. "Don't you believe me? Do you
think I killed him? Do you——"

"Now, pet, calm down," said Julius in a steadier voice.
"Of course you didn't kill him—I'm quite sure of that. What I
want to point out is that he must have been killed because he
was Lovelace, and therefore someone did know he'd come back to
England. That someone followed him to our flat and killed him
—ugh!" He grimaced. "I've never seen anything like his face."

"Don't!"

"I'm sorry, I'm sorry," muttered Julius. "I *am* talking sense
though, aren't I? No one broke into the flat to see a Mr. Smith
who called casually. They must have known it was Lovelace. I'm
beginning to think we were wrong."

"Wrong about what?"

"Not to tell the police."

"With everything against us?" demanded Anne. "With *our*
bread knife used, with——"

"*Don't!*" cried Julius in turn.

"Then for heaven's sake don't talk like a fool," said Anne. "If
the truth had come out, in court or in the newspapers, do you
think Teddy would still contemplate marrying me? Of course he
wouldn't! He would back out, which would be easy enough, and
if that happened where would be our money?"

"I know. I know what you mean," said Julius.

"It's so much better this way," Anne went on. "They can't trace it to us, they won't be able to identify the body. As soon as it's dark we'll take it out." She gave a mirthless laugh. "The Inspector kindly told me that the River Ord is quite deep, and we've only got to row along the river at the end of the garden and get near the Ord and throw it overboard with some stones tied to it. Why, it may never be discovered; no one will ever know, no one will look for Lovelace. If we took any other course we would be ruined. Julius! I'm not doing this only for myself, I'm thinking of you. If we don't get some money soon we shall be in serious trouble—we're inundated with debts, *your* debts. Teddy was the only hope, and his family is trying desperately to make him break the engagement. If the body had been found at Chelsea, if we'd told the police, the family would have been too strong for him. Why, you agreed to all this last night, when you were only half sober!"

"Perhaps that's why I agreed," sighed Julius.

Anne said coldly, "I see. You're too frightened to go on with it. All right, Julius. *I'm* not enjoying it, you know. We haven't disposed of the body yet. We can tell the police everything and explain that we were in a panic and decided to come down here early. We'll tell them why and say that we couldn't carry on with it. On the whole, I think it would be better. I don't particularly want to marry Teddy. I don't particularly want to see you in jail for obtaining money on false pretenses, either, but that would be better than a life sentence, I suppose."

"Pet, don't talk like that."

"I thought it was what you wanted me to say," said Anne.

"You know it isn't. I won't let you down."

"I'm not a bit sure that I can trust you," said Anne. "I don't like the way you keep harping on not letting me down. You think I killed him, don't you?" When he did not answer immediately she raised her voice: *"Don't you?"*

"Now—"

"Stop calling me pet!" cried Anne. "What a fine specimen of manhood was wished on me for a brother! I've done everything for you. If it weren't for me no one would have heard of Julius Stafford, the rising young composer. I've saved you from prison more than once; I've often kept you when you've squandered your money right and left, because I thought you had a spark of genius. And what do I get in return for it? You think I killed Lovelace! All right, let's send for the police at once. I don't mind sacrificing what there is left of my life for you, but I'm not going to go on while you think that I killed Lovelace."

"It isn't true," protested Julius, but he would not meet her eyes. "Don't lose your head now, Anne. You're quite right, there won't be any reason for the body to be connected with Lovelace, and even if it were, no one would know that he had come to see us, except—" He broke off.

"Go on," said Anne.

"Except the man who killed him," mumbled Julius. "That's what you seem to forget, and that's what I can't understand about it. If you didn't kill him——"

"*If* I didn't?" Her voice rose to a scream. "That's the end of it, I can't bear any more!"

She rushed outside, half sobbing, and Julius followed her, not aware that Mildred Castle was watching the scene in astonishment. He had the sense, however, to keep his voice low.

"Pet, don't lose your head, I'll stand by you. I don't really think you killed him; it's just that I can't understand it, that's all. Don't lose your head, for both our sakes."

"For yours, you mean!"

"No, I'm not such a beast as all that," said Julius, with a catch in his voice. "I'm thinking of you as much as myself. Come back and be sensible. There's a boat at the end of the garden—we'll get everything done tonight. Now come inside and rest."

After a long pause, Anne gave way and let him guide her back to the house. By that time Harry Castle had hurried upstairs to his wife's room, summoned by a tapping on the floor with a stick, to which course she resorted only in an emergency. Together they watched the Staffords, and then Harry looked at Mildred, his face a study in bewilderment.

"Do you know, my dear, those people are in some kind of trouble, serious trouble. I'm sure of it. I couldn't understand why they had moved in such evident haste, and the man's manner, to say the least, was abrupt. Then there was Foster's visit, a remarkable thing. I wonder if I can help them?"

"Harry, it's no business of yours."

"I don't know, my dear. If I can help, I should do so. After all, they have come to live in my parish. When I saw Foster, I left the loaf on the kitchen window sill. It seemed more tactful. But I must watch for another chance to speak to them. If you see anything that might help, tell me at once, won't you?"

"If you really insist, my dear."

"I do insist." Castle smiled. "It's a very good thing that Agnes has been delayed. If she had seen that—" He broke off. "I don't think we'll say a word to her about it, do you?"

"Most decidedly not," declared Mildred.

Castle laughed. "Poor Agnes! We needn't worry about Maude. She can't see anything from the kitchen, and even if she could I don't think it would convey anything to her." He laughed again and then heard footsteps in the garden. "I wonder if that's Agnes? For once I shall be really pleased to see her—I'm getting hungry. You know how she carries on if I start my supper before she gets in."

"You let Agnes domineer too much," said Mildred.

"You're a fine one to talk! I— *What on earth is that?*"

He turned toward the window, startled. From Spindles there came music, wild, frenzied playing of some strange yet fascinating melody.

"Imagine playing the piano with the house in that condition," gasped Castle.

"Harry, go down and talk to Agnes, or she'll be going next door and protesting about it. We mustn't let that happen tonight. Hurry, dear!"

Castle bolted from the room, and Mildred listened to the strains of music—so out of place in that quiet village and, even to her, so disturbing—tumbling, cascading out, as if the tormented spirit of the player were struggling for freedom.

· 4 ·

INTO THE RIVER

JULIUS OPENED the back door of Spindles and peered out. Only the stars broke the darkness, except for a gleam of light from a window next door and, in the distance, the glow from the village.

"Is it all right?" asked Anne.

"Yes, I think so."

"Then let's go," said Anne.

"All right—I'll take him, pet."

He turned to the kitchen, which was lighted by a single candle. On the floor was a sack, and beside it a small suitcase, filled with bricks that would be put in with the body of the murdered man. They had walked down the straight garden path several times, twice when darkness had fallen, to make sure that they could reach the river without stumbling. The boat was tied to a small, rotting landing stage.

Julius hoisted the sack, which contained Lovelace's body to his shoulder, grunting with the effort, and then went out. Anne followed with the case of bricks. By the time they reached the stream Julius was breathing heavily and Anne was exhausted, holding the case with both hands. There was a soft lapping of water against the boat, which they could see swaying gently.

"Rest a minute," Julius said.

Soon he bent down. Anne went on her knees to steady the boat, which rocked perilously as the heavy sack fell into it, and water splashed into her face. Julius wiped the perspiration from his forehead, blew his nose softly, and then picked up the case and put it in the stern, to balance the weight in the bow. Cautiously they stepped into the little boat, and Anne took the rudder rope. Julius carefully pushed off from the bank and then lost his grip on an oar; it was held secure in the rowlock, but the splash made their nerves scream.

"Be careful!" Anne hissed.

"It's no use, we'll be heard if we go on like this," Julius said. "We'll have to tie rags round those rowlocks."

"We haven't any."

"I'll get some sacking from the shed," said Julius. "I won't be a minute."

He left her alone with the corpse in the swaying boat, which made little creaking noises when it moved against the landing stage. The house was just visible, but a square of light from a window in the vicarage gleamed over-brightly. The village was visible from the river, and it seemed to be all light—the yellow glow stretched as far as she could see. There were sounds distinguishable now, footsteps in the village streets, voices from the inn, and music from a radio.

Julius was a long time gone.

Anne sat still, her hands gripping the sides of the boat. Suddenly her body went tense. There was a light coming *along the river*. At first she thought it was a boat being rowed toward her, but as she saw the way the light wobbled from side to side she realized that it was a cyclist. So there must be a path running alongside the stream on the opposite bank. Now she could hear the bicycle, little tinny noises and the soft sound of tires on the path. Nearer and nearer it came, and suddenly the light shone toward her. She put her hand to her mouth to stop a scream. Then the light receded, and her breathing grew shallow. She started when she heard Julius' voice just behind her.

"What was that?"

"A cyclist."

"It nearly made me jump out of my skin," whispered Julius hoarsely. "It's all right, I've got the rags."

It took nearly five minutes to tie them onto the rowlocks and leave room for the oars to move freely, but at last they were ready. Julius pushed off, got to midstream, and then began to row steadily; once on the water he seemed to have more confidence. They turned a bend in the river, with high ground on either side, and only the stars lighting their way.

"How long will it take us?" breathed Anne.

"About half an hour, now."

"Half an hour!"

It seemed an age. Sometimes they passed near other villages and then lights seemed to be everywhere. But soon the stream broadened, and Julius strained his eyes to see the landmark which would tell him they were near the Ord. He had been to the spot after a scratch supper and seen a white bungalow close to the river's edge. At last he saw the faint blur of its walls.

"We're nearly there," he said.

They were now in a swift-running current where the two rivers met, and the little boat swung wildly. Julius steadied it. But as they passed the bungalow, a sudden light blazed from an opened door. Surely they must be seen! There were voices and a burst of laughter; then finally the door closed. Two people were walking from the bungalow, shining a light. The two in the boat waited until the last sound of their footsteps had died away, and then Julius spoke swiftly.

"Now we won't be long. Open the case."

Anne's fingers fumbled with the catches, and at last she had it open. She handed him the bricks, and he put them into the sack and tied the neck with stout string.

"Sit quite still," he said. "Don't move, or we'll capsize."

He lifted the sack, and, straining every muscle, managed to lean forward so that he could ease it into the water without making too much noise. The boat was dipping sharply, and water slopped over the side.

"Now," grunted Julius.

He pushed the burden over, but it caught fast on something. The weight on his arms was almost unbearable, and he was gasping helplessly.

"Shift it your end—shift it!" he muttered.

Anne put her hands beneath it and heaved until the sack went over, with a loud splash, which sent spray into her face and drenched her chest. The boat swayed wildly to and fro, and Julius balanced himself precariously while Anne leaned over the side trying desperately to get at something in the water.

"What is it?" gasped Julius. "Sit still, for God's sake!"

"It's the case!"

"What?"

"The suitcase, it caught against the sack—Julius, I can't get it!"

"Be quiet!" he hissed.

He sat down, fuming. The suitcase was just out of reach and floating away rapidly. By the time he had turned the boat it was out of sight. He peered in one direction, Anne in another, but although they rowed on for half a mile they saw no trace of it.

"It must have sunk right away," said Anne in a strained voice.

"What case was it?"

"That cheap fiber one you borrowed from Tony."

"Was our name on it?"

"It wasn't inside, but there was a label."

"A sticky one?"

"Yes."

"It'll come off in the water," Julius said. "We can't stay any longer. It will be the devil going against the current."

She did not answer, and he turned the boat again and began to row back the way they had come. As they drew nearer the village, which was still lighted up, Julius was breathing harshly, making no attempt now to subdue the sound.

Anne turned toward him. "Can I take over?"

"No, we're nearly there."

It took them twenty minutes to reach the landing stage, where, for the first time, things went smoothly. They tied up the boat and walked back to the house, Julius breathing heavily and muttering under his breath; she heard the word "case" and walked on tight-lipped. He reached the back door first and turned the handle and pushed.

"Why don't you open it?" Anne demanded.

Julius said, "It's stuck."

They pushed together without avail, and at last Julius muttered, "We'll go to the front."

"Have you got the key?"

"Yes."

They walked quickly to the front of the house, no longer trying to hide their presence. They turned the corner, and then stopped dead in their tracks, staring at a patch of light that shone onto the neglected lawn. The light was coming from the front room!

"What on earth——" Anne began.

"Be quiet!" hissed Julius.

He crept forward, keeping close to the wall. Anne could hear her heart thumping as she followed him. He reached the window and peered through cautiously, ready to dodge back at any moment. No one was in sight. Emboldened, he went farther forward and saw in the light from an unshaded lamp that the room was empty and that part of the floor was wet. Furniture had been moved, and there was some sort of order at one end of the room. Anne stared wide-eyed and saw that there the floorboards were damp but nearly dried out, although at the sides they were still very wet.

"Who on earth—?" she began.

"It's that damned Vicar! I'll wring his neck!"

"Don't be a fool, he wouldn't break in. Someone must have a key." She gasped. "You did lock the front door?"

"Of course I did. I—look out!"

They heard footsteps inside the house and dodged out of sight. A tall man in his shirtsleeves entered the room, smiling with evident satisfaction. He carried a bucket of water and a mop. Lighter footsteps followed, and a girl appeared, young, fair-haired, looking thoroughly happy. She was comely and a little plump, and there was an infectious gaiety in her manner as she spoke to the dark-haired man, whose laughter sounded clearly to the ears of the watching couple.

"Well, I'm damned!" exclaimed Julius. "Tony and Gillian!" He glared at Anne. "You said they wouldn't get here until Friday!"

"You read the letter!"

"Well, at least it could be worse," growled Julius. "We'll tell them that we've been out to dinner."

"But we're both wet through—at least I am, and you're not much better." Anne stared at her brother, her hands clenched in front of her. "Everything possible has gone wrong!" Her voice held a note of hysteria. "Look at them, making fun of it—fun! Julius!"

"Now who's losing her head?"

"Never mind that!" Anne gripped his wrist tightly. "Julius, did you scrub out the trunk?"

"The—" he began, then turned pale and stared back at her. "No," he muttered, and gulped. "No, I didn't think I need worry about it then; I was going to do it as soon as we got back. It—it wasn't very stained, I took particular notice. They can't have seen anything."

"We must go in," said Anne. "It doesn't matter what we look like, you must get upstairs and lock the trunk before they look into it: *it's their trunk!*"

"It was Tony's suitcase," Julius muttered.

"Fancy using that when we'd several of our own."

"No one could have foreseen this," muttered Julius. "Come on, we'll put a bold face on it and tell them that we stumbled into the river by mistake; they'll believe anything, that's one advantage."

Anne said, "I'm chilled through. I— Just a minute, Julius! Let's bang on the window. It will scare Gillian, she's always nervous, and then they won't have their wits about them when we get in."

She went forward, keeping to the side of the house, and then clenched her fist and banged loudly on the window.

• 5 •

TONY AND GILLIAN

TONY AND GILLIAN ABBOTT were enjoying themselves in their own particular way. Gillian, sister to Julius and Anne, had always been lighthearted and gay, with a serious streak in her which she never allowed to gain the upper hand for long. She did not approve of Julius, but she admitted that there were times when she was fond of him. She was younger than both Julius and Anne, of whom she was really fond. She had often told her that she made too much fuss over Julius, who traded on being hailed in some quarters as one of the most promising composers of the day. It had been chiefly due to Gillian's influence—exerted with some reluctance, for she was by no means sure that it would work out successfully—that they had bought Spindles, mostly with Tony's money.

When he had agreed to put up the lion's share of the capital required—nearly five thousand pounds with legal and agent's fees—he had been quick to declare that they must look on Spindles as belonging equally to each couple. Gillian knew that he was sincere in his eagerness not to create a situation which might give rise to jealousies and petty quarrels, which he disliked above all things. He was not particularly fond of Julius, but he liked Anne, who was the business head of the family. He knew that she had nursed Julius skillfully and guided Gillian through difficult days of school and adolescence.

He had tried, unsuccessfully, to buy a small house in the country. He disliked London, and the small suburban house on its outskirts, where he and Gillian had lived since he had left the hospital after a car crash, had become anathema to him. After his failure, Anne had suggested buying a large house where they could all live and reduce their expenses. If Gillian's reluctance had been marked, his own had been even greater, but once he had realized that it was the only reasonable hope of getting away from London, he had agreed.

Spindles had attracted them both. It was well built, the quaint plan of the three floors interested them, and the large studio in the roof would be ideal for Julius' piano. His own small study, he had decided, would be in the wing farthest away from the attic windows, a little morning room where he could write in peace. His circle of readers was not unduly large, but his publishers were content to go on publishing his novels, and he made a living with the help of occasional articles and crime stories. One day, Gillian said, he would write a really *great* novel. His reply was always the same:

"I don't think I've got it in me."

"If only you had more confidence, darling!"

"Confidence doesn't make literature," Tony would say.

"You're so sure of yourself in every other respect."

He would laugh at her and dismiss the subject.

In the middle of that morning they had gone to see Anne and Julius in their Chelsea attic flat, and learned with surprise that they had already left for Spindles. The landlady said they had been up all night packing, and had telephoned the movers asking them to send the van on Wednesday instead of the following day. The landlady just didn't know what had come over them; they had lived in her house for two years; you would think they could bear it for an extra day.

Had it been anyone else they would have been surprised and perhaps piqued, but it was impossible to guess what Julius would do next. There were times when he left London, declaring that the atmosphere stifled him. He would hide himself in a little village pub, usually drinking heavily, for a week or more, until he ran out of money, usually borrowed, and return truculently, refusing to answer questions. Gillian had learned that it was a waste of time to reason with Julius; he merely became offensive, later apologizing in maudlin fashion, calling her Sweetie Pie or his Little Angel. In such moods Julius was revolting.

At Spindles, however, they would have their own apartments and meet only for meals, perhaps not even then. The house was quite large enough for two families. The two sisters could run it with daily help, and the men could concentrate on their work. Tony would plug away steadily, and Julius would work erratically, sometimes hardly sleeping for days on end, and sometimes doing nothing for a month. If Julius had Tony's application to his work, or Tony had the touch of genius which many people saw in Julius, either of them could become celebrated. Gillian thought it unfair that a measure of fame had been given to her brother, who took it for granted that he was the best composer in England, and not to her husband.

Tony had been before a tribunal about his insurance, as he had lost his left leg from the knee, and although he managed remarkably well with an artificial one, there could hardly be any argument about the cause of the amputation. He had attended one sitting and been told that he would be called to another that Thursday, which was why they had not been able to plan to travel to Spindles until Friday. Then they had received a curt notification that the insurance would be paid, and that no further appearance before the board was necessary. It was that which had sent them hurrying to Chelsea, to say that they could, after all, travel on Thursday with the others. Their furniture had been warehoused by the firm which had done the moving, and

all they had to take with them were a few personal belongings.
Finding the Staffords had already gone, however, they decided
to follow them down that afternoon.

They had not really been surprised, on arriving at Spindles, to
find it deserted and in such a state of dirt and disorder. Doubtless
Julius had grown tired of work and carried Anne off to the nearest inn for a meal—and to see what the local beer was like. Had
they been left on their own, the Staffords would probably have
slept in this mess and waited for Tony and Gillian.

They had been at Spindles for nearly an hour. Two small
bedrooms were now reasonably clean and tidy, and inroads had
been made on the drawing room, which had two red brick fire-
places and enormous windows overlooking the village and the
wooded hills beyond.

"Every square yard wants a fresh bucket of water," Tony said
as he walked with Gillian to the kitchen, "and the mop wants
washing out every five minutes. I'm beginning to wish we hadn't
started on the drawing room, sweet; we haven't done too badly
upstairs."

"We can't very well stop now," Gillian said practically. "As for
those lazy beasts, I'll tell them what I think of them when they
come in." In spite of her words, she laughed. "I suppose this is
how it will work out. Anne will have to mother Julius, and——"

"You'll do the donkey work," said Tony, frowning. "I've always
been a little afraid of that."

"Ass! I'm not serious, and *Anne* isn't afraid of work."

"No, that's true."

"As for Julius, can't you imagine him sitting at the piano surrounded by dirt and cobwebs, banging away as if he were possessed by a thousand demons?" said Gillian.

That had started the laughter that had annoyed Anne. They
had set to work with a will, unsuspectingly, and then suddenly
the quiet was broken by a great bang on the window. Gillian
started violently and Tony swung round.

"What the—the *fools!*" he exclaimed.

"What—what was it?" gasped Gillian.

"Anne and Julius. I thought Anne had more sense," said Tony
angrily.

"I expect they thought it was funny," said Gillian, who had gone white. She had not yet fully recovered from the shock of the car crash and was more than ordinarily nervous. "Don't let's start off with a tiff with them, darling."

In the hall, Tony kissed her. "I won't," he said.

"Hallo, hallo!" boomed Julius, flinging open the front door. Anne looked contrite.

"I'm sorry we banged like that, Gill; I forgot for the moment that you were so jumpy."

"That's all right," said Gillian. "Well, you're a fine couple, I must say. The place looked like a pigsty. Why on earth didn't you tell us about the change of plans? And what have you been doing—you look as if you've fallen into a pond."

"No pond, a river," declared Julius heartily. "We took a wrong turning—on our way back from the village pub—and I fell into the river. No damage done, though, but I must go up and change. So should you, Anne."

"Yes," said Anne. She looked at the room, and to Gillian's surprise, because she was notoriously undemonstrative, she stepped forward and kissed her. "You're both too good to be true," she said. "I won't leave it all to you. Sit down and have a cigarette until we come down—*Julius* is going to pull his weight until we're settled or I'll know the reason why."

The rest of the evening—or what was left of it—went smoothly. The success of their trick had reassured Julius and Anne, and a further inspection of the trunk had shown that there were only one or two brown stains, which became very faint when washed. They locked the trunk again and went downstairs. Julius was in his best mood and on such occasions was likable and amusing. A surprising amount was put straight before they had had enough. They had made beds in three rooms— Gillian and Tony's at the back of the house, just across the landing from Anne's; Julius had selected one farther along the passage.

Julius was coming out of Anne's room, when he heard Tony say, "Gill, do you know where I put that old fiber suitcase?"

"No," said Gillian. "Why?"

"I think I had my pajamas in it."

"They're in the leather case," said Gillian.

"Oh, so they are. It's funny about the other one, though. I can't imagine where it is."

Julius stood quite still, listening. When they had changed the subject, he turned as if to enter Anne's room again but changed his mind and went to his own. He looked very thoughtful and pre-occupied, and the telltale signs of strain were at his eyes and lips. It had been a severe effort to keep boisterously cheerful, and whenever he thought of the missing suitcase he had a shivering fit. Of all the damn fool things to let happen, that was the worst. True, it was Tony's, and he appeared to have forgotten that he had lent it to Julius, but the name Stafford and the Chelsea address had been on the label. If by some freak of chance the case had been washed to the riverbank and the label was still deci-pherable, there were bound to be inquiries, and the police were likely to hear about it.

He mixed himself a nightcap, smoked two cigarettes, and then got ready for bed.

When he woke up it was broad daylight, and he could hear movements about the house. He was filled with a curiously buoy-ant sense of security and satisfaction; nothing had happened dur-ing the night, and this lulled his fears and put him in a good humor, and he went along to the bathroom whistling.

Gillian, drinking morning tea with Tony, smiled as she heard the whistling.

"It looks as if we're off to an auspicious start. I suppose I'd better go down to the village this morning and try to get a daily woman. Anne and Julius will be anxious to get the studio ready, and you can put your study shipshape, darling. I want you to be able to start work by Monday."

She left him, obviously pleased and humming cheerfully. To complete the genial circle, Anne was downstairs preparing break-fast.

At the table, Julius was in great form, chiefly on the subject of the Vicar and, he presumed, the Vicar's wife. He made great fun of Agnes Blackshaw's sour visage and her harsh, obviously reluc-tant invitation to rest in the vicarage, and of Maude's red face and shuffling feet until at last Anne put in gently:

"I thought he was charming and really sincere when he said he

would like to help us. If the other woman was his wife, I feel
rather sorry for him." She frowned. "But it wasn't his wife—he
told me she was confined to her room."

"Poor soul," said Gillian. "I wonder if he can preach?"

"You'll have to let me know one day," said Julius, grinning.

"It wouldn't do you any harm to find out for yourself," said
Gillian, unruffled. "Here and now I declare that Tony and I are
going to church on Sunday mornings, whether he can preach or
not."

"I can never understand anyone taking that seriously," said
Julius. "No offense meant, Tony, but religion always strikes me
as being a sop to one's conscience."

"Well, we've all got something to learn," said Tony with a quiet
smile. He looked thoughtfully at Anne. "If the Vicar was so helpful, he might be able to suggest a suitable daily woman."

"I shouldn't get too friendly with the old boy," said Julius, "or
you'll have him wandering in when you're trying to write. And I
certainly don't want to have him wandering in when I'm trying
to compose."

"I think you two had better call on him," said Anne. "We created a poor impression yesterday, and you can put it right. If you
can fix up with a charwoman it will be splendid. I think Teddy
might come down sometime soon, and you can never be quite
sure that he won't drag one of his relations with him."

"I'm going to look round the garden," said Tony. "Coming,
sweet?"

"Yes, and we'll go next door afterward," said Gillian.

The garden had been kept in order until quite recently and
needed only clearing to put it right.

Suddenly they heard sounds from next door and a voice hailed
them from a window. They looked up, to see a man whom they
immediately assumed to be the Vicar. His gray hair was untidy;
his brown, leathery face, rather too thin, was creased in a smile,
and he attracted both of them immediately.

"Good morning! I've been telling my wife that you don't look
like the people I saw yesterday."

Tony laughed. "We're not. Are you the Vicar?"

"I am." said Castle.

"I wonder if we can come and see you for a few minutes?"

asked Tony. "We'd be very grateful for a word of advice and—"

"My dear sir, I'm delighted," declared Castle. "Come round at once—or take the shortcut through the hedge. That's what I usually do." He pointed to the gap near the house and disappeared.

When Gillian and Tony reached the front door of the vicarage he had brushed his hair, but his coat collar was rucked. He wore a loose-fitting tweed suit, and both Tony and Gillian—quick to observe little things—saw that the knees of his trousers were patched, that his cuffs and collar had been darned, and that he needed a haircut. The garden of the vicarage looked neat, but the house needed painting nearly as badly as Spindles.

"Come in," said Castle, offering his hand. The hall was furnished with heavy Victorian furniture and needed papering. He bustled ahead of them into a room on the right. "This is my study," he said. "You must forgive the mess—I'm the most untidy creature imaginable."

His rolltop desk was littered with papers, and the wastepaper basket was overflowing. It was a dingy room and looked at its worst because the morning sun was shining through a large bay window. There was an assortment of pipes on the desk, and he picked one up; the stem was bound with adhesive tape and the bowl had been burned down to little more than half its original size. There were several prints on the faded walls, and two shabby leather armchairs, one on each side of the littered fireplace.

"Do sit down," said Castle. "Don't think me curious, but are you living next door, too?"

"Yes," said Tony. He introduced himself and Gillian and explained the situation at Spindles. Then he asked about a daily woman, and Castle frowned.

"They're not easy to find," he said, "but I think I know one who might look after you, a Mrs. Kelly. But she does have a young son, not yet at school, and wherever she works she has to take him with her."

"That wouldn't matter a bit," said Gillian.

"Good! I'm going down to the village this morning, and I'll ask her. If she's willing, I'll tell her to come along and see you."

He asked few questions, and Gillian got the impression that

he was anxious not to appear too inquisitive. He told them about Mildred, and said that his sister-in-law lived with them, and that her husband had built Spindles.

"I knew it wasn't very old," said Tony, pleased.

"Only about twenty-five years," said Castle. "It was designed to look older, of course, but give me a new place every time— this vicarage is just an invention for collecting dirt."

"I've been intrigued by the name Spindles ever since I saw it," said Gillian. "Do you know why he chose it?"

"Yes," said Castle. "He was a Lancashire millowner, a self-made man and originally a cotton spinner. By spindles he made his fortune, and in Spindles he proposed to live. He was quite a good amateur artist. He—"

Castle broke off, so abruptly that Gillian was puzzled. There was a forced heartiness in his voice when he went on to say that after the house had been sold several people had rented it, but none had stayed for long. Then, perhaps in explanation of his change of tone, he added a little awkwardly, after glancing at the door to make sure that it was closed:

"My sister-in-law has a rather curious fixation about Spindles. Her husband lost his money, and she had to sell soon after his death, but ever since she has been rather—well, intolerant of people who have lived there. It's only fair to warn you. She may appear to be rude and cut you in the village. I do hope you understand."

"Perfectly," said Gillian.

"Of course," Tony murmured.

"You encourage me to say that she is tone-deaf and rather hostile to musical people," said Castle with a rather uneasy smile. "I heard——"

"Was Julius playing yesterday?" exclaimed Gillian.

"And he played very well," said Castle. "My wife and I were entranced. I do hope you understand that what I say goes only for my sister-in-law, and I do hope you won't take anything she may say or do too seriously."

"You're very thoughtful," said Tony. "Now we mustn't take up any more of your time.

"At least Tony won't worry her," said Gillian. "He works in his study all day, and——"

"Now, Gill!"

Gillian laughed. "We may as well get all our confessions over while we're at it, Mr. Castle. Tony is a novelist. So you will see that a very queer bunch of people have come to live next to you."

Castle lifted a protesting hand.

"Queer, Mrs. Abbott? Certainly not! I've often wanted to write a novel myself. As a matter of fact," he added, after a moment's hesitation, "I've nearly got one finished. I haven't dared to show it to anyone, not even my wife. I wonder if—" He broke off.

"I'm no expert," Tony said quickly, "but if you would care to let me have a look at it one day, I might be able to give you an opinion."

"I'd be very glad if you would." Castle turned to his desk and pulled open a drawer, rummaging inside. "Ah, here it is." He held up a thick bundle of papers covered with close handwriting. "I haven't even mentioned it to anyone else; I don't know why I should have started to talk about it to you."

Tony stood up and stretched out his hand. "Let me take it with me."

"That's very good of you," said Castle.

"Nonsense! I shall probably be a week or two," warned Tony. "If I bring it back too soon, it might mean I'll have a depressing opinion to give you."

"Then I'll expect it back tomorrow," said Castle gaily. "I don't seriously think anything will come of it. It must have been the fact that you're a professional author, Mr. Abbott, which made me lower my defenses. I don't mind being told that I've been writing nonsense by someone who should know, but an amateur opinion frightens me. I haven't licked it into the shape that I would like, but it's all there."

"Leave it with me," said Tony.

"I will, gladly." Castle went to the door with them, and as they strolled along the hall, he said, "Oh, there's one thing I should mention. I don't think it amounts to anything, but I think your boat was taken out last night."

"Our boat?" said Tony.

"Yes. My sister-in-law went to see a friend who lives in a cottage a little way along the river—and when she came back she told me that she thought she had seen someone in the boat, just pushing off. I had a look—you can see the landing stage from the garden here—and I saw that it was wet and that the oars were shipped differently. Probably some youngster decided to have a jaunt, as it was a fine night. Still, I thought you should know."

"Yes, thank you," said Tony. "We'll keep our eyes open."

· 6 ·

MRS. KELLY

As THEY LEFT the vicarage Tony said that he was short of tobacco and that it might be a good idea to see what kind of stock there was at the village shop. The village green was surrounded by attractive thatched cottages, and there was even a small duck pond. Beyond it was the river bridge.

He bought some tobacco and placed a regular order for his favorite brand, and they started back.

"It's a queer thing," he said abruptly.

"What is?" asked Gillian.

"The boat business," said Tony. "It would be different if it had been stolen, but it isn't likely that anyone would take it for a spree by night and return it—in the daytime would be more understandable. Anne and Julius said that they had been to the village, but it was quite late before they got back. Then they said they'd stumbled into the river. I noticed last night that the upper halves of their bodies were wet, and there were damp patches on Julius's trousers and Anne's skirt, but their shoes looked dry. If they'd stumbled into the river they would have been wet from the knees downward."

"I suppose you're right," said Gillian, a little troubled. "I didn't notice as much as you did, but I did think it funny that their shoes weren't wet. So you think they went out in the boat?"

"Well, it does look rather like it," said Tony. "There's another thing, too. I was thankful that Julius was in a good mood last night, but it was so good, for such a long time, that it wasn't natural."

"I noticed it," said Gillian. "I thought it might have been because he felt guilty at having left the place in such a mess, and not telling us that they'd decided to move yesterday. Tony, if you're right, why on earth did they want to take the boat out at night? Julius is fond of boating, but there wasn't even a moon. Even he isn't as eccentric as all that."

"No," admitted Tony. "I suppose it's foolish of us to worry about it; we'd better not say anything. If they want to tell us they'll need no prompting."

"Yes," said Gillian. They walked on in silence for a few minutes, and then she glanced at him quickly. He appeared to be in a brown study.

"I wonder if we have been wise," she said at last. "We're both very conscious of the need for—well, studying Julius' feelings. It isn't going to make a very healthy atmosphere."

"We came into it with our eyes open," said Tony. "When we've settled down we won't see much of him, remember. If he runs true to form, he'll go off from time to time for a week or two, and the atmosphere will be clear enough then. Anne on her own is a very different proposition. I wonder why she mothers him so much?" he added. "I think she's going to marry Teddy Barr because it will enable her to help Julius financially. Teddy isn't the man for her."

"I've often thought the same," said Gillian. "Anne is a different person when she isn't worrying about Julius. I think she really believes that he is brilliant, and is afraid that if he is left on his own he'll just run wild and never do any work. She's probably right, too."

"Yes. Well, we'll say nothing about it," said Tony.

When they got back to the house, Julius and Anne were in the studio. The piano was standing in one corner, highly polished, like a thoroughbred among cart horses. Julius was brushing down the walls, which were covered with dust and cobwebs, and Anne was sprinkling water over the floor to lay the dust. Gillian and Tony had just started on to the morning room when there was a knock on the back door. Gillian went to answer it, and found a short, fat woman, a headscarf tied under her chin, standing on the doorstep. She had a broad smile and a fat, red face, and she was breathing heavily.

"Morning, mum," she said. "The Vicar sent me, mum."

"Oh, for daily work?"

"That's right, mum. Kelly's me name, but don't make any mistake, I'm not Irish—Lunnon's my 'ome town, mum. I come 'ere because my boy Archibald needs the country air. I ain't afraid o' work, mum, that's a fact—good work for good wages, that's wot I always says." She looked at Gillian hopefully.

"What do you call good wages?" asked Gillian, restraining a laugh.

"Three and a tanner an hour for odd days, mum, three and threepence for reg'lar work every day eight to twelve except Sundays—come Sundays for special occasions, like, I wouldn't mind doing that, an' I wouldn't charge you any more."

"We certainly want someone every day," said Gillian, "and this week we could do with you for more than four hours a day. The place badly needs cleaning."

"Don't I know it!" declared Mrs. Kelly. "Took a look through the winders I did, as I come in. Crikey, it ain't 'arf a mess, I thought, I dunno what they was a doing of, coming before it was cleaned aht. Still, it's no business o' mine, I said to meself, and I ain't afraid of work. I'd 'ave to bring Archibald, mum."

"Is Archibald your son?"

"That's right, the one I told yer abaht—don't you get me wrong, mum, he ain't *ill*, it's just that he's a bit delicate, like the doctor says. You'd like me to start today, I suppose?"

"If you can," said Gillian.

"I dessay I can," said Mrs. Kelly. "S'arternoon—it's a bit late for this mornin' now. Like me to work mornin's an' arternoons this week, would you, mum?"

"Please," said Gillian.

"Yer got everything, I suppose?"

"If there's anything you need that we haven't got, you can get it from the village store," said Gillian.

Mrs. Kelly's blue eyes sparkled. "Then that's settled, mum," she said with satisfaction. "There's one thing I will say for meself,

I'm a worker and I don't talk like some people—I gets on wiv me work. I likes to do it me own way, mind—I don't mind *trying* your way, but I've found me own way's usually the best, mum."

"We'll have to give both ways a trial," said Gillian, struggling to keep a straight face.

"Well, you couldn't say fairer than that, mum, I will say," declared Mrs. Kelly with a beaming smile. "Two o'clock suit yer? I'll be along, then, wiv Archy. Good mornin', mum!"

"Good morning," said Gillian, "and thank you."

As soon as Mrs. Kelly had disappeared, Gillian started to laugh and was startled when Tony's laughter echoed hers. He had been in the hall, listening. Their laughter reached the couple upstairs, and Julius came to the landing to ask what the joke was about.

"You'll see," said Tony. "We've got a daily woman."

"Then that's finished me," declared Julius after a short pause. "I'm parched, and I'm off to have a look at the village pub."

Tony stopped smiling and exchanged glances with Gillian. The same thought occurred to them both; Julius would not have said that he was going to have a look at the village pub if he had been there the previous evening. By mutual assent, they made no comment, and they were busy in the study when Julius banged the front door and went along the drive. The sun caught his fair hair as he disappeared into the road. Anne volunteered to prepare lunch while Gillian scrubbed the morning-room floor. By lunchtime the room was thoroughly cleaned and did not look at all bad. From the window they could see the window of Mrs. Castle's room, not knowing that by sitting up she could see into the study-to-be.

Mrs. Kelly came promptly at two o'clock with a plastic apron tied about her ample waist and Archibald by her side. He was tall for his four years, and he looked delicate. There was something appealing about the child. He was quiet and reserved, and although Gillian knew better than to assume that his behavior on the first day was a criterion, she was surprised that he was the son of Mrs. Kelly. There was an air of refinement about him, too, until he opened his mouth, when he spoke in a slow country voice. Silent, he looked unusually intelligent; speaking with his slurred voice, he seemed almost simple. He came to the morning room, which in a few hours would become a study, while his mother received instructions from Gillian.

"All right, mum, I'll start on the 'all," said Mrs. Kelly. "Come along, Archibald. 'E'll be as good as gold," she confided. "I got 'im a comic."

"Does he read already?" asked Gillian, surprised.

"Read, mum? Bless yer 'eart, 'e don't do nuffink else. 'E's a bright boy, my Archibald, aren't you, Archy? Percoshious, that's 'im," declared Mrs. Kelly. "Archy! Don't stand there starin' at the gentleman—that's rude!"

"Odd little chap," said Tony as Archy went obediently to the hall, holding his comic. "Mr. Kelly must be a remarkable man."

Whatever her husband was like, Mrs. Kelly proved herself a remarkable woman. She worked with concentrated fury, and while she was working she hardly said a word. Between jobs she talked so much that Gillian could hardly keep pace with what she said. Archy stood watching Mrs. Kelly while she was talking, and sat in a corner while she was working. On the first afternoon they thought that the lad had not yet grown accustomed to strange faces, but he was the same during most of the next week, while a transformation was wrought at Spindles, thanks largely to Mrs. Kelly.

It needed twice as much furniture, of better quality than that which they had, to set off Spindles as it deserved, but when it was clean and fresh the general appearance was pleasing.

Tony spent most of his spare time in the garden. Toward the end of the week, when he was already making progress, he invited Archy to come and join him. The child skipped out by Tony's side, flung himself on the grass, and watched Tony steadily. After a while he got up and leaned against an oak tree in the middle of the lawn, as if he were tired of sitting. Tony made no comment, but suddenly Mrs. Kelly let out a bellow and came running from the house. Tony looked round in alarm.

"Archy! Archy! Come away from that tree!"

The child moved away hurriedly.

"Why, what's the matter with the tree?" asked Tony curiously.

Mrs. Kelly, breathless from her exertions, looked at the tree with a curious mixture of indignation and apprehension.

"Why, Mr. Abbott," she said. "*That's* the tree wot Mr. Blackshaw hung hisself on! Archy! Don't you never let me see you leanin' on *that* tree again!"

· 7 ·

A PARAGRAPH IN A NEWSPAPER

TONY GLANCED at the tree's spreading branches and imagined a body swinging from it. He smiled, chiefly to allay Mrs. Kelly's fears, and declared that it made no difference to the tree; good English oak had been used for far worse purposes than that. His remarks shocked the daily woman, who called Archy to her and, taking his hand, led him away from a man who could make a joke of such things. Tony smiled as they went off, the woman waddling—she really was incredibly fat—and the lad so thin and graceful by her side.

Then he caught sight of Anne.

Obviously she had been in the garden, but he had not seen her. Now she appeared from behind the beech hedge that separated the kitchen garden from the front. She was deathly pale. She looked toward him without appearing to see him, and he saw her glance toward the tree. Before she disappeared into the kitchen he saw that she was carrying a newspaper.

"Well, well," said Tony aloud, "I wouldn't have expected it to affect Anne like that."

He hardly knew what moved him to go after her. It was early afternoon—the last one on which Mrs. Kelly would come, for it was Friday, and from tomorrow onward she would work only in the mornings. Gillian was in the kitchen, cutting out a linen frock. As Tony went through the scullery Mrs. Kelly tossed her head, and he wondered a little uneasily whether what he had said would make her give notice. Gillian looked up.

"What on earth happened to Anne?"

"Did you see her?"

"She looked like a ghost."

"Well, I hope you don't feel the same about it," said Tony with a grimace. "Do you remember that Castle hemmed and hawed a bit the day we first saw him, when he was talking about Blackshaw?"

"Yes," said Gillian, puzzled.

"Mrs. Kelly has just told me that Blackshaw committed suicide," said Tony. "He hanged himself on the tree on the lawn. It must have happened seven or eight years ago, but Mrs. Kelly still fears an evil influence on her Archy."

"Well, that isn't surprising," said Gillian practically. "I've never known anyone so superstitious, and dread of violent death often goes with that. I'm surprised at Anne—did she hear it?"

"Yes."

"She's always been unaffected by death," said Gillian. "I think she is rather hard. I suppose the fact that he committed suicide explains it." She raised her hands. "It's a pity, but it would be absurd to let it affect us, wouldn't it?"

"That's my opinion," admitted Tony. "I——"

The kitchen door swung open and Anne appeared. She was a little less pale, but her eyes were very bright and she looked as if she had suffered a considerable shock. She did not appear to have heard what they had been saying, for she snapped, "Where's Julius?"

"I don't know," said Gillian.

"If yer wanter know where 'e is," said Mrs. Kelly, appearing from the scullery with Archy by her side, " 'e's in Mr. Abbott's den, that's where 'e is. I seed 'im through the winder." She gave Tony a smile that indicated that his flippancy was forgiven, and went through to the hall.

"Tell him I want to see him upstairs, will you?" Anne asked.

Gillian came out of the kitchen, quite bewildered by this turn of events. Tony, who suspected that Julius had run out of cigarettes and was raiding his supply, went to his den and opened the door.

Julius was sitting at Tony's desk with his feet up, reading a manuscript. He looked round with a broad grin.

"Tony, you scoundrel! The *magnum opus* of the Reverend Harry Castle, and you didn't tell me that you had it." He hooted with laughter. "Listen to this: 'It has always been—' "

He broke off as Tony moved round him and roughly pushed his feet off the desk; there were several scratches on the polished wood, made by Julius' heels. Had Julius taken some of his cigarettes it would not have worried Tony, but to find him at ease, prying into the papers on his desk, was a different matter. He went pale, and Gillian saw the portents of a coming storm.

"Take it easy!" protested Julius.

"Get out!" said Tony, keeping his voice steady.

"Damn it, man, it's a joke in a thousand. He—"

Tony said, "Julius, I do not want to hear your opinion of Castle's work or any work you find in this room. I don't want you to enter this room without permission. If I find you here again, I shall lock the door when I'm not working."

"Well, well," sneered Julius. "The worm turns. I'm damned if I like your attitude."

"That hardly affects the matter," said Tony.

In a few seconds, unless Julius went out, there would be a furious quarrel. Gillian's sympathies were all with Tony, but she knew that any interference might only make matters worse. There was a tense pause. Anne appeared in the doorway, speaking as if she had heard nothing of what had passed between them.

"Julius, I want to see you upstairs."

Julius got up with alacrity; obviously he had been looking for a chance to go without appearing to lose dignity. He scowled at Tony, ignored Gillian, and followed Anne. Tony stood staring after him. He took a cigarette from a box on the desk, without noticing that the box was half empty although he had filled it that morning.

"What a hateful brute he can be!" exclaimed Gillian.

"Silly of me to see red," said Tony with a rueful smile. "It was the fact that he meddled with the Vicar's stuff which really riled me—not to mention his feet on the desk." He examined the wood and rubbed the scratches with his forefinger. "Not too bad," he said. "Sorry, Gill."

"I was as mad as you were," said Gillian.

"You're not capable of it," said Tony, and there was a queer expression in his eyes. "I used to think I was a fairly even-tempered individual, but recently I've been on the point of losing my head several times."

It was true that he had felt bedeviled, thrown out of gear, since the crash; just as Gillian's nerves were edgy, so his temper was likely to break out with fierce, bewildering suddenness. He had raved about the insurance difficulties and afterward admitted that he felt as if he had suffered a brainstorm. He was back to normal now, except that he still remembered how he had felt; knew how close he had been to flinging himself bodily at Julius.

"Warn me when you see the danger signs," he said.

"It's the reaction," said Gillian, "and Julius isn't the easiest of persons to live with at any time. I don't think he'll come here again in a hurry," she added, and looked at the manuscript. "I'd forgotten that, darling—so you didn't have to send it back to the Vicar after a day or two?"

"There's some good stuff in it," said Tony. "I'm thinking of asking Snub to read it."

Gillian opened her eyes wide. "Is it as good as that?"

"It wants pruning," said Tony, "and the Vicar has one or two ideas which I think ought to be toned down, not necessarily because they're wrong, but because he spoils his effect by over-emphasis. It's in novel form, but it amounts to an attack on some forms of ecclesiastical control and on ritual and charlatanism inside the Church, and it gives a pretty grim insight on the conditions of some of the clergy trying to live on miserable stipends in barns of houses. As far as I can see, if it were published as it stands now—and I think Snub could find a publisher for it—it wouldn't be believed. It can stand quite a lot of toning down without losing effect. Of course, much depends on whether the conditions he describes still prevail widely. In any case, it isn't going to be popular with the Ecclesiastical Commissioners!" Tony was turning the pages of the manuscript thoughtfully. "Shorn of its wilder criticisms it's the story of a man who has one great desire, to see Christianity brought to the masses, a man who wants a practical religion based on the New Testament teachings. I think a lot of people could learn a great deal from it."

"Have you told him what you think?" asked Gillian.

"No, I thought I'd rather see what Snub says."

"But darling, you've had it for ages and the Vicar will be eating his heart out! Now I know why he's had that wistful look in his eyes whenever I've met him—he's been wanting to ask me about the book."

"I hadn't thought of that," said Tony. "I'm so used to waiting for a month or two before I get opinions on my own stuff. I'll go over and have a word with the old boy now, I think. I won't raise his hopes too much, in case I'm wrong."

"I think I'll come with you, if you'll wait ten minutes," said Gillian. "I promised to pop in and see Mrs. Castle."

"All right," said Tony.

He sat at his desk, pushed the manuscript away from him, and remembered the rage which had taken possession of him when he had come into the study. In such moments he felt capable of anything, and the moods frightened him. Anything in the way of injustice affected him deeply, but he knew there was nothing normal about the spasm through which he had passed. He had not mentioned his worry to Gillian, but he had talked to Snub Savory, a lifelong friend and literary agent of acknowledged acumen. Snub had agreed that a spell in the country would probably put him right, and had encouraged him to put his money into Spindles.

"Ready, darling?" called Gillian.

He smiled and stood up. Gillian's companionship was the most soothing thing in his life; she more than made up for hard knocks, for the rudeness of her brother, and the curious manner in which Anne sometimes behaved. Whenever he was alone with Gillian he felt content, and the knowledge that she was in the house was always satisfying. He felt quite normal as he walked with her along the drive. The gap in the fence had been repaired at Julius' insistence. They heard Castle digging in the back garden of the vicarage and decided to walk past the house and call him, but as they passed the front door it opened and Agnes Blackshaw called out:

"What do you want?"

Tony turned, and Gillian said quickly, "I think Mr. Castle is at the back, and——"

"You might have the common *courtesy* to knock," said Agnes sharply. "Just because you've bought Spindles that doesn't give you the right to wander at will over other people's property."

"Oh," said Tony, "I'm sorry."

"I don't know what manners are coming to," grumbled Agnes. "The language I hear from next door is a positive disgrace!" Tony and Gillian exchanged swift, surreptitious glances.

It was not their first encounter with Agnes Blackshaw, and they knew the "language" had come once or twice from Julius.

"I am sorry," Tony repeated.

"I should think so," said Agnes.

She flounced off down the garden path, and then a quiet voice called from a window:

"Is that Mr. Abbott?"

"Hallo, Mrs. Castle!" called Gillian.

"I'm so sorry about such rudeness," said Mrs. Castle, "you will never know how it vexes me. Please do forgive her."

"That's all right," called Tony and Gillian in unison.

Soon Castle came hurrying up, smiling. He had not heard Agnes' greeting, and insisted on taking Tony and Gillian upstairs. Mildred Castle said nothing more about the incident and was soon smiling as Tony went into detail about the antics of Mrs. Kelly and Archy. Neither Gillian nor Tony mentioned the story of the hanging.

"Well, Abbott," said Castle with a conspiratorial wink, "let us go downstairs and smoke a pipe in peace and leave the ladies to their chatter, eh?" He laughed and led the way downstairs.

In his study he picked up his old pipe and began to fill it from a jar which, Tony saw, was nearly empty.

"Try some of this," said Tony, handing the Vicar his pouch. "It's good stuff, although not everyone likes it."

"No, I—"

"Go on," said Tony, smiling.

"Well, if you insist." Castle filled his pipe carefully, talking about the weather, the village, and the fact that the lot of a country Vicar was often hard. He could not afford a man to do anything in the garden. How were they getting on in the garden next door? The man's anxiety not to broach the subject of his book was almost pathetic, and Tony fought against the temptation to plunge into it too enthusiastically. He veered the conversation round to his writing, and then said, as if it had only just occurred to him:

"Oh, that reminds me, Vicar—will you mind if I send your manuscript away for a second opinion?"

Castle's eyes lit up. "Have you read it?"

"Yes. I think it might have possibilities," said Tony. "My agent will gladly read it, and he's a better judge than I."

"My dear fellow, I'm delighted that you should think it's worth worrying about," said Castle. "When you didn't bring it back in a day or two I began to weave dreams, you know. Foolish of me, I know, but we old men are like that."

"Young men, too, in writing," said Tony. "I think it might find a publisher and have a small market." He was deliberately cautious. "Of course, these things take time, and I think that if my agent decides to handle it he'll probably suggest some revision. He'd give you guidance as to the kind of thing that would be needed, of course."

"I've been working on it for five years," said Castle, "and I won't mind another year or two if there's a gleam of hope." He drew on his pipe and added a little too ingenuously, "Supposing it did find a publisher, what—er—what are they likely to pay for it?"

"That would depend on sales," said Tony. "You would get a ten per cent royalty on the first few thousand copies—that's if it sold as many as that—and a higher percentage afterward. And you'd get a small advance on royalties when it was published."

"Oh," said Castle. "Fifteen pounds or something like that?"

Tony smiled. "If it had any luck at all you would get an advance of a hundred and fifty, I think."

"A hundred and fifty!" exclaimed Castle. "By George!" He seemed stunned. "I don't mind admitting, Abbott, that a hundred and fifty pounds would make a world of difference to me. There just isn't enough money to go round. Forgive me talking about my own troubles," he added, "I don't often let myself go, but—well, you can imagine how it is. My wife is an incalculable woman; her patience in these trying days is remarkable—I never cease thanking God for it. But her illness is an added expense. Every penny I can earn will be spent on her," Castle added quickly. "I sometimes *cannot* believe what Anderson tells me. You haven't met him, I suppose? He's not a local man but comes out from Milton once a fortnight."

"How long has she been ill?" asked Tony.

"For nearly eighteen months now," said Castle. "It's incurable, according to Anderson, and yet it's devilish hard to believe. It only seems yesterday that she was as active as you or your wife. I little thought when she had the seizure that she would never get up again. I don't think Anderson did, either."

"I'm terribly sorry," Tony said awkwardly.

"My dear fellow, we've grown used to it now, and she isn't in much pain, which is a blessing. I really can't think why I've unburdened myself to you," he added. "It's a relief to talk sometimes, you know. I find it difficult in Bray. The people are very kind indeed, but they're not church-minded. You were in church on Sunday morning. How would you like to preach to a congregation of about nine people every Sunday, morning and evening? Sometimes I blame the people for not being alive to the need for religion in their daily lives—and sometimes I blame the Church for its wrong approach to ordinary people, as you will have seen from my book. And sometimes, more often these days, I blame myself. I lack something, some spark which would help me draw people to church. The village élite are not very helpful, I'm afraid. There are only four families, and one of those goes into Milton Parish Church; they'd rather travel nine miles than come into the village. The others—well, I haven't seen them at church for years. I don't think they go anywhere. I was surprised, and I don't mind admitting it, when I saw you and your wife there. You were the talk of the village."

Tony smiled but was at a loss for words.

"What *was* wrong with my sermon on Sunday morning?" asked Castle abruptly. "Don't mince your words, Abbott."

Tony's eyes were somber for a moment, and then he smiled and settled back in his chair. "You've asked for it," he said.

"Yes, go on. You won't hurt my feelings."

"This is only an opinion," said Tony carefully. "You preached as if you had a full church—you *preached*, in other words, whereas what that little congregation wanted was a homely chat. Here you have a little community working from dawn to dusk, doing its duty by its neighbors, I imagine, and needing reassurance and encouragement rather than condemnation for their black deeds. You know, Vicar, the deeds of a little community like this probably aren't very black. If I hadn't read your book I might not have understood, but as I see it, you feel a great bitterness about the indifference of people to religion, and you show it too plainly. Bitterness freezes ordinary people, doesn't it? It erects barriers which they can't climb. Now *I'm* letting myself go, and without the slightest authority," he added a little awkwardly.

"I don't know about authority," said Castle, "I think it's sound common sense. I agree with you, but I've tried the homely chats. They don't work any more than the impassioned orations, and with the orations at least I feel that I'm putting my best into it. I think the people *like* me," he added. "They've come to accept me, but they don't come to church."

"Have you ever thought of trying stunts?" asked Tony.

"Stunts!"

Tony laughed. "Don't sound so shocked, I don't mean anything outrageous. Why not try to get a well-known singer to sing solos at a special afternoon service and give it good publicity beforehand? Then, perhaps, tea in the vicarage grounds, and——"

"I know, Abbott, I know, but I can't *afford* to dispense teas, and I haven't a single member of the congregation who will come up to scratch. We have a garden party once a year, and since my wife has been laid up that has been a failure. You've got to have a hostess for these things, and you've got to give a good spread. What point is there in inviting the villagers to tea when you have to go round a fortnight beforehand and beg contributions for the table?"

Tony said nothing.

"I don't mind humbling myself, but they just won't play. If my wife were well I would try to find another parish, but I can't move her, I'm anchored here for the rest of her life, and, please God, that will be a long time yet." He paused and then smiled. "Abbott, you've been a greater help than you know. I've wanted to get these things off my chest for a long time."

"Good!' said Tony. "And who knows, Gillian and I may be

able to help from time to time. What kind of a village is it for social occasions? Is there a cricket club?"

"No. There's quite a lot of work attached to that, you know, and I don't think there's a man in the village who would be prepared to accept the secretaryship."

"Yes, there is," said Tony. "I would, gladly. I used to play a bit. I can't get about quite so well now, but once a cricketer—" He laughed. "The posts of secretary and scorer are filled, you see. All you need are a dozen men and some gear."

"We've got some gear," said Castle, suddenly eager. "I keep it upstairs. It's a bit late for this season, and yet I know there are several clubs in the district that would like to get more fixtures. Shall I call a meeting and see how many we get? The pitch isn't bad—it's been cut and rolled each year. Abbott, you've put new life into me! When can you come to a meeting?"

"Anytime," promised Tony.

"Good fellow! Do you know, I think the spell over Spindles has gone at last—" He broke off, dismayed. "What a clumsy oaf I am!" he added angrily.

Tony smiled. "Don't worry; Mrs. Kelly told me all about the tree with the gruesome past."

"Well, I should have expected it," Castle said. "Does it worry you?"

"Not seriously," said Tony. "If it ever did, we could have the oak cut down, but at the moment I'm against that. It would give the place a sinister touch which it hasn't got at the moment. I don't know how the others feel, mind you; I can only speak for Gillian and myself."

"It's the sensible point of view," said Castle. "I haven't heard the piano much lately, by the way."

"The spark of genius isn't working," said Tony.

The conversation recalled the incident in his study, and he was glad when he heard Gillian coming downstairs. In the domestic regions someone was banging pots and pans about; it was not the daily, who came down the stairs after Gillian.

Gillian and Tony walked back to Spindles, and Tony did most of the talking. At the word "cricket" Gillian pricked up her ears. She had not known Tony when he had played before they were married, but occasional comments had proved how wrapped up he was in the game. If he could interest himself in a local club it would probably help him a great deal. She knew the effect of the sudden moods of rage, and although he had not discussed them freely with her, she had talked to Snub Savory and got a clear idea of what effect they had on Tony.

When they were out of earshot of the vicarage he went over the rest of his conversation with Castle, mentioning the Vicar's eagerness to know how much the book might earn.

"I hope I haven't raised his hopes unduly," said Tony. "I'll pack that manuscript up and get it off to Snub tonight." They were walking round the house to inspect his afternoon's work on the garden and were immediately beneath the attic window. Suddenly they heard Anne's voice, sharp and angry.

"Don't be a fool!"

"Be quiet!" said Julius. "Why on earth you have to go into a panic over a paragraph in a paper, I don't know!"

Gillian and Tony looked at each other in surprise, then shrugged their shoulders and went inside. Tony packed the manuscript and went to the post office, while Gillian prepared tea. She and Anne shared the catering, each having a day on duty.

The post office was combined with a little general store which sold everything, and Tony bought the last remaining copy of the *Milshire News,* a local paper. He was thinking that there would probably be room for some articles on the Bray Cricket Club, if it was restarted. Walking back along the road to Spindles, he glanced at the inside headlines, and eventually turned to the stop press. There were some racing results, some county cricket scores, and badly smudged at the foot of the column, the words:

BODY IN THE ORD

The body of a man which had obviously been in the water for some days was found by two boys bathing near the lido at noon today. The face was mutilated. The police, it is understood, suspect foul play.

· 8 ·

THE BODY

CHIEF INSPECTOR FOSTER had a good reputation in Milshire. It was a small county, and he was second in command to Superintendent Mellor at police headquarters. Mellor had been on sick leave for some weeks and was likely to be away for at least another month. The Chief Constable of the county, Colonel Harrington, had a soft spot for Foster and a deep respect and regard for the sick Superintendent. Police headquarters, in fact, was generally an efficient, well-oiled machine, in which the relationship between senior and junior officials was excellent. The only exception was the other inspector on the C.I.D. section, a man much older than Foster and one who resented the younger man's promotion.

Foster refused to allow himself to be seriously affected by Inspector Garth's hostility, however. At most it gave rise to a series of pinpricks which Foster, happily married and conscious of success in his chosen vocation, hardly felt. In fact, Garth gave him grounds for mild amusement, which he hid from everyone but his wife.

Now trouble might flare up in a more serious manner.

There was no doubt that the section of the town which included the public lido was in Garth's domain. It was south of the river, and Foster looked after everything to the north, which included all the villages on the way to Bray. That day, however, Garth had been giving evidence in the County Court, and had gone straight home to lunch; consequently only Foster had been on duty when the discovery of the body had been reported. The story came from a reporter on the *Milshire News*, a go-ahead young man who was friendly with Foster and had little time for Garth.

Foster hurried down to the lido, getting there soon after twelve o'clock.

The chief attendant of the lido, which was fairly empty at that time of day, had been called by two excited but frightened boys who had seen something floating in the river. He had telephoned the *Milshire News*, knowing that he would receive a useful payment if he gave them the story. When Foster arrived the body was on a bench in the attendant's dressing room, covered with a large bathing towel.

Lancing, the reporter, looked round at Foster with a grin.

"I'm glad it's you, Mark. As soon as Sam rang off, I called you."

"Good. Well, let's have a look at it."

Murder was unusual in Milshire, but bodies were found in the river half a dozen times a year. Usually they were suicides, but one glance at this bloated, disfigured face convinced Foster that there was no question of suicide here.

The body was naked. About the neck was a piece of cord, with scraps of sacking adhering to it. Another piece of cord, and more sacking, were tied about the ankles; the feet were inside the sacking. No clothes had been found.

"Looks to me as if someone tied him in a sack an' pushed him in," said Sam, the lido attendant.

"It might be that," said Foster. "Ugh!" The thing was nauseating. "How long has it been in the water, Sam?"

"About a week," said the attendant.

"No longer?"

"Not much," said Sam.

As he spoke the little dressing room was invaded by more police, including a photographer. When they had finished their work the body was removed to the mortuary at the police station. The other policemen had gone back by car, but Foster chose to walk. There were bowling greens and a recreation ground near the lido, between the river and the town itself. Milton was a small market town with about twenty-five thousand inhabitants, and although it was the county seat of Milshire, there were three larger towns within the borders, all of them seaside resorts, thirty or forty miles to the south.

"You aren't very talkative," said Lancing.

"No policeman is to the press," said Foster with a grin. "Don't overdo this, Lancing."

"I'll be good," said the reporter. "When can you tell me some more about it?"

"I'll see what I can do in the morning."

Lancing grimaced. "Nothing for a special edition?"

"I doubt it. For one thing," Foster went on, "I can see parochial trouble brewing over this. If the body had been brought out on this side of the river it would have been all right. You may have to deal with Garth."

"Not if I know you," said Lancing. "This is your murder."

"Don't be too sure about murder," said Foster.

"I couldn't be too sure," said Lancing. "A man doesn't tie himself up in a sack and throw himself in the river, you know that as well as I do. Is there anyone missing?"

"Not locally," said Foster. "I'll have a look at the records when I get inside."

There were several reports of missing men, information about whom was required by Scotland Yard or by the authorities of other counties. Foster, who had used a tape measure in the dressing room, shook his head when he saw the details; the body they had found was that of a man below medium height, five feet five, and broad in proportion. It was impossible to give a description of his face, and there was little else to go by. The police-surgeon, Dr. Anderson, would make a closer examination, and until then Foster would not waste time on speculation. He sent reports to Scotland Yard and neighboring counties, and then he telephoned Colonel Harrington. The Colonel, said a maid, was in Milton, and would probably be found at the White Horse, which was the one good hotel. Foster telephoned his wife to warn her that he might be late for lunch and went round to the hotel.

Harrington was in the dining room with two men unknown to Foster. The Colonel beckoned and Foster went over.

"There's a nasty business turned up, sir, and I'd like your advice as soon as possible."

"What kind of nasty business?" asked Harrington.

"Murder, I think," said Foster, "and not a lunchtime murder, either."

"Nonsense!" said Harrington. "Sit down and tell me all about it. Have you had lunch?"

"No, sir."

"Then join us," said Harrington. "My friends won't be put off by the grisly details." He introduced his companions, and then Foster began his report, while the Chief Constable listened attentively.

Harrington was a tall, leathery man, with a whippetlike face, bright grey eyes, and a caustic tongue. Those who knew him well ignored it. He believed in letting his men get on with their work and interfered as little as possible. In spite of his sharp tongue and his reputation as a martinet, he contributed a great deal to the unity which reigned at headquarters.

"Well, you haven't got much to go on," he said.

"That's my own opinion," said Foster with a grimace. "Identification won't be easy. The body might have been put into the river anywhere between the lido and Grasling. It isn't likely to have been put in north of Grasling Lock, nor very near the lido, or it would have been seen before."

"It could have been put in the Mille," said Harrington.

"Yes, possibly. It looks as if it had been tied up in a sack and weighted to make it sink. The ends near the cord are badly worn. I think the body wanted to float and the weights wanted to stay on the riverbed, so they parted company."

Harrington glanced at his friends. "A police inspector with a pretty wit," he said, and the others laughed. "Yes, Foster, go on."

"The sack was probably badly worn in places," said Foster. "The lido attendant thinks the body had been in the water for a week. He isn't unused to these things, and I've never known him to be more than three or four days off," he added. "I imagine that the sacking held for several days before it finally tore away, so the body probably hasn't been floating for more than a day or two."

"How long would it take to come down from Grasling Lock?" asked Harrington.

"Well, we've had a lot of rain and the current's running fast," said Foster. "A day would probably be enough. I don't know that we're going to get a lot of information from what I've been saying, sir, but something might crop up. Shall I carry on?"

"Of course, man."

"It was Inspector Garth's side of the river," said Foster.

Harrington stared. "What difference does that make? It might have been put in on your side. Garth has plenty to do already," he added. "He'll be at court this afternoon and tomorrow morning, anyhow. I'll have a word with him. You go ahead and find out what you can."

"Thank you, sir." Foster did not try to hide his pleasure. "I'm not very optimistic, but the sooner we spread our net the more chance we have of catching something quickly. I've asked the Yard and other county headquarters for information."

Harrington laughed. "You'll do! I'll have a word with them on the telephone this afternoon. You've nothing at all to go on, you say?"

"Nothing," said Foster, "but I'm expecting to be busy as soon as the *News* comes out. Mysterious noises on the river will be reported by the dozen if I'm not mistaken."

He left the White Horse, hurried to his own house, which was not far away, gave his wife a résumé of what had happened, and went to Dr. Anderson's house.

Dr. Anderson was a character admired in Milton and the surrounding districts. The truth was that he inspired confidence in all his patients and that he readily sought other opinions when there was the slightest doubt of his diagnosis. He was one of a partnership of four doctors, each of whom specialized in some way or other. Anderson, with his amiable laugh, admitted that he was the sawbones. He was a fattish man of sixty, with luxuriant white hair which gave him a venerable appearance. He dressed immaculately, and that was a match for Foster. He had a rubicund face, round and weather-beaten, and his large mustache still had streaks of black.

"Now what's the matter?" he demanded as Foster sat in the surgery armchair.

"Urgent work for you," said Foster, and told him.

Anderson frowned. "Can it wait until after four o'clock?"

"I'd rather it didn't," said Foster. "I want to try to get the approximate time of death and then set inquiries going along the river."

"I'll get someone to take my afternoon round for me," said Anderson, "and I'll be with you just after three o'clock."

The police-surgeon was not optimistic when he reached the morgue and went in with Foster and two sergeants. Foster's regular aide was on leave but would be back on the following Monday; Foster hoped that things would not really get moving until then, for it was difficult to change sergeants in the middle of investigations. Feelings were apt to be hurt and continuity disturbed.

No one in his senses, Anderson said, would try to guess when the man had died. It might be possible to judge about how long the body had been in the water, but there was no doubt of the cause of death.

"Whoever used that knife must have gone mad," said Foster. "Look at the slashes over the face, neck, and shoulders."

"Or he could be a cold-blooded customer intent on preventing recognition," said Anderson.

"Possibly. If the wounds were caused after death, though, why are there so many on the shoulders and the side of the neck? It looks to me as if he was attacked with the knife by a man who completely lost his head."

"I am not a believer in brainstorms," said Anderson. "Well, I'll do what I can. You're after marks for identification chiefly, I suppose? Seriously," he added, when he saw Foster's expression, "you mustn't expect to know what day he died, even within a day or two—not from the body, at all events." He frowned as he continued his examination. "If it was an attempt to conceal his identity, it was badly done. See these short little fingers? That'll be a great help. H'm," he went on, casting a professional eye over the bloated corpse. "Operation in the neck, probably for a cyst or a cancerous growth. It's quite a commonplace—I don't suppose that will tell us much, except that it could've showed above his collar. No marks on the body that I can see; let's turn him over."

"Sharp!" called Foster to a sergeant.

He watched the doctor and Sharp raise the body and turn it so that it lay face downward. Everyone in the room stared at the man's back. There was no doubt that it had been cruelly lacerated. There were even ridges where the flesh had healed.

"That's a nasty piece of work," said Anderson.

"A flogging," said Foster.

"Something worse than a flogging," said Anderson. "Something more brutal than a cat-o'-nine-tails was used, too. A *very* nasty business," he repeated.

"How long ago was that done?" asked Foster.

"There's no way of telling. It could have been at any time."

"Have you ever seen anything like it before?" asked Foster. He stared at the dead man's back; it was easy to imagine the state of it after the beating up.

"Not actually on a body," said Anderson. "I saw some photographs which came from Germany and were taken after men had been flogged, as they called it, in concentration camps. It is the same kind of thing. Those marks were made by a beating up of calculated savagery. It just isn't conceivable that he received such treatment in this country."

"Oh," said Foster heavily.

"Why that grunt?"

"If he's a foreigner it's going to make it ten times more difficult," said Foster. "There's been a constant traffic to and from the Continent, and we no longer keep a close watch on aliens, provided their passports are all right. You haven't given me a lot of encouragement yet," he added with a grimace.

"If I were you I'd ask Harrington to consult the Yard," said Anderson.

Foster smiled. "He is doing so. That doesn't mean I wouldn't like to have identified the body by the time they arrive, or find out where he was put into the river. There might be something on the rest of the sack," he added hopefully. "I've got a river patrol looking for it. If it comes to a point, I shall ask for some dredging to be done. I wonder where his clothes are? We won't get much help at all until we know who he is and when he died," he continued with a touch of irritation. "It would turn out like this, wouldn't it?"

"Turn it over to Garth," said Anderson, laughing.

"That's another headache brewing," said Foster. "How long will you be here?"

"Several hours, as presumably you want to make sure that he died from the wounds and not from drowning," said Anderson, "and I may as well do a thorough job of the post mortem while I'm at it. You go away and play. I don't need you. You might tell them to open a window," he added, and made a wry face.

He had finished soon after five o'clock and went to Foster's office to report. Death had been caused by the knife wounds; the primary cause was the severed carotid artery, and death had been almost instantaneous. The body had, he estimated, been in the water a little over a week. He could give Foster no further definite information.

The Chief Inspector sat at his desk and studied the reports he had already received. They could hardly be less encouraging.

Then Garth came in.

The older Inspector was a handsome man, much larger than Foster, with a face marred by a perpetual frown and eyebrows which he allowed to grow bushy, giving him a forbidding appearance. He was dark, with an olive complexion and very fine brown eyes. He went to his desk in the office he shared with Foster, and after looking through some papers, said:

"I see you're not above poaching, Foster."

"Don't be an ass!" Foster said mildly. "I was on the spot and you weren't. I reminded Harrington that——"

"Knowing quite well that he would prefer you to handle the matter," said Garth. "It is a great asset to have better table manners and a public school education, as I well know."

"Come off it, old chap. It's simply that I was on the spot. That's all there is to it."

Garth's mouth closed like a trap, and the two men worked in an uneasy silence for half an hour. Garth was the first to leave the office. Foster sat back, with the end of his pencil between his teeth, and then his eyes brightened. Although relations between him and Garth were often strained, his wife and Mrs. Garth were on good terms. It would probably help things if Mrs. Garth were warned what to expect. Garth lived several miles out of Milton, and there was time to set the wheels of peacemaking going. He called his home and was relieved when his youngest daughter, aged four answered him. She was always with her mother.

"Listen, Laura," he said when he had finished talking to the child. "Garth has got a sore head over this business, like the ass he is. Have a word with Mrs. Garth, will you, and warn her to be prepared for a sermon on the evil deeds of his fellow inspector?"

"All right, Mark— No, don't *shout*, Wanda—sorry, Mark, she wants to say good-bye. What time will you be home?" Laura asked.

"Unless something turns up, about seven," said Foster. "If I'm not there by half-past, you carry on. 'Bye—good-bye, Wanda."

He was smiling when he replaced the receiver, but the smile soon faded.

There was a curiously depressing influence exerted by the discovery of the dead man. That lacerated back, the possibility that Anderson was right and that the man had been tortured, added to it.

The telephone rang as Foster was about to leave the office, and he was surprised to hear Anderson.

"I didn't tell you before," said Anderson. "I know you of old, Foster, and I wanted to be quite sure of my ground. I took Lumley round to see the *corpus.*"

"Lumley—oh, the dentist. Yes?"

"He agreed with the impression I got of the state of the jaws," said Anderson. "His teeth were removed by an amateur. Proper dental instruments weren't used."

"Oh," said Foster heavily. "You're backing your theory hard, aren't you?"

"Well, people in concentration camps were beaten up and their teeth were pulled with pliers and pincers," said Anderson. "You would be quite safe in putting it up as a possibility. You needn't give me any credit; let the Yard think you worked the miracle all by yourself."

Foster replaced the receiver. Facts were facts, and reluctance to accept them was a fault in a policeman. The man had been tortured; there was no reason to assume that it had happened in Germany, but it had happened somewhere.

The telephone bell rang as he was going out of the office. It was twenty minutes to seven. He was looking forward to talking to Laura, whose calm common sense was invaluable, and he hoped this caller would not detain him for long.

"P. C. Grimes of Riversmeet would like to speak to you, sir," said the operator.

"Put him through," said Foster.

Riversmeet was a little hamlet where the Mille ran into the Ord, about four miles out of Milton. Grimes was a reliable man, and there was little doubt that this was the first story to come in response to his telephoned instruction to all village police-men; the flood of volunteered information from the general pub-lic would not start until the next morning.

"Hallo, Grimes," he said. "What have you got for me?"

"Some sacking floating on the river surface, sir," said Grimes promptly. "It's anchored to summat, sir—I don't know what. I thought you would like to come along and see it yourself."

"I would," said Foster. "Well done, Grimes."

He replaced the receiver and then lifted it again and was put through to the sergeant's office. He would have to take a man out with him, and he arranged for Sergeant Sharp to join him outside the police station.

We might get something fairly quickly after all, mused Foster as he went for his car.

· 9 ·

THE RIVERSIDE BUNGALOW

RIVERSMEET WAS a charming spot, one of the loveliest in Milshire, the clear shallow stream of the Mille flowing gently between its rush-lined banks into the deeper, more opaque waters of the Ord. Near the confluence was a little hamlet with old, thatched cot-tages resplendent in new cream color wash, and only one mod-ern building within sight, a white, creeper-clad bungalow, with a red-tiled roof and a well-tended garden. The bungalow was a café, but the sign hanging above the rustic woodwork was painted attractively and fitted into the general scheme. Beyond the rivers, on either side, was rising land, some fields already high with green corn, others newly ploughed. In the distance tractors were work-ing, and from a field near the humpbacked bridge that spanned the Ord came the smell of new-mown hay.

A crowd was beginning to gather on the bank of the Ord, a

hundred yards or so from the point where the two rivers met. Mrs. Kelly was there, and two or three middle-aged couples also watched with interest as Sergeant Sharp emerged from the riverside bungalow with a mackintosh over his swimming trunks.

Foster and P. C. Grimes, a burly man of few words, stared at a piece of sacking floating on the water. Grimes said that it had been there for two days—several people had noticed it. A boy bathing in the river had tried to move it, but it was tied to something on the riverbed. Grimes himself had remembered it when the request had come through, had cycled over to make sure it was still there, and telephoned Foster from the bungalow, the owner of which was watching from his garden.

Foster drew on a pair of waders that the efficient Grimes had borrowed, and was ready when Sharp came up. Grimes also wore waders. Sharp took off his coat and plunged into the river, which was flowing fairly fast because of a recent spell of rain. The sacking was about ten feet from the river's edge. Foster waded in until he was knee-deep, halfway between the bank and the sack. Sharp reached the sacking and stood upright; he was up to his waist in water. He took the sacking carefully in one hand and tugged gently. After a pause, he called:

"It's fast, all right, sir."

"Can you see what's holding it?" asked Foster.

"I'll try, sir," said Sharp.

A ragged cheer rose as he dived. His feet waved in the air for a few seconds, and then disappeared. He seemed to be under for a long time, and Foster was getting agitated, but suddenly the water swirled and he reappeared, gasping, holding something aloft. It was a brick. A louder cheer greeted him.

"Coming, sir," he called, tossing the brick past Foster to the bank. "Shall I get them all, sir?"

"Yes, but take a breather. How many are there?"

"About a dozen, I'd say. It looks as if they're in the bottom of a sack, sir."

"The sack is as important as the bricks," said Foster. "Look here, Sharp, you'd better have some help. I— What was that?"

A splash not far away was followed by a second and a third, and suddenly he saw the lithe figures of youths, little more than boys, swimming rapidly from the opposite bank. The boys trod

water around Sharp, and he took the unexpected interruption
good-humoredly.

"All right, try your luck," he said, "but don't go and drown
yourselves, and leave the last brick to me, understand? If you let
that bit of sacking float away you'll all come up before the magis-
trates."

One after the other the boys went down, brought up the bricks,
and tossed them to the bank. Suddenly something floated to the
surface—another piece of sacking. Sharp roared and went after
it, but one of the boys caught it and swam with it toward Foster,
holding it up in front of him.

"Thanks very much," said Foster. "Take it to the bank for me,
will you?" He waited for Sharp to come out. "They did save you
a lot of trouble, Sergeant. It's been good work all round."

Mollified, Sharp hurried to the bungalow. Grimes and Foster
examined the bricks, which, as far as Foster could see, were ordinary yellow ones, of good quality. Grimes took the pieces of
sacking and spread them on the grass. Foster had brought a piece
from the morgue, and a comparison proved beyond all doubt that
it was the same material; it even fitted to the torn parts taken
from the river.

"Satisfied, sir?" asked Grimes.

"I'm very satisfied indeed," said Foster, "although I wish we'd
found the clothes. There isn't much doubt that the body was
dropped in here. Have you made any enquiries?"

"I thought I would leave that to you, sir," said Grimes.

"Good. The bungalow is the nearest place, isn't it?"

"Yes," said Grimes. "I've asked them to put a room at your disposal, sir, and there'll be some supper, if you'd like it." Foster
nodded approvingly.

Symes, the owner of the bungalow café at Riversmeet, was a
one-legged, powerful man. He ran the café with the help of a
manageress and two girls. Foster knew that it had a good reputation for food and service. A small sitting room had obviously
been made tidy for him, and a gateleg table with ink, paper, and
blotting paper was in the middle of the room. Foster looked at it
all appreciatively, and Symes asked him whether he would have
supper.

"Yes, please," said Foster.

"Then it won't be ten minutes, Inspector."

"Thanks. Well, you've a fair idea of what I'm after, I suppose?"

Symes smiled. He was a big, slow-speaking man, running to fat, and he used a crutch. There were noticeable scars on his cheeks and forehead.

"I'd rather you told me," he said.

"You've heard about the body we found drifting on the river," said Foster, and when Symes nodded, went on: "It was in a sack, and the sack was almost certainly dumped in the Ord about the spot where we found the bricks. I think it was put there a little over a week ago. It would almost certainly have been by night. You live nearest to the spot; have you any recollection of hearing a boat within the past ten days?"

"It isn't a thing I could be certain about," said Symes. "There wasn't a moon ten days ago, and there have been several storms which would cover any noise."

"That's true," said Foster, "and I don't want you to invent anything, but if you can recollect the slightest thing out of the ordinary and tell me on what night it happened, I would be grateful." He thought Symes had something to report but was making sure that he was not called upon to swear it on oath.

"Well," said Symes, "there was a little thing, exactly ten days ago, Inspector. It was the night that you'd been in to see P. C. Grimes—I remember him telling me."

"Oh," said Foster. "What was it?"

"I'd had some friends in from Milton," said Symes, "and they stayed for supper and left a couple of hours afterward—about half-past ten. It might have been earlier, but it was well after dark, I do know that."

"Yes," said Foster.

"When I opened the door to let my friends out," said Symes, "I *thought* I heard a boat on the river, and I *thought* I heard whispered voices. I couldn't be sure. Voices and sounds travel clearly over the water especially if the wind is blowing across the Mille, as it was that night."

"I can check up with the meteorological people with your information to give them a good start," said Foster.

Before Symes went on, the manageress bustled in with a tray of attractively prepared food: sausages, bacon, fried tomatoes, a fried egg, and a heap of crisp, golden-brown chipped potatoes in another dish.

"Why, this is magnificent!" exclaimed Foster.

"We do our best," said Symes, with a gratified smile.

Grimes was standing by the door, and it opened suddenly to admit Sharp, equipped with notebook and pencil.

"Grimes," Foster said, "give Sergeant Sharp a résumé of what Mr. Symes has told me, will you?"

He began his meal, taking the opportunity to think deeply and recall everything that had happened on his tour of the village police stations. The one thing which stood out in his mind was his interview with the Staffords at Spindles. He had noticed that there was an atmosphere of strain in the house, but he had put it down to annoyance on the part of the Staffords at receiving a caller when the house was in such a mess. Julius Stafford's rudeness he had dismissed as being the result of too much to drink, but his sister had struck him as both attractive and intelligent. While waiting for her brother, he had amused himself trying to draw her out. He had seen the many changes in her expression, and now that he thought back he wondered if there had been any unusual significance in her manner. There was a risk of imagining too much, of course, and at the time he had seen nothing to make him suspicious.

"Well, now," he said at last. "You think you heard voices and a boat. Did you mention it to anyone?"

"Yes, to my friends," said Symes. "We all looked toward the river, but we couldn't see anything—that is, I couldn't be sure we did. We thought we saw a dark shadow on the water, but it might have been imagination. There wasn't much sound, that's a fact. The voices could have come from the opposite bank, too, and I think that sack was dropped overboard from a boat."

"So do I," said Foster. "Did your manageress think she heard it?"

"She was with me at the time," said Symes. "We stood waiting for five minutes after our friends had gone, but we didn't see anything for certain. There *might* have been someone there."

"I see," said Foster.

"It's rather a lonely spot here," said Symes slowly, "and there

were some burglaries a few months back. Grimes always thought
the thieves came from the river, sir. Do you remember them?"

"Yes. We never caught the beggars," said Foster.

"They stopped working when you got busy," said Symes with
a faint smile. "Well, I thought they might have started again, and
I kept looking out of the window and opening the door, to make
sure that they didn't come into the garden. I suppose it was
about half an hour later, but it might have been a bit less, when
I *thought* I heard a boat pulling upstream."

"Up the Mille?"

"Yes," said Symes. "I stood at the door watching. It was pretty
dark, but clearer than it had been earlier. I think it's certain that
there was a boat then, but it needn't have been the same one, sir."

"No. Do you often notice boats at night?"

"Not very often. You get them on moonlight nights, of course,
and sometimes couples take a boat out after dark if they know
the river. None of the boathouse men will let a boat go after
dark unless the people *do* know the river," said Symes. "You'll be
able to check up on that, sir, won't you?"

"Yes," said Foster smiling. "You're very careful."

"A man's life might depend on what I say, sir," Symes reminded
him.

"You're also wise," said Foster. "I wish everyone told a story as
well as you do, Symes. Well now—did you discuss this with anyone apart from your friends?"

"No," said Symes. "I didn't forget it, but no one else mentioned
it, and so I didn't see that there was any point in starting a rumor
that the thieves were busy again."

"Good!" Foster looked at Grimes. "That's a job for you, Grimes.
I think you'd better start now and ask everyone in Riversmeet if
they heard anything that night. There aren't any buildings on the
other side of the river, are there?"

"There's old Martin's cottage," said Grimes.

"A cottage—oh, yes, in the hollow; you can't see it from the
river. He isn't likely to have noticed anything; he couldn't see, and
he's pretty deaf, isn't he?"

"Yes," said Grimes, "but he's often at the riverbank o' nights. He
stays there at the end of his garden and smokes his pipe. I think

we ought to have a word with him, sir. If you don't mind my saying so, sir," went on Grimes stolidly, "it wouldn't be a bad idea if you and the sergeant saw old Martin. He hasn't been very friendly towards me lately—not since I had him up for poaching last autumn. You'd probably get more out of him than I would. I shouldn't take much notice of his deafness—he's not as deaf as all that."

Foster laughed. "All right, I'll tackle him. Let me see—" He looked first in his diary, then enquiringly at Symes—"ten days ago. That would be May 12?"

Symes nodded.

"Right," said Foster. He stood up. "Sharp, Sergeant Willet is outside, isn't he?"

"Yes, sir," said Sharp.

"Tell him to take the bricks that are still by the river and call on all the builders in Milton and ask if they can identify them. I want to know where they were made and in what houses they've been used in this district for the last few years."

Sharp went to speak to Willet, while Foster telephoned the station and asked them to check on the direction of the wind on the evening of May 12, between ten and eleven o'clock. Five minutes later the two men were setting off to see old Martin.

"Well, Sharp," said Foster as they began to walk over the bridge toward the opposite bank. "Do you know this man Martin?"

"I've come across him," said Sharp without a smile. "A surly old customer who's got his knife into Grimes."

"Grimes is a bit of a tartar, is he?" asked Foster.

"I wouldn't say that," said Sharp. "He's let Martin have the benefit of the doubt for a long time. Martin's a poacher, all right, and it was time he was stopped."

"I see," said Foster.

The door of the little cottage in the hollow was open, and the firelight was flickering inside. It was getting dark, and the sky in the west was a glorious golden red with the setting sun catching little fluffy lines of clouds. The light spread over the whole countryside, softening the hedges and the trees; it even made the dilapidated cottage with its huddle of outbuildings look picturesque. Old Martin kept his garden well; there were vegetables, sturdy and healthy looking, at the front and sides. A little bed of wallflowers and forget-me-nots made a splash of color beneath one window.

There was no movement as they reached the door, and Foster called out, "Is anyone at home?"

"He's seen us, all right," said Sharp.

There was no response, and Foster called again. At last an old man came from the kitchen at the back of the cottage. He was short and bent, but his weather-beaten face and clear blue eyes had a look of health, and there was a hint of strength in his wiry body.

"What do 'ee want?" he asked in a querulous voice.

"I am Chief Inspector Foster," began Foster.

"I know 'ee," said Martin. "What do 'ee want?"

The hostility in his voice and expression made Foster thoughtful. It might be due to Martin's quarrel with Grimes, but long experience of questioning witnesses had taught Foster that often little guilty secrets worried them and made them hostile.

He stepped inside. The small room was crowded with oddments of furniture.

" 'Ee've no right to come in wi'out bein' asked," said Martin angrily.

"Now, come, Mr. Martin," said Foster with a broad smile. "We haven't come to make trouble for you; we only want a little information." He stepped across the room and sat in an old saddleback chair. "I'm told you have a very good memory," he went on.

"It's none so bad," agreed Martin grudgingly.

"Do you remember the evening of May 12?" asked Foster.

"Oh, *dates*," said Martin scornfully. "I don't hold wi' *dates*. What night o' the moon were it?"

From the glint in the old man's eyes, Foster thought that Martin considered he had scored a triumph. When Foster had looked at his diary, however, he had noted the period of the moon; it had been three days past the last quarter and had risen at about half-past four in the morning.

"It was nearly down," he said. "The last quarter was May 9."

"Oh, aye," said Martin, nonplussed. Then: "Well, what about it, mister?"

"Do you remember what you did that night?"

"Maybe I do, maybe I don't," said Martin.

Foster smothered a sigh of annoyance. "It was a Wednesday night," he said, "a fine night, with the wind blowing across the river towards the café bungalow."

"Oh, *that night!*" said Martin with sudden eagerness. "It were the night when there was someone on the river. Late it were. I was watching, standing by my gate. I recalls it clear. Two people was in the boat, and it come downstream."

"The Mille?"

"From the Mille to the Ord, and back again," said Martin, who now appeared convinced that his own petty offenses were not the subject of the inquiry, and had livened up considerably. "Two there were—I seed 'em."

"Men?" asked Foster quickly.

"Might've been, and then again they might'nt. Boat hung about for half an hour, mebbe more, that's what I remember, an' then off they went again."

"Do you know what time it was?" asked Foster.

"Half past ten it were when I first saw them," said Martin. "Or as near as makes no matter."

"You've been a great help," said Foster warmly. "Do you often see anyone on the river at that time of night?"

" 'Ee be thinkin' o' them thievin' varmints," said Martin with a cackle. "Earlier, they always was. If Grimes had done what I told 'im an' watched about seven o'clock, mebbe you wouldn't have lost them thieves, mister. I told 'im often enough; he wouldn't listen to me. He's nowt but——"

"We'll talk about that another time, shall we?" said Foster, standing up. He walked across the room.

Until that moment Martin had been quite happy, his fear all gone. Sharp had stood by the door without speaking, writing occasionally, a fact that had not worried the old man. Now, however, Martin stiffened. He even put out a hand as if to stop Foster, and then he stood watching with his eyes rounded.

In front of the window was a sofa, and behind the sofa was a fiber suitcase.

· 10 ·

INSPECTOR FOSTER PAYS A VISIT

FOSTER WAS SILENT as he drove back to Milton with Sharp, dropped the sergeant at the station, and then drove to the Chief Constable's house on the outskirts of the town. It was on a hill, one of many houses built among trees. When he pulled up outside Harrington's front door he stopped the engine and sat for a moment looking over the town. The neon lighting of the cinema cast a red glow over the center of the town, and he could just see his own house, where Laura would be listening to a symphony concert while knitting or sewing for the children. Four-year-old Wanda and seven-year-old Iris would be asleep in the nursery. Kathleen, aged ten, was probably reading in the little room she had to herself; she was allowed to read until nine o'clock, when Laura would go up and say good night and turn out the light.

Foster gave an involuntary sigh; there were times when he felt almost sad because there were three girls and no boy. Laura was thirty-eight and had not had an easy time with Wanda; was it fair to hope?

"This won't do!" he exclaimed aloud, and hurried to the Chief Constable's door.

He had telephoned for the appointment from the bungalow and was expected. A maid showed him to Harrington's study, a pleasant and homely room, with a store of books which Foster greatly envied. There was a single table lamp, by the light of which Harrington had been reading; a book was open by his side. A wood fire gave the room a cheerful look; it was chilly for late May, and Harrington, who had spent most of his life in India, could not get used to cold out of season. He wore a smoking jacket over dinner clothes, and his feet were in pumps. The firelight shone on cut-glass decanters, glasses, and a syphon of soda by his side.

"Hallo, Foster, what will you have?" The Chief Constable's hands hovered hospitably over the decanters. "Whisky, brandy, or—"

"A tot of whisky will suit me nicely, sir, thanks." Foster sat down in a chair already pulled up for him, and accepted the glass.

"You've got some good news for me, I gather?" said Harrington, genially.

"I know where the body was dropped into the Ord," said Foster, "and there are one or two things of interest, sir—I'm not dissatisfied with the night's work." He sat back and told his story. Harrington nodded from time to time and interrupted with pertinent questions.

"I took Grimes's advice—incidentally, sir, I think Grimes should be in the running for promotion; he is a keen man and he's very thorough—and saw Martin myself. He confirms the story of people on the river that night, but he says that he didn't hear anything drop into the water. I doubt whether he's telling the truth, because I think he picked something up from the river bank and failed to report it. A suitcase." His eyes were bright, and it was obvious that he still had something up his sleeve. "I found it behind a sofa in Martin's parlor. First he denied having taken it out of the river at all, and then he said that he took it out months ago, but I don't believe him. The case had floated to the riverbank from the boat, I think; there were watermarks on it outside, but it looked all right inside. It's an ordinary fiber suitcase. A label had obviously been torn off it, and Martin denies having done it. However, there was something else." He put his hand to his waistcoat pocket. "In the first place the case hadn't been dusted out; there was brick dust and a small chipping of brick lodged in the lining. The chipping is of yellow brick, probably the same kind as the bricks which were used to weight the body."

"Hmm," said Harrington. "You're building it up well, Foster. You think the body was taken in the boat, and the bricks from the case were transferred to the sack before it was thrown overboard."

"That's right, sir. And then the case went over the side. Old Martin picked it up, thought he might make a bit on it—he could sell it on the market in Milton—and held on to make sure that no one claimed it. It isn't the kind of case one could trace easily," he added, "but——"

Harrington laughed. "You look positively smug, man."

"I suppose I feel it," said Foster. He held a little metal strip toward his chief. "That was fastened to the top of the inside of the case. It's one of the metal strips which you can punch out on machines at railway stations. It's a bit rusty, but the name is clear enough."

"'Abbott,'" said Harrington, reading. "'A. J. Abbott,' but there's no address."

"That isn't going to give us much trouble, sir; at least, I don't think it is. A man named Anthony John Abbott is living at Spindles—old Blackshaw's place."

"Abbott?" repeated Harrington in surprise. "Didn't you tell me that some people named Stafford were there? You told me an amusing story of how you'd caught them before they had even dusted the rooms."

"Yes," said Foster, "but the Staffords are brother and sister, living there with Abbott and his wife, née Gillian Stafford. I learned that from Dr. Anderson—Castle told him all about them. By all accounts the Staffords are a queer couple in some ways, the brother particularly. He's the composer, as I told you. Abbott is an author with a moderate reputation. I took one of his books out two days ago. Sound, careful stuff, not brilliant, in my opinion. It's asking rather a lot to think that we might have found a case belonging to another A. J. Abbott, isn't it? Symes—that's the owner of the bungalow café—is sure that the boat went down the Mille, and Spindles is about three miles upriver from Riversmeet. It all looks as if it's working in nicely."

"Very nicely," said Harrington. "I half wish I hadn't taken your advice to ask the Yard for help."

"As the Staffords and the Abbotts had moved from London that day, I think it's a good thing that we did, sir, even if the Yard handles only the London side of it. It's a curious thing that I called there that evening. Looking back—and making allowances for wishful thinking—it's safe to say that the Staffords were very much on edge. That wouldn't be surprising if they knew that the Abbotts, who showed up later that night, were getting rid of the body, would it?"

"No," said Harrington.

"A woman now working for the Abbotts and the Staffords was

at Riversmeet tonight," said Foster. "She prefers the pub there to the one in Bray and cycles down most evenings, I'm told. However, sir, she was at the river, together with all Riversmeet and half of Bray! I had a word with her—casually, of course."

Harrington smiled. "Yes, of course."

"I found out that the Abbotts arrived sometime after the Staffords," said Foster. "Apparently Agnes Blackshaw—you remember her?"

"She was rather affected by her husband's suicide, wasn't she?"

"Yes, and she's still very sour. At all events she makes a confidante of the Castles daily, and told her that she happened to see the Abbotts arrive—some time between ten and eleven-thirty, she thinks. And eleven-thirty would be just right, if they had come off the river. The Staffords had been there for several hours. Since midday, in fact."

"I see," said Harrington. "As far as I can make out, Foster, you're working up a rather peculiar situation. The Staffords were touchy and on edge, but the Abbotts did the job."

"They might all four have been parties to it," said Foster. "Mind you, I'm taking nothing for granted, but at least we've plenty to go on. Very much more than I thought likely a few hours ago," he added.

"What do you propose to do?" asked Harrington. "See the people at Spindles?"

Foster smiled enigmatically. "I nearly went there straightaway, and then I thought it might be a good idea if I waited for a day, at least. Mrs. Kelly, the daily woman, will be there tomorrow morning. I think she's certain to talk about what happened at Riversmeet, and she'll probably tell them that I asked questions about what time the Abbotts got there. They might get scared and get out in a hurry. If they do—" He broke off and grinned.

"So you've got men watching the house, have you?"

"Not yet, sir—except that I've told Grimes to keep his eyes open, and I think he will probably plant himself outside Spindles all night. He sees this as his big chance. I don't expect any more until after Mrs. Kelly has gossiped, so I thought we would leave it to Grimes tonight and send other men out there in the morning."

"Is it wise to assume that Grimes will keep an eye open off his own bat?" asked Harrington.

"I think so, sir, or I wouldn't have taken the chance."

"Hmm, yes. All right, Foster. You'll go out there tomorrow, I suppose?"

"I thought I might go in the afternoon to see Castle—and park my car near Spindles so that it will be seen—and then see what the position is next door. That's if they haven't flown," went on Foster, smiling again. "It would be almost too easy if they did run away, I'm afraid. I don't really expect that."

"It's worth trying," said Harrington. "Yes, do that. I—but haven't you forgotten something? Tomorrow is Sunday, not a good day for seeing Castle."

"Tomorrow's Saturday, surely," said Foster. He picked up a newspaper. "Yes, today's Friday. By George, sir, you gave me a scare: Mrs. Kelly doesn't work on Sundays."

Harrington said, "I'm getting mixed up. What about the Abbotts, Foster? Do you think you'll have enough for an arrest?"

"A great deal depends on what happens when I see them," said Foster. "I think the best thing is to go in a friendly way and just ask general questions, sliding in a sharp one now and again. By tomorrow I should have expert opinion on the bricks that were in the sack, and brick dust and chippings in the case. If they're definitely the same, then we can say for certain that Abbott's suitcase was used, but that in itself wouldn't be strong enough as grounds for arrest, and I don't think it would be wise to let them know how much we know. Don't you agree?"

"Yes," said Harrington.

"Of course, they might precipitate trouble by leaving hurriedly, or they might break down under questioning," said Foster. "In either case we might make a move and charge them, but if they hold their ground we shall need a lot more before we can talk about arrest."

"You're quite right," said Harrington. "I was a little too anxious. After the work you've done I would like to see you make a real breakthrough and clear it up quickly."

"So would I, sir," declared Foster.

"Good!" said Harrington. "Will you have another whisky?"

When Foster refused and stood up, the Chief Constable walked to the front door with him, and for a moment they stood watching the lights of the town.

"How is Garth taking it?" asked Harrington.

"He hasn't said anything," said Foster untruthfully.

"Good," said Harrington. "I wish we could find a way of getting round his dislike of you. Do you share it? Be frank with me, Foster. I know that antipathy can be an unpleasant thing, and they've asked for an inspector at Milsea. It might be a good thing to transfer Garth."

"Oh," said Foster. "I shouldn't like to think I'd been responsible for anything like that, sir. His home is here, and he's a Milton man. I hope you won't do anything on my account."

"All right, try to work it out," said Harrington.

Foster drove home in a thoughtful frame of mind. He was smiling when he put his car into the garage, but his wife found him uncommunicative; she did not press him for information. Although he had once wanted to talk the affair over with her, his mind was so crowded now that he felt it wiser to sleep on the events. There were moments of elation when he shared Harrington's optimism and thought that he might be able to make an early arrest. Before he could prove a case, however, he had to have a motive and to know the identity of the dead man. He wondered if there had ever been a murder charge arising from the finding of the body of an unknown man. He set that thought aside and asked Laura how she had got on with Mrs. Garth.

Laura, dark, slim and tiny, laughed.

"She telephoned half an hour ago—Garth had gone out for his usual constitutional. She says he's a bit down, but she's often known him worse. Can't you get him to help you?"

"The trouble is that he would think I was dispensing charity," said Foster. "He's so confoundedly proud. If something turned up for him to work on himself, behind my back, for a day or two, it would be a different matter. I hope it doesn't!" he laughed, and they went to bed.

He was talkative at breakfast next morning, and Laura got a fair idea of the situation and the extent of his hopes. When she watched him drive off, she was frowning thoughtfully. She knew he was a little afraid of acting too soon. If he failed to take de-

cisive action, it would disappoint him; the case, which had been
so shrouded in mystery at first, seemed now to be very much
clearer, but he had worked too fast for his own peace of mind.

Foster himself was trying not to be overanxious. It was difficult
to wait until midmorning, however, before sending Sharp and a
detective-constable to watch Spindles. He told them that they
need not hide; it would do the Abbotts and the Staffords no harm
to know that they were being watched.

He had an early lunch, and drove out to Bray soon after half-
past one. He pulled up in the middle of the village when he saw
Grimes cycling toward him from the direction of Spindles.

"Anything doing?" asked Foster.

"There's been a quarrel," said Grimes.

"Between whom?"

"The brother and sister—the Staffords," said Grimes. "I heard
a part of it, sir, but not all. I think Mrs. Abbott managed to
soothe them down, but I can't be sure. Then Mr. Abbott went out
looking like death."

"*Did* he!" exclaimed Foster.

"I followed him," said Grimes. "I thought something might have
happened to make him run, sir. I was there most of the night," he
added, "and I got my son to keep an eye on the place while I had
a few hours sleep; I didn't want to take any chances."

"Good!" said Foster. "Put that in your report."

"Yes, sir. This Mr. Abbott—he's very well liked in the village
already, sir, and there's some talk of him starting the cricket club
again. Old Tom Pickett was telling me about it. He got it from
the Vicar."

"Cricket" was a magic word to Foster—he played whenever he
could. In his opinion there was always some good in a man who
was keen on cricket, although he admitted it was not a rule for
policemen to follow.

"Well, where did he go?" he asked.

"To the cricket field," said Grimes, and he sounded puzzled. "He
walked pretty fast for a while, and then he slowed down and
went into the field—you know where it is, just behind The Angler.
He strolled up and down the pitch several times, and when he
came away he looked a different man. He went straight back to

the house, and I heard him talking and laughing with his wife. I didn't stay any longer, sir. Now that Sergeant Sharp is on duty, there isn't any need, is there?" He spoke a trifle wistfully.

"There'll be plenty for you to do before this is over," said Foster encouragingly. "I'll see you later."

If love of cricket was deep in a man, it was surprising what anything associated with the game could do to him. When he himself had been worked up over a particularly difficult case, or when Laura was lying in, or at other times of crisis, a walk across the Milton field and five minutes swinging a bat in the pavilion with no one to see or hear him had often worked like a charm. If Abbott's mind was in turmoil, there was nothing surprising in his jaunt.

Foster pulled up outside Spindles. Sharp was sitting on a gate nearby, and Foster waved him away when he got down. The other detective was out of sight. No one appeared at the windows of Spindles, but he thought he saw a curtain move. He got out and walked along to Castle's gate.

Castle saw him from the study window and opened the door to him. Foster caught a glimpse of Agnes Blackshaw's sour, twisted features; the woman always gave him the creeps. Before her husband had died she had been a self-indulgent, spoiled creature, proud and vain, lording it over the village and displaying her wealth ostentatiously. Then Blackshaw had lost all his money and, in despair, had hanged himself. His wife seemed to change overnight. Foster had been in charge of the enquiry, and it had hurt him to talk to the woman. Before the enquiry was finished, however, he had come to dislike her; he did not think she grieved for the loss of her husband, but for the loss of the money and position. He always felt sorry for Castle because he had to put up with his sister-in-law without any help from his wife. He was equally sorry for Mildred Castle. That the Castles were desperately hard up was generally known.

"I can't say that I'm surprised to see you, Inspector," said Castle. "I've seen your men in the village, and I know what you found further along the river, of course. A very bad business, and I'm extremely sorry about it. How is it going?"

"Slowly," said Foster carefully. "Such inquiries take time, you know."

"I suppose so. Look here," went on Castle bluntly, "do you suspect my neighbors?"

"Suspect is rather too strong a word," said Foster.

"Which means that you do," said Castle. "I'm sorry. I don't know them well, of course, but Mr. and Mrs. Abbott are a most charming couple. They'll be a great asset to the village, but enquiries such as you are making—and you have made them rather obvious, haven't you?—won't be lived down easily. You know what villagers are." Castle's manner was a bit cool, as if he thought that Foster had overstepped the bounds of permissibility.

"I must do my job," Foster said reasonably. "I can tell you one thing, Vicar—in confidence, of course."

"You know I will respect it," said Castle.

"Thank you. Well, the body was put into the river on the evening of the day the Abbotts and the Staffords moved in. There isn't any doubt about that." He would not have gone so far with many people, but he believed he could trust Castle. "I'm wondering if you noticed anything unusual that day?"

"It was a most unusual day," said Castle.

Something in his manner worried Foster. He was a man for whom the truth was part of life, and would never make an easy liar. Now he gave the impression that he had something to hide. Had Foster known of the manuscript and Tony's work on it, he might have understood more clearly. As it was, he knew only that Castle was unusually reserved and lacked something of his normal frankness. Foster wished he had not made the confidence. Perhaps he had been a little indiscreet. He should have borne in mind that Castle might become an important witness.

"I understand it was unusual," said Foster, "but I'm thinking of something even more than ordinarily unusual, if I can put it that way. Do you know if the boat was used at all? There is a boat at the end of the garden, isn't there?"

"I believe so," said Castle with feigned indifference. "I can't imagine them moving in, and being in such a muddle as they were, and leaving it all for a spell on the river, can you?" He was filling his old pipe and did not look up.

"I'm seeking facts," Foster said quietly.

"*I* noticed nothing unusual," said Castle, deliberately. "*I* saw nothing on the river. I—"

He stopped abruptly, for the door was thrown open. Agnes came into the room, her face livid. She was a tall, thin woman, and since her husband's death she had worn old-fashioned clothes, always black or dark grey. She wore her hair drawn back tightly from her forehead with a harsh, and unbecoming severity. Her skin was pale and lined, and her lips were thin and sunken in lines of bitter denunciation. There were spots of color on her cheeks, and her eyes were glittering.

"Well, Harry, I never thought *you* would be a liar!"

Castle gasped. "Agnes! What do you mean by forcing your way into my room when I'm engaged?"

"I never thought it of *you!*" she cried. "I thought you were a God-fearing man, not a *liar*. Of course the boat was used!"

"Agnes!" Castle's voice hardened. "Go out this moment. I will not allow you to interfere. Inspector, Mrs. Blackshaw has an abnormal dislike of anyone who lives next door, and——"

"Who *wouldn't* dislike them?" demanded Agnes fiercely. "A wicked, blasphemous lot they are; I wouldn't be surprised at anything they did, murder or worse. The boat was used that night, and I told you so. You went out and had a look at it; you even mentioned it to that man Abbott. Yes you did! You can't deny it."

Castle had gone very pale. He sat down heavily, but did not meet Foster's gaze. Agnes stood trembling on the threshold, and her voice must have been clearly audible in the garden next door.

"Perhaps you are thinking of a different day," said Foster calmly. "Mr. Castle would hardly—"

"He has taken a liking to the Abbotts; he'll do anything for them," cried Agnes. "Yes, *anything!* He would turn himself into a liar, he would deny his Maker for them—he must be mad!" She pointed a quivering finger at the Vicar, who sat very still, fingering his pipe. "I've heard everything you've said, and I knew what you found last night, I don't go about with my ears closed, nor does *he*. The boat was used the night of the murder. And tell me this! Why should they wait until after dark before they washed the floors? They didn't touch a spot of water until after dark, and then I saw the Abbotts scrubbing and mopping as if their lives depended on it."

Castle said, "I think you have said more than enough, Agnes. What were you doing next door, to see anything of the kind?"

"I have every right to go—it is *my* house!" cried Agnes. "No one should live there but me—it's mine, mine!" She was beside herself, and her thin, twisted features were flushed with a rage not far removed from hysteria. "I'll go there when I want to, Harry, I will, and you can't stop me. And it *is* true, they washed the floors after dark—I saw them."

Foster said, "What time, Mrs. Blackshaw?"

"As late as ten-thirty—ten-thirty at night, washing floors! I saw them with my own eyes. I thought then that there was something wrong, I couldn't understand——"

"Agnes, I have never been so ashamed of my own sister."

The words, uttered in a frail voice, came from the hall. Castle uttered a horrified exclamation and jumped to his feet, pushing past Agnes. Foster, torn between the desire to get everything he could from the half-hysterical woman and the need to help Castle with his wife, did neither, but just stood by.

"Mildred!" Castle gasped. "Oh, my dear, you should not have come downstairs. How——"

"Be quiet, Harry, please. Agnes——" Mildred Castle supported herself against the door, ashen-faced, her hair disheveled. She stood framed there, trembling so that her voice quavered, and yet her words were clear. "Agnes, you know very well that you are making this up because you dislike Mr. and Mrs. Abbott. It is sinful, *sinful!* I wish you to go to your room at once."

There was a moment of tense silence. The appearance of her sister seemed to have shocked Agnes, who stared at her with lips parted and hands trembling. Before Foster could speak she moved to the door and went along the passage. He heard her walking heavily up the stairs.

"Mildred—" began Castle.

The name stayed, quivering through the air, the sentence unfinished, for Castle's wife had fainted.

· 11 ·

A WELCOME AT SPINDLES

FOSTER TELEPHONED for Dr. Anderson, while Castle carried his wife up to her room. After Anderson had promised to come at once, Foster hurried upstairs. Castle was pulling the bedclothes over his wife. She was unconscious, and seemed hardly to be breathing. Her face now looked waxen. Castle stared at Foster distractedly but did not speak until suddenly words were wrung from him.

"It is eighteen months since she walked. Eighteen *months!*"

Foster said, "She—so she can use her legs."

"But at what terrible cost!" cried Castle. "I—" He pulled himself up and rested a hand on Foster's arm. "Please don't disturb yourself, Foster. The blame is not yours, it is mine. I lied to you." He ran his fingers through his hair, and his gaze did not move from his wife. "Agnes told the truth about the boat—it was used. I had no desire to do anything to injure a man and woman for whom I have great regard."

"Did you see them in the boat?" asked Foster.

"No. Agnes told me that it had been used. I knew nothing of the housework that was done at Spindles that night. I know that lights were on quite late, that is all." He stood looking down at his wife for a long time without speaking, and his lips moved as if in prayer.

Foster waited for several minutes, then turned and walked quietly from the room.

He did not think this was a time to try to interview Agnes Blackshaw. That she hated the Abbotts bitterly was obvious; in her hysteria she might as easily tell lies as the truth, and that was not the kind of evidence he wanted. In any case, the incident had shaken him. He knew Castle's devotion to his wife, and he felt— as he knew Castle did—that the result might well be fatal. He lit a cigarette as he waited in Castle's study.

It was some time before Castle came downstairs.

"Have you telephoned for Anderson?" he asked.

"Yes, he should be here anytime."

"Thank you. Inspector, I know you understand the situation. I will gladly put myself at your disposal at any time, but just now—"

"There is no hurry," said Foster. "Is there anything I can do?"

"No—no, thank you. Perhaps you will telephone when you are coming again."

"I will," promised Foster.

He left the house and walked slowly along the drive. Sharp was standing by his car.

"Did you hear anything?" Foster asked.

"I couldn't catch what was said, sir, but I heard some shouting," said Sharp. "I think it was something about a boat."

"It was," said Foster.

"Have we got 'em, sir?" Sharp asked eagerly.

"We're getting them," said Foster tonelessly. He had to restrain himself from speaking abruptly, although he had the fairness to admit that Sharp was hardly to be blamed for showing eagerness. In fact the round, fresh-complexioned face of the sergeant, with its guileless expression, looked more intelligent than usual; contact with murder was probably sharpening his wits.

Sharp obviously noticed nothing amiss.

"I know one thing, sir," he said. "The people there heard it." He nodded toward Spindles. "Stafford was leaning out of a window, and the Abbotts came to the front door. I don't think they missed much. It ought to be a good time to have a go at them."

"As good a time as any," admitted Foster, cursing the man. "Keep your eyes open, Sharp."

"Yes, sir." The sergeant was obviously disappointed at being left behind, but he did not say so. Foster walked slowly to the gateway of Spindles. He saw a face at a window at the top of the house and thought it was Anne Stafford's. He was halfway along the drive when Sharp called "Sir!" in a curious half tone, suggesting that he wanted to attract his attention but not that of the people in the house. Foster turned. Cycling at a good speed along the road was P. C. Grimes, waving toward Sharp.

Foster went back to the gate.

"Well, Grimes, what have you found now?" he asked, forcing a smile.

"I thought you ought to know this at once, sir," said Grimes, a little breathlessly. "Mr. Stafford rang up just now—it proper took my breath away."

"What did he want?" demanded Foster.

"He *said* he wanted to complain about the boat here, sir; he *said* people have been taking it out at night, and he wants them stopped, sir."

Foster stared at the man, a completely new emotion taking hold of him.

"Did he, by George! That's very smart of him, Grimes."

"That's what I thought, sir."

"Do you mean he knows we're on to him and he's trying to find a way out of it?" asked Sharp incredulously.

"As we know that boats have been used by thieves along here, it isn't a bad get-out," said Foster judicially. "I see. I think I'll be very careful with Mr. Stafford—you're sure it was Stafford, not Abbott?"

"Quite sure, sir. I wouldn't make a mistake about his voice—he nearly always shouts, and Mr. Abbott is a quiet-voiced gentleman."

"Good," said Foster. "All right, Grimes you get back. You wait here, Sharp." He heard a car coming along the road and waited when he recognized Anderson's Humber. The doctor pulled up and asked for the latest news of Mrs. Castle. Foster told him the little he knew. As he reached the door of Spindles, Anderson's car drew up outside the vicarage porch.

The door of Spindles was standing open. Foster knocked, and after a pause Tony Abbott appeared from a room on the left.

It seemed to Foster, as Tony approached slowly, that each was taking the other's measure and was aware of it. His own impression was good; in that queer, undefinable way which always puzzled him, he knew that Abbott was a man he could like. There was an air about him, partly self-confidence; it was not the look of a man who was trying desperately to cover up the traces of an evil deed. He did not even try to show surprise or to pretend that he did not know the caller.

"Good afternoon, Inspector," he said.

"You're Mr. Abbott, aren't you?" asked Foster.

"Yes. If you're wondering how I came to know you, you have been pointed out by my brother-in-law in the past half-hour." He seemed genuinely amused. "How can we help you?"

He stood aside in silent invitation, and Foster stepped into the drawing room, which was on the right. He was surprised to find it looking so well, although there had been little redecoration.

Tony offered cigarettes.

"Thank you," said Foster. "I'm not a bit sure that you can help me, Mr. Abbott. I am investigating—"

"A murder," Tony said calmly

"You're well informed."

Tony laughed. "Mrs. Kelly works here, and if you know Bray well, you will know that she is a fountain of information. I think I know everything that happened when you were at Riversmeet last evening, and I have seen the early edition of the local paper. Two and two make four. The coincidence of our arrival and the dumping of the body in the river is puzzling you, isn't it?"

"It is," said Foster, a trifle sourly.

Although the good impression remained, he felt on the defensive and somewhat aggrieved. This was not at all the kind of interview he had expected; in fact, he would not have been surprised to find Abbott and the others sullen and uncommunicative. Instead, here was this dark-haired, rather handsome man taking the whole thing into his own hands. Abbott, Foster thought, was used to command.

"And very naturally," said Abbott. "Look here, Inspector, I've killed no one. I heard something of the conversation next door, when you called there. It concerned our boat, didn't it?"

"Yes," said Foster, still more aggrieved.

"I think my brother-in-law has telephoned to the village policeman about that," said Abbott. "I don't mind admitting that I was once rather— "

He broke off because there were footsteps in the hall; a moment later the door opened and Julius came in. He raised a hand in greeting and grinned at Foster with such aplomb that the Inspector was now completely taken aback. Suddenly there was a light burst of laughter, more footsteps, and both women appeared on the scene. Gillian was flushed and looked excited; her sister was much calmer, but there was a glint in her eyes which Foster had not seen when he had first met her. The complete assurance with which all of them greeted him, amounting in Gillian's case to exuberance, was remarkable.

"Tony is about to spill the beans," declared Julius. "Shall we leave it to him, or shall I handle it?"

"You'd better leave it to Tony," said Anne.

"All right, all right, he's the word spinner of the family."

Foster got the impression that he was going to be told a carefully rehearsed story and that the bright atmosphere was being deliberately created for his benefit.

He was not altogether right.

A little after twelve o'clock that morning, Mrs. Kelly had let off her broadside. The whole story, including the fact that Foster had questioned her about them, was poured out into Gillian's startled ears. Anne, who had been washing some clothes, kept her face averted. She went off before the recital was finished, and when Gillian had gone to tell Tony, Julius' bellowing voice sounded from upstairs. Anne and Julius were still touchy, especially with each other. Between Julius and Tony there had been a state of armed peace, and no further outward signs of trouble, and Gillian had been busily intent on preserving that peace, even though Julius obviously vented his ill temper on Anne.

While the quarrel was at its height, Gillian had told Tony all that Mrs. Kelly had said. Each of them thought immediately of the boat and Castle's warning.

"It's beginning to worry me," Tony said.

"Tony, you *can't* think they know anything about it."

"They've been behaving very queerly," Tony said, and then seeing his wife's expression, drew her to him and kissed her forehead. "I'm sorry, darling, I'm talking nonsense. There must be a simple explanation of it. Supposing we come out with it bluntly and tell them what's been passing through our minds? We'll wait until they have settled down a bit and then bring up the matter about the boat, shall we? Luncheon will be a good opportunity."

"All right," said Gillian doubtfully.

She went back to the kitchen, and Tony went upstairs to change his clothes. There had been a period of quiet for some time, but

now he heard Julius speak again in a high-pitched voice; he was
in Anne's bedroom

"I tell you it's not impossible!"

"But——" Anne began.

"For crying out loud!" roared Julius. "Do you think I'm taken
in by that scribbler? Of course he was capable of it!"

"But, Julius, he——"

"Oh, have it your own way!" cried Julius. "I tell you that he's
quite capable of anything; it wouldn't surprise me if he committed the murder."

"Be quiet!" cried Anne.

Tony heard nothing of what followed; he was standing outside
in the grip of an ungovernable rage, greater than any he had
so far experienced. When the worst had passed he turned on his
heel and went out of the house, striding toward the village at a
fast pace. He found himself in the cricket field, where he walked
up and down until peace came to him.

Meanwhile Julius went on in a quieter voice:

"Oh, you make me sick. Why in the world did you wait until
today to remember that Tony called at the flat when Lovelace
was there?"

"But he couldn't have seen Lovelace."

"How do you know what he saw? He knew the man, didn't he?
He actually introduced Lovelace to me. How do you know what
passed between them? How do you know that after you had gone
out, leaving Lovelace alone in the flat, he didn't come in and kill
him? Don't you tell me he wouldn't do such a thing. I tell you
that there's been murder in his eyes more than once when he's
looked at me. His hands have itched as if he would like to strangle
me. The man's liable to fits of insanity which could well be homicidal."

"Don't be absurd, Julius!"

"My dear, trusting, innocent sister," said Julius in a voice suddenly silky with sarcasm, "I may be a fool in some respects. I may
not be a genius. I may be a lazy good-for-nothing who has caused
you a great deal of heartbreak. But—*I am not a congenital
idiot!*" He stepped forward and glared into Anne's eyes. "Have
the goodness to admit that, my dear. I am not entirely witless.
Tony knew Lovelace. You left Lovelace in the flat. Shortly after-

ward, Tony called on some trivial excuse about the moving. Tony might have had a better reason for wanting to kill him than either you or I dream of. Oh, don't misunderstand me, *I'm* not going to accuse him of being the killer, but it certainly wouldn't surprise me." Suddenly he roared with laughter. "Here's a pretty situation! We worry ourselves stiff and risk getting hanged for a murder which Tony Abbott committed. That's rich! That's——"

"I am beginning to think that you are a worse beast than I thought," said Anne in cutting tones, "and I knew you were bad enough."

"Well, you've got to admit that he could have done it," Julius said, aggrieved.

"I don't believe it is possible," said Anne. "It's true that he knew Lovelace, but, as far as we know, they weren't friendly enough. He hadn't any reason to hate Lovelace, as we had."

"You mean that we don't know that he had any reason to hate Lovelace," said Julius, but he did not return to the attack on Tony immediately. "What are we going to do—that's what I want to know. I think it's time we started making sure that even if they find out that our boat was used, they can't blame it on to us. Supposing we complained that the boat had been used by someone else——"

"Tony and Gillian know that it hasn't, and they won't lie," said Anne.

"Oh, no, they're too smug for words! But how can they tell whether the boat's been used? It may surprise you, my dear sister, to know that I am always first up in the mornings in this household. It is not unusual for me to walk in the garden before breakfast. It is quite possible that I might notice what your impeccable Tony does not."

"It would have to be remarked upon at breakfast time," said Anne.

"Not at all," said Julius, his voice syrupy again. "We now have Mrs. Kelly's story about the finding of the sack in the river, and therefore we know that a boat was used—we didn't before. There is no reason why I should not pretend to be horrified by the possibility that our boat was used." He stared at her with narrowed eyes, and she watched him closely. He was certainly no fool, and there were times when he was brilliant. She could almost see his mind working, and she waited patiently.

"I think I see a way in which we can present a happy and united front to the police," he said at last, "and make the others rejoice at a change of heart on my part. It will demand great magnanimity, my dear, and I have no liking for it—there are times when I would like to knock my hypocritical brother-in-law through the wall. However, we must study the family interest first, mustn't we? Here is the situation as I see it. In order to save ourselves, and because we lost our heads—let us admit it, my dear—we have placed ourselves in a position of acute danger. The police will find it hard to believe that we took the body from London and dumped it into the river simply because we were innocent, but afraid that the murder would be laid at our door."

Anne said, "Why don't you say what you mean? *I* made you do that."

"My dear sister, possibly I was drunk when I agreed to help in the conspiracy, but I have never seriously doubted that it was the wise thing to do, even when I have been sober. Both of us were shocked when we first realized what had happened. We were not normal. We did what we thought was best, and now it appears at least possible that at the same time we saved Tony a great deal of trouble." This time she ignored the barb against Tony. "Let me proceed," said Julius with heavy sarcasm. "A united family can, I think, be created if I apologize to Tony for going into his study. His temperament will not allow him to reject the olive branch. Then we need to explain why we have been somewhat on edge during the last few days. We have, you know. Even I admit it. Well, what is the matter with us? This: we knew that the boat was being used that night. We assumed that Tony and Gillian had taken it out for some purpose of their own they would prefer us not to know about. When the boat was used again, this time at an hour we knew Tony and Gillian were in the house, and could not possibly have been responsible, we were filled with remorse at our vague suspicions. Do you think they'll bite?" he added with a touch of anxiety.

"I don't see why not," Anne said thoughtfully.

"There is one other thing that might cause trouble," Julius went on. "That is the fact that the suitcase was lost. I don't think the police have found it, but they may have been lucky. It will be better if we have an answer for all questions before they are actually put to us. So, I'll discover in the grounds some oddments of clothing which I'll say were packed in the case. I will remember that, in the rush on the day of our arrival, the case was left by the back door—or the front door, it doesn't greatly matter— and that it was stolen. I had completely forgotten about it until I made the discovery in the grounds. How does that sound?"

"It sounds all right," said Anne.

"It *is* all right," declared Julius. "Let us prepare for a sentimental *rapprochement* during luncheon."

Julius was more fortunate than he expected, for when he was going into the grounds with some ties and other oddments in his pockets for him to "discover," he overheard a brief exchange between Tony and Gillian. Tony was speaking lightly, as if he did not take it seriously. "He must be crazy, but he actually said that he wouldn't put it past me. I nearly gate-crashed, and that would have caused a real shindy."

"But it's absolute nonsense!" Gillian protested.

"There must be some reason for it," said Tony.

Julius hurried off, very thoughtful.

He made sure that he was not seen at the end of the garden, where the river came over a muddy bank and lapped at the rough grass near the landing stage. High hedges hid him from the houses, and there was no one on the other side of the river nor in the vicarage garden. There was a muddy pool close to the landing stage and he dropped the things into it, ground them down under his heel, and then retrieved a few of them. These he took back with him, and there was water dripping from them when he went into the kitchen. Gillian and Anne were dishing up lunch.

"What on earth have you found?" demanded Gillian.

"There's some funny business going on around this place," declared Julius. "Some *very* funny business. Where is Tony?"

"Here," said Tony, coming from a cloakroom near the kitchen. "Now what's the trouble?"

He came in slowly, half-expecting Julius to make a more public statement of his suspicions, and he was taken aback by Julius' opening sentence, which seemed so sincere that he himself colored a little.

"Tony, I know I have been pretty bearish during the last few days. I'm sorry. The truth is that I've had something on my mind and it's worried me a great deal." Julius uttered a short laugh. "I was even working myself up into a frame of mind where I was capable of suspecting *you* of funny business."

"Me?" exclaimed Tony mechanically.

"Yes. The first morning we were here I strolled down the garden and saw the boat had been used," said Julius. "I thought you'd been out for an early morning airing and didn't take much notice of it, of course. Then I saw that it had been out several times afterwards. There were rumors in the village about thieves working after dark, from the river. Oh, I know it was crazy," he added, looking shamefaced, "but once or twice I saw you coming up the garden fairly early in the morning, and—well, especially after the row over old Castle's book, I wanted to believe the worst of you. Then this morning Mrs. Kelly was blabbing about a body in the river," Julius went on with a short laugh. "Like a damn fool I mentioned my earlier suspicions to Anne, and when she saw what I was driving at, she nearly bit my head off." He gave a rueful smile. "I started to put in some heavy thinking. As a matter of fact the boat was out last night, and I happen to know you didn't take it out, because I was awake and I would have heard had you gone out, after the rest of us had gone to bed. I *stayed* awake, to find out," he added, with another sheepish smile. "One way and another, I've been a pretty lousy specimen, old chap. I'm damnably sorry."

"Oh, forget it," said Tony awkwardly.

"I'm afraid we can't dismiss it as easily as that," said Julius seriously. He held up the muddy articles. "I've just found these, in the garden—they'd been thrown away. I remember they were packed in a case I'd borrowed from you a few days before we moved."

"Oh, *that's* where the case went," said Tony. "I remember now."

"I also remember that I took it out of the removal van. I forgot it until I found these things. I distinctly remember putting it by the back door," went on Julius, "and presumably I left it there overnight, and it was stolen. Why anyone should want to steal the case and throw away the contents I just don't know, but there it is. I think it would be wise to tell the police, don't you?"

"I do," said Tony.

"Surely that can wait until after lunch," said Gillian, who had been cooking. "It's getting cold now."

"Oh, there's no hurry for half an hour," said Julius. "I'll dump these things in a shed," he added. "Can you spare a moment, Tony?"

Gillian turned to the stove, feeling flushed but relieved. She had been afraid that Tony's calmness, after the fit of fury which he had just admitted, would be a brittle one, liable to break. Now there were no fears of that, for he was so made that he could never refuse to accept an apology. This one, so frank and open, and uttered in Julius' humblest manner, might go a long way toward healing the breach for good. She felt angry that Julius had harbored such absurd suspicions, but it did not really surprise her. Probably Julius had taken Tony into the garden to put the finishing touch to his apology; she would know as soon as they returned.

She was right; Julius was talking in a confidential undertone in the little potting shed where he was putting the "recovered" oddments.

"I don't mind admitting, Tony, that it worried me no end. You're a secretive kind of customer, you know, and when you flared up at me in the study the other day I jumped to the conclusion that you had something to hide in there. I can see now that it was quite unforgivable of me. I don't know what came over me."

"Well, you can forget that, anyhow," said Tony.

"That's very sporting of you, old chap. As a matter of fact, it wasn't until Anne really let herself go—she's got a soft spot for you, you know—that I pulled myself up. Earlier this morning I'd been inventing all manner of wild theories. You know the police have been watching the house, don't you?"

"I've seen two or three men about, and the constable has been within sight most of the morning," said Tony. "I did wonder if it was connected with the murder. As a matter of fact—" It was his turn to feel sheepish. "I'd noticed that the boat had been out once or twice, and I rather thought that you—"

Julius stared, then guffawed with laughter. "What a precious pair of fools we are!"

"I'm beginning to think so," admitted Tony. "I think the police will come to see us, and we can mention the case then."

"That's a good idea," said Julius.

During lunch there was a more genial atmosphere than at any other meal since the first breakfast. Tony and Gillian admitted to each other that they felt greatly relieved, and even when they saw the police car drive up, and Anne and Julius pointed out Foster, they were not unduly worried. The loud voices from the vicarage had rather startled them, but by now nothing that Agnes Blackshaw did or said caused surprise. It was a good thing, thought Tony, that Julius had already telephoned to the sergeant in the village about the mystery of the boat.

As it happened, Tony was alone in the drawing room when Foster came along the drive, and in a mood almost of elation he prepared to welcome the Inspector.

· 12 ·

INSPECTOR FOSTER IS BOTHERED

FOSTER RETURNED to his headquarters in a very puzzled frame of mind. The theory he had built up appeared to be demolished, but he was by no means satisfied that he had heard all the truth from the people at Spindles. For one thing, Julius Stafford had shown a new aspect of himself; his geniality and good humor had been remarkable, and Foster could not rid himself of the suspicion that a conspiracy had been hatched to confuse and outwit him.

All of these things had been subservient, for a while, to Mrs. Castle's condition, and he was still worried about her. Before he left Spindles, Anderson had gone, and Castle had not been in any shape for talking. As soon as the Abbotts learned what had happened they hurried next door, and Foster found himself out in the cold. He left Sharp and the other plainclothesman on duty.

The first thing he did was to telephone Anderson.

"I don't think I can commit myself," said Anderson frankly. "I was astonished to hear that she had walked down the stairs without assistance—I did not think she would ever have the use of her legs again. I'm getting another opinion, of course. She was still unconscious when I left, and if she comes round today I think she may have considerable pain. I've given the district nurse instructions to inject morphia if it seems necessary, and there isn't much else I can do."

"You don't think there's any immediate danger then?" said Foster.

"I can't see where it could come from," said Anderson. "I want to try to get Trevelyan down from London."

"Isn't he consultant pathologist to the Yard?" asked Foster.

"Now you come to mention it, I think he is."

"Leave it to me," said Foster, suddenly more cheerful. "If he comes down here to look at our corpus, you can ask him to look at Mrs. Castle as a matter of professional interest."

"Good idea," said Anderson. "See what you can do."

Saturday afternoon was not a good time for such endeavors, but two hours later a return telephone call from the Yard brought the hoped-for news; Sir Alexander Trevelyan would come to Milton the following day, and Superintendent Folly would accompany him. That Folly was coming puzzled Foster; the Superintendent had a reputation for rarely leaving London.

That information finally sent Foster to his Chief Constable. He found Harrington in the clubhouse at Milton Downs golf course, benignly pleased with himself after a round inside his handicap. He was having tea with his wife, a tall, willowy woman, apt to instill diffidence by height alone. She went to join another table after Foster arrived; it was part of her creed to have nothing to do with the more sordid details of her husband's profession.

"You got in touch pretty quickly," said Harrington. "By that I gather things haven't gone as well as you hoped."

"Certainly not according to plan," admitted Foster. He lit a cigarette as he marshaled his thoughts. "I can't make up my mind whether the people at Spindles have been pitchforked into this business accidentally and really know nothing about it, or whether they are an unusually clever lot who are intent on cheating us. I'm glad we called in the Yard, after all—and there is a curious development up there, sir."

"What?" asked Harrington.

"Folly is coming."

"Folly, by George! That's most unusual—he's got a reputation for not stirring from his office. I wonder what's bringing him."

"So do I," said Foster ruefully. "On the face of it there's nothing to attract him. I'm wondering if the fact that we've suggested that the dead man might be an alien has anything to do with it."

He plunged into a recital of the afternoon's events, including the fact that he had asked for Sir Alexander Trevelyan, and why. Harrington raised no objection and seemed sympathetic, although he did not know the Castles very well. He was far more interested in the developments at Spindles.

"Well, what do you make of it?" he asked. "Did they realize that you knew their boat had been used when you put men to watch, and try to get a step ahead by reporting an imaginary unknown user?"

"It wouldn't surprise me," said Foster. "But there was something else that makes it seem less likely. Stafford told me that a suitcase which he had borrowed from Abbott was stolen on the day he moved in. He showed me some things which had been taken out of it and were thrown away at the bottom of the garden. I don't think he could know that I'd found the case. Martin is too scared to open his mouth about it."

"Hmm," said Harrington. "Stafford or Abbott might know that the case was used."

"Unless he thought we had it, he would hardly put up an explanation like that," said Foster. To his surprise, Harrington laughed.

"Folly won't stand much nonsense," he said. "Now don't misunderstand me, Foster—but he has a reputation for being merciless and very heavy-handed. I haven't met him," he admitted. "I'm rather looking forward to it; he is the lion of Scotland Yard, all right. I wonder how you'll get on with him."

Foster grimaced. "Well, I made my own bed."

"Don't let him be heavy-handed with you," said Harrington. "I'm not going to let my officers be browbeaten—but you know that."

Foster was in better humor when he left the clubhouse, reassured of the Chief's support. But although he told himself he was not even slightly anxious about working with the great Folly, the truth was that he would be on edge until he discovered what the man was like.

He went back to the office, not expecting to find much there. To his surprise, there was a man waiting for him in the hall, accompanied by Sharp, who should still have been at Spindles. Foster recognized the caller as the manager of a Milton firm of builders. He thought of the bricks and made a mental note to reprimand Sharp for leaving his post.

Sharp, however, was obviously ill, sneezing and running a temperature. Foster sent him home, telling him to stay there until he was better. He, himself, would telephone for a replacement.

Wylie, the manager of the building firm, smiled at Sharp's departing back. He was a tall, well-dressed man of middle age.

"It's about this brick," said Wylie, as Foster led the way to his office. "I don't think there's much doubt where it came from, Inspector."

"Where?" asked Foster.

"It's a special brick, much dearer than most used for building in this district," said Wylie, "but old Blackshaw wouldn't have anything but the best—he knew exactly what he wanted, too. We built Spindles, you know." He smiled into Foster's unblinking eyes. "I shall be very surprised if any other builder in the district says he's used that brand. I've been looking up the report from the foreman after Spindles was built. There were a few dozen bricks left on the site."

"Oh," said Foster.

"I hope that's what you want," said Wylie.

"Yes, thanks," said Foster. "I suppose they could have been taken away from the site by unauthorized people."

"Obviously," said Wylie, "but I can't see why, unless they were to be used." He smiled, as if he suspected that Foster was trying to be more noncommittal than he felt. "Is there anything else I can do for you?"

"Not just now," said Foster, "but you may be called to give evidence."

He saw the builder out and then looked thoughtfully at the

brick that the man had left on his desk. Everything he needed to prove that the body had left Spindles was now at hand. He telephoned Laura, and, when she answered, said, "I can't get back for an hour or so. How would you like to bring the children for a ride as far as Bray?"

"They'd love it," said Laura.

"Good, I'll pick you up in ten minutes or so."

Half an hour later, Laura and the three children got out of the car by the village green, and Laura, only a little taller than her eldest daughter, raced with them toward some ducks waddling about the pond, laughing and waving as Foster drove toward Spindles. Grimes and the other men were talking together and had nothing to report.

Tony was working in the garden, and looked up when he saw the visitor.

"Still at it?" he asked, amiably enough.

"There are one or two things I'd like to do." Foster smiled. "I was rather worried about Mrs. Castle, and they slipped my memory. Do you mind if I have a look around the garden?"

"Of course not. Can I be your guide?"

"Thanks," said Foster.

"My wife's in the village," said Abbott as he dusted his hands on a rag, "and I think my brother-in-law is in the last stages of germination."

"Germination?" asked Foster, startled.

"Yes. At any moment weird and wonderful sounds may come from his piano, and by tomorrow we shall probably have to listen to the new masterpiece," said Tony. "He's a curious fellow—I think you ought to know that, Foster. He often does things which no normal human being would dream of doing, and trivial things upset him."

"Defense of a brother-in-law," said Foster lightly.

"Nonsense," said Tony. "Guidance for the police."

They both laughed.

Foster, who had brought a walking stick, poked about the long grass which grew near the river and at the sides of the large garden. Now and then he touched something hard, but it proved to be only a stone. Then, behind some bramble bushes, he saw a little shed. The water had come up to it recently, and there was mud on one side. He saw footprints on a patch harder than the rest, but when he went down on his knees he came to the conclusion that they were not clear enough to give him any help. He forced a way through the brambles toward the little shed, with Tony helping him to hold the branches back.

He found a clearing and saw that the shed had been approached from the river several times, for the earth was churned up and branches were broken and trodden down. By the side of the shed was a patch where the grasses were white and delicate-looking—as if they had grown beneath something standing there, out of the light of the sun. Then he saw a part of a brick buried in the ground.

"Is this what you're after?" asked Tony.

"I'm after anything I can find," said Foster.

He was satisfied, after a few minutes' inspection, that a dozen or so bricks had lain at this spot. Then he tried to open the door of the shed. It was fastened with a wooden staple and hasp, and it had jammed tightly. He took a handkerchief from his pocket before he grasped the wood firmly and tugged at it.

"Surely you won't find fingerprints on that," said Tony.

"You never know where you might find 'em," said Foster. At last he drew the wooden peg out. The door swung open.

"Look here, you aren't looking for another body, are you?" asked Tony.

"No," said Foster, "but nothing would surprise me." He bent down, peering into the little shed, but it was dark inside. He had not brought a flashlight with him, and before daylight was let into the place the bushes would have to be cut down. There was something on the floor near the door, and he put his hand inside and pulled at it.

He took out a piece of sacking; there were other pieces beyond. Some of them looked almost unused, although they were rotting in places.

"The sack!" exclaimed Tony.

Foster snapped, "What do you know about the sack?"

"What I read in the paper," said Tony promptly.

"The papers say too much," growled Foster.

He examined the sacking closely. He could not be sure until he had compared it side by side with the sack taken from the river, but it looked to him as if it was of the same material; it was fairly closely woven. Expert opinion would be easy to obtain. He had certainly justified his second visit.

He did not give up his search then, but looked for some of the oddments which Stafford said were still missing from the case. He found nothing. The pool where the goods had been discovered was thick with mud, and even Stafford's footprints were vague and confused. It was not likely that Foster would find any clues to help him there, but he decided to send for a sergeant who was an expert on footprints, in the hope that he could get one or two casts.

He told Tony so, and added, "I'm afraid we're being a bit of a nuisance. I'm sorry about this, but it's got to be done."

"Not at all, I'm deeply interested," Tony assured him. "Do you think he was killed on the grounds?"

"I wouldn't like to go as far as that," said Foster.

He had another look at the boat, which was still tied up to the landing stage. He had examined it thoroughly in the afternoon, and there was not the slightest trace of blood on it. For the first time, he wondered uneasily whether he had been wise to let his men stay in such obvious places. His plan to stampede the people at Spindles had been a lamentable failure; it was the kind of thing on which Folly would probably seize as an example of the errors made by country policemen.

They walked back to the gates, and Foster tucked his finds into the trunk of his car.

"If you're going to the village you might give me a lift," said Tony. "I'll just about get to the shop before it shuts—I forgot to ask my wife to get me some tobacco."

"Gladly—hop in," said Foster.

It was only half a mile to the village, and when they reached it the sun was shining, touching the thatched roofs of the cottages with gold. On the green, still bright from the recent rains, two women were standing by three little girls who were calling the ducks, now swimming sedately in the middle of the pond. One of the women was Gillian. Nearby stood a poorly dressed boy, who watched the scene gravely.

"Hallo, there's Archibald Kelly," said Tony, smiling. "It looks as if he's attached himself to my wife. Poor kid." He glanced with kindly interest at the woman to whom Gillian was talking. "That's a pretty girl."

Foster laughed. "That's my wife!"

"Oh!" said Tony.

Obviously the two women had been chatting together, and Gillian was startled when she learned who the other was. She had been watching the ducks when Mrs. Foster and her children had arrived, and soon afterward, Archy had come hurrying to her side. Now he greeted Tony with grave politeness, and then his mother called him.

Archy trotted off, watched curiously by the little girls. Tony, on his way to the shop, looked back and thought what a pleasant scene it made. Gillian and the Fosters were talking animatedly, and a burst of laughter followed Tony into the shop. His first good impression of Foster increased, and he was attracted by his tiny, vivacious wife.

He bought his tobacco and rejoined the group. The Fosters drove off, and Tony and Gillian waved until the car was out of sight, for the three children were pressing against the rear window, their arms gyrating wildly.

"There's nothing sinister about them," said Tony.

"No," said Gillian. "I like her." She was frowning in spite of her words. "Darling, is that man trying to attract your attention?"

She looked toward The Angler, outside which a man was standing with his hand half-raised. At first Tony thought it was someone who knew of the interest he was taking in the village cricket club—for there was a notice about a meeting posted outside the inn and the village shop. There was something different about this man, however. He looked as if he were a townsman, dressed as he was in a blue suit that was a shade too bright, with a cheap trilby on the back of his head and yellow-brown shoes.

"I don't think so," he said. "He's a shifty-looking customer, isn't he?"

"He's following us," said Gillian.

Tony glanced round. The man was fifty feet away, walking slowly, and his shoes were creaking.

"Not he!" said Tony. "You're imagining things."

As he spoke, however, the stranger raised a hand, and this time there was no doubt that he was waving to him. Tony waited. Gillian glanced round and started when she saw one of Foster's policemen standing quite near, certainly within earshot.

The man drew up. His thin features had a furtive look, and when he spoke it was out of the corner of his mouth. He looked up at Tony with a leer.

"Reckernize me?" he asked.

"I do not," Tony said, sharply

"Yer'd better, mister." The man's voice was low-pitched but penetrating. Gillian glanced at the policeman, who had come a little nearer and seemed intent on what the stranger was saying.

"What on earth are you talking about?" asked Tony.

"Come orf it, mister," said the little man. "You know me as well's I know you. I wanter word wiv you."

"About what?" asked Tony.

"About"—the man took a step nearer, and there was a look of great cunning on his face—"about Jerry Lovelace, mister."

"Lovelace?" echoed Tony. "I don't know a man named—"

He stopped abruptly and caught his breath. Gillian looked at him in surprise, and the policeman drew a little nearer still, while the sharp-faced man gave a short laugh and said;

"I thought yer'd reckernize '*im*, mister. Where can we 'ave a nice quiet little chat?"

· 13 ·

A MAN NAMED LOVELACE

"AND THAT's all I heard, sir," said the detective-constable who had listened to the conversation on the road from the village. He was sitting in the pleasant lounge of Foster's house and had a self-important look. "He mentioned the name—a man named Lovelace, Jerry Lovelace. Abbott said he didn't know anyone of that name, and then he caught his breath. He looked as if he could kill the little fellow, sir."

"Aren't you exaggerating?" asked Foster.

"No, sir, I assure you I'm not. He looked real wild, and then he ticked the little man off, sent him off with a flea in his ear, all right. I've never known anyone look so surprised—that's a fact. I thought they were going to have a quarrel there and then, but the little man was frightened, and I don't blame him, sir. Abbott and his wife walked back to Spindles, and the stranger went to The Angler. I made one or two enquiries at once, sir, and the little man is named Albert Hibbett, and he's staying at The Angler for the weekend. In the register he's given his address as Clapham, London. I've told Grimes to keep an eye on him."

"Grimes will need a dozen pairs of eyes if we go on like this," said Foster. "All right, Smith, thanks—you've done very well."

When the man had gone, Foster put in a call to headquarters. Mentally he went through the names of the men on duty, one of whom would have to be sent to The Angler to keep an eye on the stranger. Foster was still undecided when the operator said, "Milshire Police Headquarters."

"This is Chief Inspector Foster." Foster made a last-minute decision. "Put me through to Sergeant Guy."

"Sorry, sir, he's just gone out. There's been an accident in the High Street. Sergeant Buckingham's just come in, sir. Will he do?"

"Buckingham!" exclaimed Foster. "Yes, please!"

He was greatly cheered, for Buckingham was his regular aide. The sergeant was a Milshire man who had gained rapid promotion and was earmarked for the next inspectorship; he would probably get it if Garth was transferred to one of the coast towns.

Laura came downstairs, and when she saw her husband's face, she said, "Found a sovereign, darling?"

"Buck's back," said Foster "I—hallo, Buckingham? What are you doing back already?"

"I heard what was up, sir," said Buckingham, who sounded eager, "and I thought you might find me useful so I came straight back. Can I do anything?"

"You can! Come round and see me."

Buckingham stayed to supper, during which he became fully acquainted with the facts of the case. He was to watch Hibbett, and Foster had already telephoned for accommodation for him. Hibbett would have recognized the man who had reported about him; Buckingham was unknown to everyone at Spindles as well as to Hibbett.

A little after eleven o'clock the telephone rang. Foster exclaimed in annoyance; late calls often meant he would have to go out during the night. He was feeling pleasantly tired and hoped, as he picked up the receiver, that this one was a report. Then he heard P. C. Grimes' voice.

"Grimes reporting, sir," said the constable. "A message from Sergeant Buckingham, sir."

"Yes," said Foster.

"The man Hibbett has gone up to Spindles, sir, and is prowling around. Sergeant Buckingham has gone after him. He thought you would like to know, sir."

"Yes," said Foster. "Thanks. I'll be at your house in half an hour."

The encounter with the furtive little man had been upsetting for both Gillian and Tony, and Tony had not improved matters by the way he behaved. He had said nothing to her about it, but she had seen his face go pale and his eyes harden—as happened sometimes when he was furiously angry. These moods of intense anger were worrying; Snub Savory had told her that Tony admitted how badly they affected him, and she could see that he was fighting to keep his composure. She did not worry him with questions, however, but the rest of the walk home, and the first half-hour back in Spindles were uncomfortable. The only relief was that neither Anne nor Julius was downstairs. Now and again there was a furious burst of sound from the piano, the same bars played over and over again, with slight variations; Julius was obviously in the throes of composition. At such times Anne was always at hand with suggestions, which her brother often used but rarely acknowledged.

After they'd had supper together, Tony lit his pipe, stood up, and said, "Let's go to the study, Gill, I want to talk."

When they were settled he smiled. "That little customer gave me a shock."

"I know," said Gillian.

"I don't ever remember seeing him before," said Tony, "and for the moment I'd forgotten that Lovelace ever existed. He was one of the nastiest pieces of work you're ever likely to meet." He seemed to be talking to himself as much as to Gillian, and his voice was low. "I liked him once—in fact, we were good friends. He handled some of my work before I met Snub. He wasn't an agent, but a music publisher with contacts all over the place, and he wasn't a bad judge of books as well as music."

Gillian did not interrupt.

"As a matter of fact he published some of Julius' early work," Tony went on. "That was on my recommendation, although I often wished I hadn't done it. It's hard to believe that I knew Julius before I knew you, isn't it? I've known him for ten years, and he's almost a stranger."

Gillian said nothing.

"Well, as I say, Lovelace handled some of my articles and stories," said Tony, "and he placed several of them in England. It wasn't until I happened to pick up an American magazine and see one of my stories, under a different name, that I began to think he might be a bit of a rogue. I asked him about it. He tried to pretend that someone in the States had been selling for profit without his permission or knowledge," Tony continued. "But I made some enquiries, and it proved that Lovelace had been doing the same thing with the work of other authors. Goodness knows why, for he had a decent income from his legitimate business and a host of contacts. I suppose there are some people who can't keep straight." He was silent for a while, and Gillian kept quite still, watching his face and seeing the shadows in his eyes. The recollections caused him pain, and she did not think it was because Lovelace had been found out. He sighed, and straightened up, then went on more briskly. "I was young, you know. I hadn't much money. The proceeds from those American sales would have made a world of difference to me. I suppose, in all, he robbed me that way of eight hundred pounds over a period of eighteen months or so. Like a fool I went to see him at a time when the story was being spread by everyone who had suffered. He wasn't in a mood to apologize—he knew that he would either be boycotted and cold-shouldered altogether or else that some of the more angry victims would prosecute. Do you know what that unpleasant fellow outside reminded me about?"

"No," said Gillian.

Tony said, "He reminded me of something I have almost forgotten. One of my damnable fits of temper. It came back vividly as I stood there. I remember going into Lovelace's office, in a grim, determined mood, intent on making him pay me for the stories he had sold. He sneered at me. I flew at him."

The room was very quiet. Tony's face was set, and Gillian understood the mental torment which he was undergoing. These paroxysms had not been started by the crash but had grown worse, perhaps been reborn, because of it.

Suddenly the spell was broken by an outburst on the piano, and Tony sat up briskly.

"Well, that's that part finished," he said. "I haven't talked much to you about it, but I fancy you had a word with Snub." He smiled. "Quite rightly, darling, I'm glad you did. To complete the story, I can remember from boyhood having a temper that all my relatives said would lead me into serious trouble. My father taught me to check it. He was a lovable man," added Tony with a reminiscent smile. "He reasoned with me, persuaded me to stand quite still and not move whenever anything happened to upset me, and after a while I was able to control not only paroxysms of violence but also the temper itself. By the time I went away to school I was fairly normal, and I'd forgotten the evil urge when I started to write. The first outburst came that day in Lovelace's office. It might have been serious, for I think I would have strangled the man if one of his secretaries hadn't come in. Then, while I was recovering and Lovelace was getting up— oh, I had him on the floor—in came a policeman."

Gillian gasped.

"A plainclothesman, of course, and elderly, a rather acid-tongued fellow," said Tony. "He saw that there had been trouble and probably heard the shouting, but he didn't ask me any questions, and I doubt whether he got much out of Lovelace. He had come to see Lovelace about complaints that other people had lodged against him. Eventually the matter was dropped, although there was talk of action, and of course Lovelace faded out of music publishing and agency work. He went to South America looking for diamonds and disappeared. There's little doubt he caused more trouble there. A change of scene rarely results in a change of character."

Gillian said tensely, "Tony, did Julius lose anything?"

"I'm quite sure that he did not," answered Tony. "Although Lovelace went out of business, they were good friends. I think Julius was one of the few people who believed in Lovelace. I never heard him say a word against him, and he often defended him in my hearing. I kept quiet, of course. I didn't see that the man could do him any harm, and I was determined not to take any further part."

"I'm glad," said Gillian. "Just for a moment—"

Tony laughed. "You're getting as bad as Julius himself. I suppose it's crossed your mind that the dead man might be Lovelace?"

"Yes."

"Let's forget it," went on Tony. "I've got it out of my system, thanks to you. I don't think Julius will come down again to-night, so let's spread ourselves in the lounge, shall we? There's a Beethoven concert, I think—or have we just missed it?"

"It's started," said Gillian, "but we'll hear most of it."

The concert finished before the nine o'clock news, and Gillian went to make some coffee, while Tony, tiring of the program, switched off the radio and picked up a book. He intended to get to bed early, but he lost himself in the book, and Gillian was content to knit and read. It was nearly eleven o'clock before Tony yawned and put the book down.

"Hallo, who's going to wear navy blue?" he demanded.

Gillian smiled. "It's a jumper for Archy. The poor little chap is short of clothes, for I think Mrs. Kelly spends most of her spare time in the bar at Riversmeet. It's curious about her and Archy, isn't it? I can't imagine him being her son."

"Let's not get involved in other mysteries," said Tony. "Let's go quietly to bed. All is silent upstairs. Julius is probably prostrate and Anne smoothing his fevered brow."

When Tony was in the bathroom, however, the piano started off again, and he thought they might be in for an all-night session.

Then he heard a scream.

It came in a lull in the music, and he heard it quite clearly, then thought he heard his name called. He rushed out of the room toward the bedroom, with the froth from the toothpaste still at his lips. He heard a thud. Then the piano went off into wild movement, drowning any sound, but he saw shadows on the wall, shadows of struggling people.

He rushed into the room.

The man saw him coming and released Gillian, uttering a high-pitched scream and putting up his hands, for there seemed to be madness in Tony's eyes—and the froth from the toothpaste was at his lips. Tony struck the man on the side of the head and sent him reeling against the wardrobe. Gillian staggered away. Tony reached the man again and put his hands about his throat and began to throttle him. The face in front of his eyes seemed to be going round and round and changing color. He saw the man's tongue pushing between his lips. He heard a shout, and then felt something beating at his head and shoulders, but he did not let go. He felt his thumbs sink deeply into the man's neck.

"Tony!" screamed Gillian. "Tony! Tony! Tony!"

· 14 ·

ATTEMPTED MURDER

SERGEANT BUCKINGHAM first heard the screaming as he was examining a downstairs window and found that it was unlatched. He lost no time but opened the window and climbed in. He found himself in a small cloakroom which led into the hall. The piano was playing, but he thought he heard shouts and hurrying footsteps. He hurried upstairs, and as he turned into the main passage he heard a woman scream:

"Tony! Tony!"

A little way along, a door was open and light streamed into the passage. Buckingham raced along, and when he reached the room he saw a woman standing over a man and beating at his head and shoulders with her clenched fists. The man had his hands about Hibbett's neck; Hibbitt's face was mottled, his tongue was protruding, and his eyes were starting from his head; he was obviously unconscious.

Buckingham thrust Gillian to one side and drove his fist into Tony's face. The blow was so powerful that Tony lost his footing and released his grip. As he fell, Buckingham saw his white face and glittering eyes and the froth at his lips. The sergeant prepared for a renewal of the attack, but Tony leaned against the wall and stared at him, the glitter fading from his eyes.

Buckingham snapped, "Get hot-water bottles, quickly!" He lifted Hibbett to one of the twin beds, then began to apply artificial respiration. After ten minutes he stopped for a moment, perspiring freely.

"All right, I'll take over," said Tony.

"You—" began Buckingham.

"Don't be a fool," said Tony sharply. "I won't hurt him."

By the time Gillian returned to the room Hibbett was breathing noisily. Buckingham took off the man's shoes, and when Tony stopped work, bundled him into the bed, piled blankets on him, and inserted the hot-water bottles underneath.

"He'll be all right," he said. "A lucky thing for you." He stared at Tony.

"Yes," said Tony crisply. "Who are you, and what are you doing here?"

Buckingham showed his card and repeated: "It was certainly a lucky thing for you. I was downstairs and heard the shouting, so I broke in."

"I see," said Tony. "Thanks." He brushed his hair from his forehead and smiled wanly at his wife. "Can you make some coffee, Gill?"

She nodded and hurried out, suspecting that he wanted to be alone with the policeman.

Hibbett was breathing wheezily but was in no danger. His face was purplish red, and his lips were open. Tony offered cigarettes.

"No, thank you," said Buckingham. He was a tall, well-built man, with attractively curly hair, a snub nose, and very full lips which were almost Negroid. "Are you Mr. Abbott?"

"Yes."

"What happened?"

"I was in the bathroom and I heard my wife cry out," said Tony. "I hurried here and saw this man trying to prevent her from calling for help. I flew at him."

"You flew at him, all right," said Buckingham. "You very nearly killed him. Who is he?"

"To the best of my knowledge I have never seen him before this evening," said Tony. "He stopped me in the road and said he knew me and asked for an interview. I disliked his manner and told him to clear off. That's all I can tell you about him."

Buckingham looked curiously at Tony, who now seemed calm and self-possessed—finding it difficult to believe he was the same man who had been so intent on throttling Hibbett.

"Would you telephone Grimes, the local policeman?" Buckingham asked. "Ask him to telephone Chief Inspector Foster and request him to come here. And ask Grimes to come here too."

Tony shrugged and went downstairs.

He was surprised to hear Foster's voice when he rang the local policeman's cottage. He passed on the message, and Foster made no comment but said that he could come at once. Gillian was coming out of the kitchen with a tray of coffee.

"Foster is on his way," said Tony. He went with her into the kitchen to get another cup, but there was a restraint between them, and he could not break it. Neither of them spoke until they were halfway up the stairs, and then Gillian said:

"Tony, I—"

"It's all right, my sweet," said Tony, gripping her arm. "I know what you're feeling, and I know what a fool I was, but I couldn't control myself when I saw the little swine manhandling you. Don't worry, it will all work out all right."

"I suppose so," said Gillian. "You'd better wash your face, Tony. You've got some toothpaste on your lips."

"Have I?" asked Tony.

When he got to the bathroom he saw the coating of dried paste on his lips. It did not occur to him that he had looked like a maniac as he had rushed into the bedroom, but he washed quickly and went back to Buckingham. The piano was being banged upstairs, and now and again Julius started to sing. Apparently he and Anne knew nothing of the incident.

As he turned into the bedroom there was a ring at the front doorbell.

"I'll go," he said.

He admitted Foster and Grimes, the former looking at him inquiringly.

"As you've gathered, we've had a spot of bother," said Tony. "I'm afraid that your chap upstairs thinks I tried to murder a man whom I've never seen before."

"Oh," said Foster. He did not entirely succeed in hiding his surprise. "Did you?" he asked rather heavily.

"No. The man was molesting my wife. I attacked him, and I might well have killed him," Tony went on. "I don't think I would have let him go if your man hadn't been on the spot."

"Oh," said Foster again. "Where is he now?"

"Upstairs," said Tony

Foster found it strange to walk beside this calm, self-possessed man, who spoke almost with humor of the unusual situation. They entered the bedroom, where Gillian was pouring out coffee. She too seemed composed.

"Will you have some coffee?" she asked.

"No thanks," said Foster.

The sight of Buckingham was reassuring; Foster would get a thorough report. He called Grimes, who had followed him as far as the passage, and made arrangements quickly. Hibbett obviously did not need a doctor, so Foster left Grimes with the man and led the others out. On Tony's suggestion they went to the study. Buckingham sat at the desk with a notebook and pencil, and Foster asked Gillian for her story. She told it clearly. She had gone into the bedroom and opened the wardrobe door to get a hanger for her dress. The little man had been inside and had jumped at her. She pointed to the red marks under her chin, where his fingers had gripped her. There was a small tear on the shoulder of her dress, where a button had pulled out, and it was obvious that there had been a struggle of some kind. Foster appeared to accept her story at its face value and asked Tony for his. Tony told it as clearly as Gillian had, but with more restraint.

Foster said, "Having dragged the man off your wife, Mr. Abbott, why didn't you stop?"

"I wasn't quite myself," said Tony.

"You remember trying to throttle him?"

"Of course."

"You were beside yourself with anger, is that it?"

"Yes."

"How long did this fit of rage last?" asked Foster.

"Not very long after your man hit me." Tony looked at Buckingham and rubbed his chin with a rueful smile. "Inspector, I don't want to evade your questions. I want to tell you the truth as simply as I can. You know what caused me to attack the man. I can only tell you that once I started to grip his throat, I had no thought except to make a job of it. It would be folly to pretend otherwise. If your man hadn't interfered, I think I would have killed him."

"I see," said Foster. Buckingham was writing quickly, and Foster looked at Tony for a few seconds to give his man time to get everything down. Then: "Have you ever seen Hibbett before today?"

"No."

"Earlier this evening I was told of the encounter you had with him in the road outside here," said Foster. "I had a detailed report. The man said you knew him as well as he knew you. At the time, you appeared to lose your temper with him, and he went off. That is not corroborative evidence for your present statement, Mr. Abbott."

"I can't help that," said Tony. "I'm telling you the truth."

"I see. When Hibbett spoke to you, he mentioned the name of a man—and it was that other name which appeared to make you lose your temper," said Foster. "The name was Lovelace. Who is this Lovelace?"

"A man whom I once knew in business."

"You told Hibbett that you knew no such man."

"It is six or seven years since I had dealings with Lovelace," said Tony. "I had almost forgotten the man's existence—and it isn't unusual to be unable to call to mind even a once familiar name after a lapse of time."

"I see," said Foster. "What were your relations with Lovelace?"

"I don't see what that has to do with it," said Tony.

"It might have a great deal. What were your relations with Lovelace, Mr. Abbott?"

"Unfriendly," said Tony.

"Why?"

Gillian said, "Tony, need you answer questions like this?"

Foster could have slapped her. He thought that Abbott was on the point of making a full statement, but now he saw the way the man's expression altered, as if all he needed was a little moral support.

"I don't think I need to," Tony said. "I will gladly tell you about my relations with Lovelace if you can show me that they are relevant to the point at issue," he said. "At the moment I imagine you are more interested in my relations, which are non-existent, with the man you say is Hibbett."

Foster managed to hide his vexation as he said, "Very well, Mr. Abbott, but at all times frankness with the police is advisable. Have you heard the name Hibbett before?"

"No."

"You have had a good opportunity of seeing the man at close quarters now. Are you sure that his face is unfamiliar?"

"Quite sure."

"I see." Foster turned to Gillian. "Do you know Hibbett?"

"Of course not," said Gillian. "I'd never seen him until this evening, when I thought he was trying to attract Tony's attention."

"Thank you," said Foster.

He was inclined to believe the stories, but there might be collusion. The torn dress and the red mark under Gillian's chin could have been caused when she tried to drag her husband from Hibbett. There was more satisfaction in the fact that Foster had now good reason to pursue his enquiries inside the house. A charge of attempted murder might not be necessary, but it was a good opportunity to gain admission whenever he wanted to. He wished that the attack had concerned Stafford, and that thought made him ask:

"Where is Mr. Stafford?"

"Upstairs in his studio," said Tony, "and Miss Stafford is with him there."

"Isn't it strange that they heard nothing?"

"No," said Tony. "Julius is composing, and the noise of the piano would probably drown out any sound from the floor below."

"Possibly," said Foster crisply. "Buckingham, go up for Mr. and Miss Stafford, please."

"Let me go," said Gillian. "If a stranger goes, Julius might lose his temper, and—" She broke off, at the rather tense smile on Foster's face. "Well, that wouldn't be unreasonable," she snapped. "Nothing is more exasperating than to be interrupted when you are working, especially such work as his."

"I think we shall have to risk another show of temper," said Foster dryly, "but I will draw it on my own head. You stay here, please."

Tony shrugged, Gillian looked angry, and Foster went upstairs briskly. The piano was silent. When he reached the second floor, which was new to him, he thought he heard voices. He listened outside the door for a minute but could not distinguish the words. Without tapping he went in.

He stood on the threshold, astonished.

There was a grand piano in the center of the room, and the top of it and the floor were littered with music sheets. Some had been written on, some had been screwed up or torn into pieces. On the piano were a bottle of whisky and a glass, standing on some brown paper. There were music racks all round the room, and in one corner was a settee.

Julius Stafford was lying on the settee, with his head propped up on cushions. He was flushed, and his eyes were closed. Anne Stafford was sitting on a hassock by his side, bathing his forehead. She had heard the door open and looked round.

"Oh!" she gasped.

She went white and stood up so abruptly that Foster was astonished, and his surprise at the scene quickened his sense of perception.

"You—you quite startled me," said Anne with a catch in her voice. "What on earth are you doing here at this time of night?"

"I am on official business," said Foster.

There was something in the woman's manner which held his interest; she was not only surprised, she was frightened. She stood rigid, with her hands clenched, staring at him fixedly, with eyes wide open and bright. Foster felt instinctively that if he could find the right question he might start a landslide.

Then Julius opened his eyes.

He wore yellow corduroys and a pink shirt open at the neck. His hair was ruffled and damp at the front, and his forehead also looked damp. There was a smell of eau-de-Cologne in the room, together with a strong odor of whisky.

"What the devil do *you* want?" demanded Julius, sitting up with a start. "My hat, have we got to be plagued with policemen day *and* night?" He swung his legs from the settee, pushed Anne aside, and advanced threateningly. "Well, what do you want?" he shouted.

"There will be no advantage in losing your temper," said Foster coldly. The feeling that if he asked the right question he would create consternation in these two people grew stronger, and he sought desperately for one. If he flung one of the names at them it might work, but there was no time to lose.

"What do you know of Albert Hibbett?" he demanded.

He knew almost as soon as the name was out of his mouth that he had picked a loser. Anne relaxed, and Julius stared at him wide-eyed.

"Never heard of him. Who is he?" Julius still sounded aggressive.

"He is a friend of—" began Foster.

He was about to say "Lovelace," in the hope that it would start something, but he was interrupted by a shout from downstairs. This time it was from Grimes, and there was something in the man's voice which sounded an alarm. Foster hurried to the landing and saw Grimes standing in the middle of the landing below, disheveled and wide-eyed.

"Sir! Sir!" cried Grimes. "Inspector—"

"What is it?" called Foster, hurrying downstairs.

"What's the matter up there?" boomed Buckingham from the downstairs hall.

Grimes gasped, "He's got away, sir. Hibbett. He—I——"

"*Where?*" roared Buckingham. "Which way did he go?"

"Out the window," said Grimes.

"After him!" roared Buckingham, and rushed to the front door. Grimes was almost distraught, and Foster did not harass him but went into the bedroom. The window was wide open, and the curtains were blowing inward.

"It's too late!" wailed Grimes.

"What the devil's happening here tonight?" roared Julius, striding into the room. His sister was passing the door on her way downstairs.

"I'll explain later," said Foster.

"You'll explain *now!*" snapped Julius.

"Oh, don't be a fool!" said Foster, pushing quickly past him. Grimes was halfway down the stairs, but Foster caught up with him and gave his back a friendly slap.

"Don't let this upset you, Grimes. What happened?"

"He—he came round, sir," said Grimes, trying to steady his voice, "and complained that his foot was hurting. I thought he looked so ill that there wasn't any danger. Suddenly he hit me with a hot-water bottle, sir—it caught me on the back of the head and nearly knocked me out. Proper dazed for a minute, I was. When I saw him going out of the window I shouted, but he was too quick for me." Grimes wiped the perspiration from his face. "I can't tell you how sorry I am, sir."

"I'm sure you are," Foster said. "Do you feel well enough to have a look round for him?"

"I'm all right now," said Grimes, "but I don't think we'll see *him* again tonight."

While he telephoned headquarters, Foster could see Gillian, Anne, and Julius talking in the study. Gillian was doing most of the talking. He thought that the others were genuinely surprised. He gave instructions for a general call to be put out for Hibbett, and when he finished telephoning, went toward the study.

Julius was asking, "What did the man look like?"

Gillian gave a fair description of Hibbett. Foster would have interrupted then, but he saw Julius start, as if he had realized something unpleasant. Julius and Anne shot quick glances at each other and then made an obvious effort to appear unperturbed. Once again Foster felt that if he could put the right question he would be able to learn a great deal. They were both worked up, but a few hours' rest would probably enable them to regain their nerve. He went forward determinedly, calling from the passage:

"Oh, Stafford, do you know a man named Lovelace?"

"Lovelace?" asked Julius, in a steady voice.

"*Love*lace?" echoed Anne, her voice not quite so steady.

"Do you?" asked Foster sharply.

"I used to know a Jerry Lovelace," said Julius, with the same studied calm. "We were very good friends, Foster. He did a lot of business for me. Why?"

"Hibbett, the man who escaped—mentioned the name."

"Well, fancy that," said Julius with a sneer.

The day will come when you'll change your tone, my man, Foster thought, but he was aware of the weakness of his position and did not pursue that line of enquiry. Buckingham and Tony returned from their fruitless search, but Grimes remained outside for some time. Before he returned there was another visitor—Castle, wrapped in a dressing gown and looking even more gaunt than usual, with his hair on end and his eyes dulled with sleep.

"I heard movements and wondered if I could be any help," he said, looking curiously about him.

"No, we're all right," said Tony. "I do hope we haven't disturbed your wife."

"She's not come round yet," said Castle. He looked unhappy and was obviously trying to restrain his curiosity. It got the better of him, however, and he asked, "Has there been some trouble?"

"Spindles has been burgled," said Foster quickly.

"Oh! I hope you've not lost anything?" Castle looked at Tony and Gillian. "I thought those burglaries were finished," he added uncomfortably. "Perhaps you'll be able to catch the fellow now, Inspector."

"I'll certainly try," said Foster.

Tony and Gillian felt grateful for his bland answer to Castle's question. Tony walked back with the Vicar, and when he returned, Foster, Buckingham, and Grimes were in the hall together.

He looked at them with a rueful smile. "Well, what are you going to do with me?" he enquired.

"Nothing at the moment," said Foster. "I hope you won't go from here until further notice, Mr. Abbott. We shall have to make further enquiries, of course. On the strength of your statement, I don't see any reason for taking immediate action."

"That's considerate of you," said Tony.

"I hope you appreciate it," said Foster dryly.

He left with the others. Tony watched them walk along the drive, then closed and bolted the door. He stood in the hall alone, with a hand on his forehead and a tormented expression in his eyes. The relief had come and gone; now he recalled the mad fury in which he had nearly choked the life out of Hibbett. The thought of what he might do in these fits of rage was frightening in itself. He had no inclination to plead extenuating circumstances; he should never have gone so far—he could well have dealt with Hibbett, who was a puny creature, in an easier manner.

Now and again he recalled Julius' talk with Anne. If the police thought along those lines, he might be accused of the murder of an unknown man. Did the fact that Foster had mentioned Lovelace mean that the body had been identified, and that it *was* Lovelace?

Anne came out of the study.

"Good night, Tony," she said. "Don't worry too much."

"I'm all right," he mumbled.

Later, in bed, he said to Gillian, "I'm beginning to wonder if I'm sane."

"My sweet, don't torment yourself," said Gillian, in distress. "It's been a horrible night, but no one could blame you for what you did. We ought to be thankful it's no worse."

"Yes," said Tony, and after a moment's silence, he repeated, "Yes. I wonder what the devil Hibbett wanted? I don't know of such a man in connection with Lovelace, and I think I would have remembered by now if I'd ever seen him before. What on earth could he want with me?" he added helplessly.

It was the question in his mind when at last he fell asleep.

· 15 ·

SUPERINTENDENT FOLLY

THE LONDON TRAIN was due in at half-past one. Foster and Buckingham waited on the platform together, silently.

There was no news of Hibbett, although all the county police had been alerted. Foster had also telephoned Scotland Yard the previous night, giving a description of him, and also mentioned Lovelace. He did not doubt that Folly would be fully acquainted with the latest details.

Buckingham and Grimes had been relieved just after dawn; nothing had happened at Spindles, and before he left for the station, Foster had been told that all four residents had been seen during the morning. He had made a full report to Harrington, who had said little but was obviously sorry that the case had taken a turn for the worse just before Folly's arrival; had Hibbett not escaped, there would have been a very different complexion on the whole business. Foster tossed away his half-smoked cigarette and grimaced at Buckingham. "We're a fine pair to be meeting a man like Folly," he said. "You look half asleep and I feel washed out. He'll rate us as country bumpkins."

"Then we'll teach him better," said Buckingham.

Foster laughed. "That's the spirit! Ah, here's the train."

It came snorting into the station, and porters crowded to the edge of the platform. Foster eagerly scanned the ranks of the descending passengers, especially those who came out of the first-class carriages. He had seen a newspaper photograph of Folly and was led to expect a big man. According to Anderson, Trevelyan, the surgeon, was tall and thin.

When most of the passengers were on the platform and the rush for taxis began, and when Foster was beginning to think that Folly had missed the train, a tall, thin man came out of a first-class carriage. He was carrying a briefcase and laughing. Then his companion appeared and squeezed himself through the doorway. He was unusually fat, and as tall as the man whom Foster took to be Trevelyan.

As he stood on the platform, Superintendent Folly opened his mouth in a wide yawn, while Trevelyan looked round for a porter. Foster approached slowly, anxious to size up the man from Scotland Yard. Buckingham was staring wide-eyed, as if he could not believe that this could be the legendary Superintendent.

Folly yawned again, noisily. Although he was so fat, his well-cut suit made him look neat and compact. He was wearing a black Homburg hat, and his heavy jowl half covered his collar and tie. His well-shod feet were absurdly small for so large a man and created the illusion that a slight push would send him over. His eyes fascinated Foster, for the lids drooped and he looked half-asleep.

"You said *I* looked tired," whispered Buckingham. "He looks dead beat. He's yawning again."

"How do you do, sir?" Foster said, stepping forward. "I'm here to meet you, and I've reserved a table at a hotel in Milton for lunch."

Folly looked at him; the idea that he was tired was an illusion. His eyes were very bright and shrewd. He stared at Foster for an appreciable time, until Foster began to feel uncomfortable; then he smiled. The smile made him look almost cherubic, and the flash of gold teeth robbed his face of the portentous solemnity which it assumed in repose.

"I am delighted to hear that, Inspector—you are Inspector Foster?" When Foster nodded, he went on: "All that remains to be proved is the quality of the hotel in Milton. I warn you, I am hungry. I may say I am famished. Sir Alexander Trevelyan is equally hungry. Who is to be the fourth? Colonel Harrington?"

"The Colonel conveys his regrets," said Foster, "but he is engaged until this evening. Sergeant Buckingham will be with us."

"Sergeant Buckingham," said Folly. He turned toward Buckingham, who blushed. Folly smiled again. "Good sergeants are the backbone of the police force," he declared. "Do you know Sir Alexander?"

"Only by reputation," Foster said faintly.

"Good physicians are ruined when they become pathologists," declared Folly. "You see here the ruin of one of our most promising physicians." He smiled again. "Trev, this is Chief Inspector Foster and Sergeant Buckingham."

Trevelyan was a younger man than Foster had expected, probably not much more than forty. He seemed mildly amused by the Superintendent; they were obviously old friends. With the luggage trundling ahead of them, the four men walked along the platform, Folly talking to Buckingham, and Foster with the pathologist.

The luggage was put into the car, and Foster was lighthearted as he drove to the White Horse. Nothing that happened during the excellent luncheon could depress him. He would get on well with Folly, who was very different from his reputation. Trevelyan was a likable man, too, and the immediate future promised well. Not once during the luncheon did they talk of the case in hand. Folly drew Buckingham out, obviously trying to judge his mettle; Foster thought he was satisfied, and felt pleased because Folly seemed to assume that he did not need testing. Immediately after lunch, Buckingham left the dining room. Folly stared after him.

"Useful man, Foster. Doesn't look a bit like a man with grandiose ideas. Where's he gone?"

"He'll be back in a moment," said Foster. "I can serve some good coffee in my office, or if you'd prefer to come to my house, we can talk there. I've all the papers ready."

"Let us sit here for a while," said Folly. "Who wants papers? I am not interested in papers. Show me people. The more the better. Bad people and good people. Trevelyan will tell you that my hobby is people. In spite of my long experience, I still have some faith in human nature. True, it is a remarkable thing. The most promising and attractive people are often the rogues. I have never really succeeded in preventing myself from being biased in favor of a decent fellow. Take Abbott, now."

Foster stared at him. "Do you know Abbott?"

"Not personally. I have made enquiries and talked to people who do know him. I am shortly to retire," announced Folly. "This may be my last case. Consequently, like all policemen, I am thinking of writing my memoirs. They will be astounding. Immediately I knew that Abbott, an author, was concerned in this case, I discovered the name of his agent. I visited this agent to discuss my memoirs." Not once during this statement did Folly smile, and his eyes were half hidden by the heavy lids. "In discussing my memoirs, I discussed promising young authors. My experience does not follow the accepted rule that authors invariably talk a great deal about themselves. They have no need to. What their publishers do not say for them, their agents do. I also visited Abbott's publishers, who, Savory suggested—Savory is his agent—were just the people for my memoirs. They were enthusiastic about my book—as yet nonexistent—but not particularly so about Abbott's work. They like Abbott, however; everyone likes Abbott. So, Abbott is the man to watch.

"Stafford is in a different category," continued Folly. "Few people have a good word for him. Even those people who publish his music are unenthusiastic about the man, but they rave about his music. I don't know an F sharp from an A flat, but I know that Stafford is considered a remarkable composer. Do you like Abbott?" he asked unexpectedly.

"I like what I've seen of him," said Foster.

"And I like what I've heard of him," declared Folly. "I imagine that our opinions of Stafford also coincide. Concerning Anne Stafford, Foster. Do we agree on her, I wonder? A woman with a mission, the preservation and glorification of her brother's so-called genius, the fostering of all the children born of his labors; not perverted—don't misunderstand me—not even abnormal, but fiercely devoted to the man's ability rather than to the man himself, her self-imposed task to shelter him from storm and trial, a woman who rarely thinks of herself. Yes?"

"I think it fits," said Foster cautiously. "I don't know her well. But how on earth did you——"

Folly held up his hand. "Do you tell others how you work? Do you allow them to learn the secrets of your success? Certainly not. I, however, do. I am untroubled by the fear that you will copy my methods. No one could do so without inviting disaster. I would not like to tell you how many times I have been severely reprimanded for *not* conforming to the police manual. I should be a sergeant. At heart I am a sergeant. I am only a C.I.D. officer because the fatter I became the less comfortable it was to walk the streets, and I had to do something about it. What was I saying? Oh, yes, about Anne Stafford. You must know, Foster, that people like Stafford have many friends and more acquaintances, hangers-on, many of them, who will gladly talk. The relationship between the Staffords is well-known. Anne is an admirable woman. She would probably make an excellent wife *or* mother, but she will almost certainly die holding her brother's hand. I can tell you that she is engaged to a man named Barr, whose parents disapprove. So they should. She is probably thinking of marriage in order to provide her brother with money. Stafford is a spend-thrift, always hard up.

"As for how I learned about her, that was not at all difficult," Folly continued. "Three times in four years Julius Stafford has been detained for motoring offenses—or other trivial offenses, I am not sure what—and each time she bailed him out. Each time, I understand, she showed a great concern for him. If she were to be taken away from him for a few months, it would make or break him—and he has been used to leaning on her for so long that it would probably break him." Folly smiled, and he looked beatific. "Now if we could detain her for a week or two—but I am driveling! You do not want to hear me drivel, but want to solve this case. What's gone wrong?"

Foster gulped. "So you've guessed that?"

"Guessed? My dear fellow, it was written all over you. If you had fitted things together, you would have waited for me in the office and received me with terrible formality."

Foster laughed. "That's not true, but something has gone wrong. Perhaps you've seen the reports I telephoned. A man named Hibbett——"

"Not Hibbett. Welch."

Foster gasped and then said, "I wish someone had warned me about you, you're not safe."

Folly chuckled. "Simple enough. Welch, or Hibbett as he calls himself, is not unknown to us in London. Nor is his reputation. He is a confidence man, a card sharp, a real rogue. He has been out of prison for two years, and that is probably two years too long. Such a man cannot keep away from crime. I was very glad that he appeared on the scene, because he is known to have visited the Staffords' Chelsea flat."

"Good Lord!" exclaimed Foster.

"It is true, and not necessarily surprising. Did I mention that he is not above a little blackmail, and certainly not beyond com-mitting violence? As he has been out of prison for so long it is obvious that he has committed none of the more obvious crimes. Therefore, he has either been conning with unusual cleverness, which I do not believe, or he has been extorting blackmail, which

I can believe, and which I think is likely. The Abbotts, according to your report, deny knowing him."

"Yes," said Foster.

"Any self-respecting person would deny knowing Welch, alias Hibbett," declared Folly. "If they are being blackmailed by him there is even more reason. That report of yours, now. It impressed and amused me. You think it possible that Hibbett was blackmailing the Abbotts. You think it possible that he was found in the room, that Abbott deliberately attacked him, intending to commit murder, or else was driven to it by some extortionate demand. Isn't that so?"

"It's obviously possible," said Foster.

"Yes. The Abbotts would tell the same story. The necessary thing is to watch them and to find out what they are like together. If the man has committed some crime of which the woman knows, she will probably feel bitter about it. In public she would present a brave front and perhaps be even more than usually cheerful. One might say exuberant. She—ah! I have scored a bull!" declared Folly complacently. "Well, is she too high-spirited?"

"At one time, all of them were," said Foster. "In my first report——"

"I remember it clearly. You are referring to the time when you first met them. That is not exactly what I mean. We must get a third party's opinion of the relationship between the author and his wife. Trevelyan, here, might get it from this clergyman, Castle—we shall see.

"But I fear I have digressed," continued Folly. "Concerning Hibbett's visit to the Staffords' Chelsea flat, now. It happened on the afternoon of Thursday—I beg your pardon—Tuesday, May 11. Yes, Foster, you are right—the day before the removal from Chelsea. You know that Stafford is not unacquainted with the police, and consequently the police are not unacquainted with him or his flat. Moreover, the noise which came from his attic while he was in the throes of composition reached the Chelsea police station whenever they were at their loudest. I have heard complaints from neighbors, too; thus the house where the Staffords lived is not unknown to the local police. Forgive me if I repeat myself, I want Trevelyan to understand." He shot the doctor a sly glance, and Trevelyan grimaced at him. "When Hibbett called there it was reported. The policeman who saw and recognized him, a most intelligent man, kept observation. Shortly after Hibbett arrived, Abbott called. He went upstairs, came out again in a few minutes, had tea at a nearby café, and then went back, after Anne Stafford had returned—both Staffords were out when Hibbett and Abbott arrived. Hibbett left after half an hour. Abbott then left. It was some time before Stafford himself returned, and he was in a very advanced stage of intoxication. It was a very fortunate thing," he added softly, "that an accident had taken place in Whitehall Place soon after Stafford left his club. Otherwise there would have been no excuse for asking you to send a man to Spindles so early. I am very glad you called in person, Foster. That must have been inspiration."

Foster said, "Confound it—*excuse* for sending me out there?"

Folly looked smug. "That is the word I used. I was delighted when I had your report. It was both factual and interesting, and so brief! You see, Foster, a short while before Hibbett and Abbott —curious similarity of consonants in those names, isn't there?— visited Chelsea, another man was seen to enter that house. Yes, you're right, Lovelace is the name." Folly beamed. "Don't say it, Foster. Pretend not to be surprised. Lovelace went to Chelsea. He was not seen to come out. The next morning there was a hurried removal—I have ascertained that, by an urgent request, the moving was put forward a day. *Why*, I wonder? Where is Lovelace?" He bellowed the question. "Where is the morgue?"

He pushed his chair back and rose majestically to his feet. Foster, a little dazed, followed him to the door with Trevelyan. As they reached it Buckingham appeared. Not until they got into the taxi did Folly speak again.

"Trevelyan knows Lovelace," he said. "That is why I agreed to bring him. We shall soon know whether Lovelace was murdered. Hurry, driver!"

· 16 ·

SUPERINTENDENT FOLLY IS SAD

TREVELYAN IDENTIFIED the body after a close scrutiny. The features were unrecognizable, but the scar on the neck and the short little fingers were definite indications, and there were other small pointers that enabled him to be quite sure.

During the examination in the cold, clammy morgue, Folly talked in loud undertones to Foster and Buckingham, explaining that Lovelace had been in South America and obviously had been badly beaten up. It was known that he had fallen foul of a remote tribe and managed to survive only after fantastic hardships. "Be that as it may," he said, "it does not affect our work."

"I don't quite follow you," said Foster.

Folly raised his eyebrows. "Indeed? Think again, Foster. You might imagine that such an eminent investigator as myself would only stir from his comfortable London office on a matter of great importance. You might think that Lovelace's sojourn in South America has something to do with the interest I am showing in him. I, however, am not interested in his past except insofar as it affects his murder." To hear the man talking now, thought Foster, it was hard to imagine that he had a scrap of humor in him. "You may conceivably have some fantastic notion that I am here because I want to find out whether Lovelace was killed by an Englishman or a vengeful South American. Is it not a fact that such notions have passed through your mind, Foster?"

"Vaguely, and I rejected the possibility," said Foster.

"So you rejected the possibility," said Folly in a vast whisper. "You imagine that I have come to Milton to investigate the murder of a man when a dozen other officers could do it as efficiently. Well! I am disappointed in you."

Foster grinned. "That's too bad. Do you think he might have been killed by a vengeful South American?"

"I did once," said Folly.

Buckingham was staring with wide-eyed astonishment. Foster could not make up his mind whether Folly was being serious or whether this was an example of his humor.

"Really," said Foster.

"Really," repeated Folly. "Come, Foster, you doubt my word. You need not. Lovelace came from Buenos Aires not many weeks ago. We did not discover it until a few days before he visited the Chelsea flat. We learned it when we arrested an Argentinian who was wanted very badly by the authorities. In an effort to save himself—a vain effort, I may say—this man told us he had come to England to seek out Lovelace, who had contrived to bring into the country a small parcel of jewels stolen from a mine in Bolivia. I understand that a man responsible for butchering tens of thousands of people was intent on buying a cattle farm in the Argentine. Most suitable! Lovelace stole the jewels which were to have financed the purchase. Naturally the victims of the robbery were angry. Also, they were now almost without means. A desperate venture was launched, no less than an effort to regain the diamonds from Lovelace. All of these things, you understand, I knew when your first report reached me. I may say that had you not asked for the co-operation of Scotland Yard I would have persuaded the Home Office to allow me to come down here. Then the fat would have been in the fire," he added with an unexpected grin. "No luncheon parties for Superintendent Folly then!

"You are interested in these jewels. You may well be. Immediately the story was known, a widespread search was made for Lovelace. He was traced to an apartment house in Bloomsbury. Some jewels were later found there—there may be others—which might be a motive for his murder. These are the reasons for my special interest in this case. At one time I thought that other adventurers might be after Lovelace's blood, but now I no longer think so. This is a local business, as one might say. Outside his Bloomsbury quarters," went on Folly with heavy sarcasm, "there waited two men who are persuaded to call themselves detectives. They made their presence known only too clearly. Lovelace did not return. He was next seen entering the Staffords' flat. Then he disappeared—or, rather, he failed to reappear.

"Had any other man and not myself been placed in charge of

these investigations—" here Folly paused, almost as if unable to contemplate the incompetent mishandling of the case that would, under such circumstances, have undoubtedly occurred—"then I have no doubt that both the Staffords and the Abbotts would have been closely questioned about him. And so put on their guard.

"In my experience, however, it is a waste of time to investigate the murder of a man if his body is missing. By interrogating the people who might have killed him, including Hibbett, we would have warned them. I succeeded in persuading my superiors to wait until the body was discovered. There appeared a reasonable hope that this was the body, and your prompt recourse to Scotland Yard gave me much pleasure, Foster, *very* much pleasure. True, the fact that it is naked creates a problem—we must find the clothes. However, let me say again, I am now sure that the motive for his murder was nothing to do with his flight from South America, or the man who pursued him. I looked upon this case, with justification, I think, as one in which I had prior rights. I rarely leave London, but I was interested not only in the murder of this remarkable man but also in a county police force which, before it had made reasonably sure that there were no prospects of making an arrest, asked for our assistance. So here I am. And now that my friend Trevelyan has confirmed that the body your people pulled out of the river is actually that of Lovelace, we are at last beginning to make progress. Have I told you how Trevelyan came to know him?"

"No," said Foster.

"That was remiss of me. Lovelace was involved in an accident before we knew that he was in the country—he used an alias. He was taken to the London hospital to which Trevelyan is a consultant. He was suffering from concussion and shock, which had temporarily deprived him of the use of his legs. Trevelyan examined Lovelace and came to the conclusion that the paralysis was temporary, and the man recovered in comparatively few days. Two days after he had been discharged from hospital we arrested the man who was looking for him. A description of Lovelace was soon circulated and Trevelyan saw it—he does a great deal of police work. Are you satisfied, Foster?"

"Quite," said Foster.

"That's more than I am," said Folly. "I want to know who killed Lovelace and why."

"What are you going to do next?" asked Foster.

"Meet the people involved," declared Folly. "There is no other course open to me."

Gillian and Tony were alone most of that Sunday. They went to church in the morning and walked back with Castle, who was obviously worried about his wife. The little church had been crowded, owing to local curiosity about the people at Spindles.

"So you see," the Vicar said, "you have found a way of filling my church for me, Abbott. I wish I had been able to take advantage of the opportunity, but——"

"Try not to worry too much," said Tony.

"From what you have told me," said Castle, "it is you who have need to worry. Abbott, please believe me when I say that if there is anything at all I can do to help you, I am only too ready. Just say the word."

"I will, thanks very much," said Tony appreciatively.

He had found it a relief to tell the Vicar what had happened, to admit to the rage that had nearly made him kill Hibbett. He had slept badly, was irritable with Gillian, and had to exert himself to behave normally. As they neared Spindles they came upon a little crowd outside the gates.

"I half expected to see Foster's car," Tony said to Gillian.

"I was half afraid that we would," said Gillian.

There were two or three policemen in plain clothes near the house, and P. C. Grimes was standing there leaning on his bicycle; he saluted respectfully as they passed him. It was a relief to get inside. Tony went to his study, Gillian to prepare the cold lunch, which, by mutual agreement, they had on Sundays. Anne came down to say that Julius had a splitting headache and proposed to spend the day in bed. She took her own lunch up to Julius' room.

Toward the middle of the afternoon a Daimler pulled up outside Spindles. Gillian and Tony were in the drawing room and looked out the window. They saw an enormous man come along the drive with Foster and Buckingham, and they saw Anderson with another stranger going next door.

"I think I know what this means," said Tony slowly.

"What?" asked Gillian.

"Foster's called in Scotland Yard," said Tony, narrowing his eyes. "Yes, that's Folly—Superintendent Folly, the big man of the C.I.D." He smiled mirthlessly. "They don't mean to lose much time."

"How do you know who it is?" asked Gillian.

"I've seen him in court once or twice," said Tony. "Police courts and criminal courts are part of my stock-in-trade. Oh, well. Folly can be a bit of a brute, by all accounts."

Folly, however, set himself out to be pleasant. He greeted them in a booming voice and bowed gallantly to Gillian. Then he proceeded to declare how deeply he sympathized with Tony in his predicament. It was natural that a man should lose his temper when his wife was attacked by a villain like Hibbett. It was a great pity that the circumstances made it necessary for him to help Inspector Foster to pursue his enquiries into the murder of the man found in the river—an acquaintance, it was known, of Hibbett. Did Mr. Abbott know a man named Welch?

Foster listened admiringly. Whatever Tony had been thinking, he certainly could not have been prepared for the casual utterance of Hibbett's real name. Foster watched Tony closely. Tony, however, showed no reaction at all.

"No," he said. "Is that the dead man?"

"Obviously you do not know Welch," said Folly. "He is, I have every reason to believe, very much alive." He went on to talk about the bricks and the use of the boat and to ask questions so blatantly intended to encourage Tony to implicate Julius and Anne that Tony began to wonder whether Folly's reputation was all deserved. It was a curious fact, said Folly, that Julius Stafford had brought forward the day of moving, was it not? Did Mr. Abbott know why? That was a pity, a great pity. Was Mr. Abbott seriously asking him to believe that during the time that they had been in Bray, Julius had behaved like a normal man? What? He rarely behaved like a normal man? Then why had Mr. Abbott denied that there was anything peculiar in his behavior? What? It would be considered peculiar in other people, but not in Julius Stafford. Surely this was asking too much of a simple policeman to believe. Stafford was temperamental, was he? Simple policemen had little time for temperament. A genius? He had heard it suggested, but he had grave suspicions of most people who claimed to be so brilliant. Where was Stafford now? In bed with a headache. How sad! And his sister? Keeping him company. How kind!

By the end of half an hour it seemed clear to Gillian and Tony that Folly had some reason to suspect Julius. He did nothing at all to try to hide his suspicions, and became more and more sarcastic until, with a sudden heave, he rose from the settee and said, "Foster, lead me to this remarkable musician."

He stalked to the door, waited for Buckingham to open it, and stepped into the passage. Then he turned round and squeezed into the room again. Something in his manner was forbidding; the man was capable of creating whatever atmosphere he wanted. He spoke softly, staring at Tony.

"Oh, Mr. Abbott, there is one other thing. Seven years ago—in April—you violently assaulted the person of a man named Lovelace, Jeremiah Lovelace. Is that not a fact?"

Tony stood quite still. Gillian caught her breath. Foster was out of his depth, but he kept his face expressionless. It was astonishing that in a few seconds Folly not only had charged the atmosphere with tension, but had blasted through Tony's composure with a statement that was obviously made with full knowledge of the facts.

Tony said, "I—"

"Did you or did you not make a violent assault upon Lovelace?" roared Folly.

"I—"

"Answer me, sir!"

"When you stop behaving like an ill-bred oaf, I'll answer your questions. Not before."

"Ill-bred—*oaf*," breathed Folly. "You have the impertinence to stand there, sir, and talk to me in that fashion?"

He paused, and no one spoke. He took a step forward, smiled with exaggerated politeness, bowed slightly before Tony, and said in a honeyed voice, "Mr. Abbott, be good enough, please, to tell me whether you once violently assaulted Jeremiah Lovelace."

"We quarreled, yes," said Tony.

"So you quarreled. You quarreled! You have the impudence to

say that you quarreled when you tried to murder the man in exactly the same way as you tried to murder Hibbett last night. Do not attempt to deny it! It is the truth! Buckingham's swift action managed to prevent Hibbett's murder, but other men have been murdered. You—"

"Don't!" cried Gillian.

"Have the goodness not to interrupt, Madam!" Folly thundered. "Abbott, the police have long memories. A policeman saw Lovelace immediately after your dastardly attack on him. At Lovelace's urgent request no action was taken; you were not charged with assault. Only a generous man like Jeremiah Lovelace would have refused to lay a most serious charge against you."

Tony said, "Lovelace was as generous as Uriah Heep."

"So you dislike him? You have a grudge against him?"

"I have had nothing to do with him for seven years," said Tony.

"In that seven years you have nursed your grudge. He cheated you. You conceived a violent hatred for him, and you attempted to kill him. That attempt failed. You thereupon determined to bide your time. You nursed your grudge, I say. You worked out a scheme of revenge, most terrible revenge, and—"

Tony said, "You're talking absolute nonsense."

"I see," said Folly quietly. "I am an ill-bred oaf and I talk nonsense. Perhaps I shall be able to modify your opinion of me, Mr. Abbott. Do you deny that you once attacked Lovelace?"

"No."

"*Thank* you, Mr. Abbott. I congratulate you on the revival of your most convenient memory. Yesterday you were asked, most civilly, whether you had any reason to dislike Jeremiah Lovelace. You refused to say. *Why*, Mr. Abbott?"

"The question was not justified," said Tony.

"I see." Folly uttered a baying laugh. "So now Inspector Foster is the victim of your weighty conclusions."

"Until ten minutes ago," Tony said cuttingly, "I had a good opinion of the police."

"Until—" began Folly. He stared ruminatively at Tony, then abruptly turned on his heel, sailed through the doorway, and disappeared into the passage. Buckingham followed him, and when Foster joined them Folly was covering his mouth with his hand and heaving; he looked convulsed. He waved his free hand toward the door, and Buckingham closed it hastily. There were tears in Folly's eyes, and Foster stood looking at him in amazement.

"Beautiful!" Folly wheezed at last. "Oh, my! Damn it, Foster, the man's a treasure! I haven't been spoken to like that for ten years. Then the man went to Dartmoor for seven, to repent." He wiped his eyes and went on in a loud voice, in spite of his precaution with the door. "A worthy opponent, Mr. Abbott. Did you observe him closely? Did you see how, at one stage, he was about to lose his self-control? Did you see how neatly he prevented himself, how differently he acted? Foster, I tell you that Anthony John Abbott is a *very* clever man."

"Surely—" began Foster.

"I have great doubts about the genuineness of those fits of rage of his," said Folly. "Think how convincing a defense it would be if he were to say that he has suffered from these paroxysms for many years, that he was not responsible for what he did during them. Think how it would affect a jury. Oh, it would not surprise me if Mr. Abbott is not cunning as well as clever, and convinced that even if the crime is traced to him he will not suffer the consequences." He pulled Foster toward him and beckoned Buckingham. "He has heard me express my doubts, of course. He may be clever, he may be cunning, he is certainly worried. Come, now, let us see Stafford."

He led the way up the stairs.

Tony and Gillian were standing looking at each other, white-faced. Hardly a word that the Superintendent had said had been lost, although they had not heard his last-minute whisper.

Gillian said, "Tony, it must be Lovelace who's dead."

"It looks like it."

"And—and they bring up a thing that happened seven years ago. It's damnable!"

"We ought to have expected it," said Tony. He was rubbing his hands together, and they were moist. "Folly probably knows, or thinks he knows, a lot more. If I could be sure that I hadn't done some crazy thing I wouldn't care a hoot, but— But I might have," he added, and drew in his breath. "I might have."

Superintendent Folly's face was quite expressionless when he reached Julius' bedroom and stood outside. There was no trace of laughter on his face now, and he seemed to have forgotten what he had said downstairs.

"Open the door," he whispered.

Foster would have knocked, but he decided to let Folly have his head, and opened the door. There was no sound. He stepped inside and saw a rumpled bed and an untidy room, but no one was there.

"Curious," said Folly. He stepped across the room and put a hand on the bed. "Cold," he said. "Not been slept in for some hours, I imagine. Perhaps the genius is at work again. Do you know the way to his studio?"

"Yes," said Foster.

"More stairs," sighed Folly.

At that moment Anne's door opened. They all looked round and saw her come from her room. She was dressed in black, which heightened the pallor of her cheeks. She stared at them in surprise.

"What are you doing in my brother's room?"

"We are policemen, Madam, with every right to search this house," said Folly. "Where is your brother? You are, presumably, Miss Anne Stafford?"

She ignored the last words and said, "He's in his room." She hurried toward them and disappeared into the room, pulling up short when she saw the empty bed. She turned round without a word, pushed past them, and raced up the stairs to the studio.

"After her!" hissed Folly.

Foster was already on the stairs, and he reached the studio a yard or two behind her. Again she stood quite still for a second, staring about the untidy, deserted room. When she turned her face was chalk white.

"What have you done with him?"

"We're looking for him," said Foster.

"Why must you hound him like this?" cried Anne. "Why can't you leave him alone? *Where is he?*"

"Now, please," said Foster. "we want a word with him and expected to find him up here."

"I left him asleep," said Anne. She pushed past him again and went downstairs, hurried into his room, and looked into the wardrobe. Folly followed her into the room and watched her closely. She pushed aside several suits, obviously looking for a particular one. Then she turned round, and her eyes looked heavy with dread.

"He's gone away," she said tonelessly. "He's gone away."

"How disappointing," said Folly, absurdly peevish. "I particularly wanted to see him. Perhaps *you* can answer my questions, Miss Stafford."

· 17 ·

THE LULL

FOLLY TREATED Anne with great courtesy, and there was little point in any of his questions. He mentioned Lovelace but didn't ask if she had seen him recently.

As they went downstairs leaving Anne in Julius' room, Folly said quietly, "The girl's thunderstruck. She must be watched. I don't think she really heard what I said; I could have got nothing out of her. If I'd asked leading questions she would have remembered them afterward and been warned. Felt sorry for her, nearly as sorry as I did for Gillian Abbott. Not a very nice case, Foster; there are some pleasant people involved. I never like it when we have to deal with decent, ordinary people who have been driven to commit some crime. Someone here *has* committed a crime, you know. Not necessarily the murder of Lovelace, although it is beginning to look like that, I must say. Hibbett could have been a party to it, and they may have moved the body under duress."

"So you think they brought it from Chelsea?"

"Someone brought it here, put it in the boat, and dumped it in the river," said Folly. "It could have been someone unknown to everyone here, but it isn't likely. Too many undercurrents of fear. Buckingham! Have you telephoned headquarters and asked for a watch to be kept for Julius Stafford?"

"Why, no, I—"

"Then what are you waiting for, man? We want to see him, don't we? That's two of them have got away from here. It looks as if your men outside want a bit of discipline, Foster. I suppose one of them might have followed him."

"There'll be trouble if they didn't," said Foster. "I'll go and see them."

In five minutes Foster knew that Julius had not been seen to leave by the front gates; Grimes, in fact, went further and swore that the man had not gone out that way. There was a plain-clothesman at the back, and he had seen nothing.

"He can't have disappeared into thin air," said Foster.

He was standing by the side of the house, immediately opposite the gap in the hedge which led to the vicarage. He heard Trevelyan's voice alternating with Castle's, but he was too pre-occupied to notice the relief in Castle's tones. Foster looked round; there was a side door from Spindles, and Stafford could have left by that and, in a few steps, got behind the untrimmed laurels near the gap in the fence.

"That's probably how he went out," said Foster.

He went into the vicarage garden through the gap. Castle was by the drive gates, still talking to Trevelyan, and Anderson came hurrying out of the house. He looked surprised to see Foster in the garden.

"Looking for something?" he asked.

"Yes. Have you seen Stafford?"

"No," said Anderson, frowning, "has he run away?"

"He's gone out," said Foster.

"Well, he can't have gone far," said Anderson. "He was in his bedroom when we came here—I noticed him looking out the window. It was an upstairs room, so I suppose it was his bed-room."

"Thanks," said Foster. "Is there anyone at the back, do you know?"

"Probably the daily is there," said Anderson. "Mrs. Blackshaw is in her room—she appears to have kept to it since the shindy the other night. I must hurry," he added, and then turned back. "Oh, Trevelyan has good news of Mrs. Castle. She'll probably be able to walk in a few weeks' time."

"Splendid!" said Foster.

He spoke mechanically as he went to the rear of the vicarage and to the end of the garden. In places the hedge was so thick that it was impossible to see the garden, but in other places there was a clear view of the river, the landing stage and the boat. The plainclothesman who had been on duty at the back was in sight, but there was no reason to believe that he had been interested in the vicarage garden. Foster went to the end of it. There was no hedge for the last few yards, and it was possible to step from one garden to the other.

Grimes came up, looking miserable. "Can I help, sir?"

"I'm thinking of striking while the iron's hot," said Foster. "We'll go to the other side and find out whether he was seen, and we'll use Spindles' boat. Come on."

Grimes took the oars, and a little crowd congregated near the bank for which he was heading. Foster started to question them as if addressing a meeting. Two or three said they thought they had seen Stafford (Foster himself had not mentioned names), but there was no general agreement. Then one old man said:

"Tell 'ee who I did see, Inspector."

"Who?" asked Foster.

"That young feller who writes for the paper."

Foster said sharply, "Do you mean Lancing, of the Milshire News?"

"Aye, that's un," said the old man. "Running, he was. I thought he'd fall in afore he'd finished, but he never." The man sounded regretful. "Running that way, he was," he declared, and pointed toward Riversmeet.

"This looks promising," said Foster. "Pull back to the other side a moment." He thanked the crowd and then waited until he was close enough to the other bank to speak to the watching plainclothesman. "Go and tell Superintendent Folly that I think I'm on to something," he said. Then to Grimes: "Now let's see how fast you can row, Grimes."

Grimes put his back into it, and within five minutes he was perspiring freely. He took off his helmet, and then bent to the oars again. The little boat skimmed the quiet river, and Rivers-meet soon came into sight. Old Martin was standing by his garden gate, and his face darkened when he saw who was coming. He did not move away, however, and Foster called:

"Have you see Mr. Lancing, of the Milshire *News?*"

"Why, that's a funny thing," said old Martin, obviously relieved. "I see him a little while back, now—crossing the bridge, he was. Run along the road and then went into the caff an' come out on a bike. Rode like mad, he did."

"Good, thanks," said Foster.

There was no point in continuing the chase, but there was every reason to hope that Lancing had seen Stafford and was on his heels. Foster took a turn at the oars, but it was stiffer going against the current and before they were halfway back, Grimes took over again. They were away from Spindles for an hour in all.

They tied up the boat quickly and hurried to the house. Folly was sitting on a garden seat smoking a cigar with his face screwed up in Churchillian fashion. Buckingham was still in the house.

"Taking the air?" asked Foster.

"Waiting for a country policeman," said Folly heavily.

"I thought I had a chance of catching up with Stafford," said Foster, "and I think we'll have some news of him soon. A local newspaperman was seen hurrying toward Riversmeet—that's the next village."

"I know it is," said Folly.

"Brilliant, aren't you?" said Foster, with a touch of acerbity. He felt sore because his men had let Stafford go, and Folly's sarcasm seemed to have a barb.

"I am a simple person, as I repeatedly tell you," said Folly. "I am also too old to go chasing about the country in search of a man who is bound to be found sooner or later." He grinned suddenly. "All right, Foster, all right—it hasn't turned out as I hoped it would. I think there's going to be more disappointment in store. I think we shall have to wait a few days before anything turns up. Let's get back." He led the way to a waiting taxi, explaining that Anderson and Trevelyan had already left in the doctor's car. There was some excitement in the medical profession, he declared, over a patient next door. He gave the impression that he did not see why Trevelyan should interest himself in anything but the case.

When they were settled back in the car, he said, "I've talked to Anne Stafford again—only for a few minutes. That girl is living under a great strain, as great as Anthony Abbott's. Abbott might be frightened because he suffers from these fits, but the girl is in a different category. She has been living on tenterhooks for a long time. She's nervous and highly strung. It's because of that damned brother of hers, of course."

"Perhaps she thinks he killed Lovelace."

"Perhaps. You should examine the evidence." Folly grinned puckishly. "That's hard—you haven't seen it, so how could you? Lovelace was seen to enter the Chelsea house on the afternoon of Tuesday, 11th May. He was not seen to leave it. Anne Stafford, Tony Abbott, Hibbett, and Julius Stafford were all known to be in the house at various times during that afternoon—although Julius left shortly after Lovelace arrived, and spent some hours at his club, not returning until about half past seven. These are the known facts. If Lovelace was killed at Chelsea, and I feel fairly confident that he was, then any one of these people could have killed him. Well, we shall just have to find out which one it was."

"What did Anne Stafford say?" asked Foster.

"What you'd expect: that there is nothing unusual in her brother going off without telling her why or where he's going. The Abbotts agree—he's often gone off for a week or ten days, and they've never known where, and never had an explanation from him. His genius had deserted him, she tells me," Folly added. "He was dissatisfied with his work. She says he collapsed last night; that's why you found her bathing his forehead with Eau de Cologne. Today, he had a headache which laid him prostrate—quite usual also, and probably not simulated. Then he disappeared. It might have been because he saw us coming— on the other hand, his sister's explanation could be the right one. We want to find out where he's gone, but I don't think it will be easy."

"Why are you so pessimistic?" asked Foster.

"Nothing pessimistic about that," said Folly. "People who go away without leaving a trace or an address *are* hard to find. Hibbett will be hard to find, unless he goes to a place where our men know him. Take my word for it, Foster, we're going to have a few days of peace and quiet. How would you like to come up to London? Have you ever been to Scotland Yard?"

"Only twice, for flying visits," said Foster.

"Come up with me and I'll show you round," said Folly. "Don't ask me why, but I think we're going to get results in London before anything else happens down here. We've done some good work. It won't do the Abbotts or Anne Stafford any harm to have a week to think about the situation. If they're guilty, they'll do something silly to betray themselves—or else they'll get worked up to such a pitch that when we come again they'll be easy game. If they're innocent—" He shrugged his shoulders. "Well, it won't make any difference."

"I'm not a bit sure you're right," said Foster.

"All right, take the chance I'm offering you. If you're worried about Stafford's or Hibbett's return, I'll promise you I'll come back with you as soon as we hear they've turned up here again."

"It might be a good thing," Foster admitted slowly.

"It will."

"I'll have a word with Colonel Harrington," said Foster. "He may think you're wrong to go back, you know. He expects great things of you."

"He won't get 'em if I stay down here," said Folly. "The scene has changed." He sat back, drawing at his cigar, and they drove through the outskirts of Milton to the police station.

Foster was puzzled by Folly's insistence about London and by no means sure that the man was right, but the thought of a trip to town attracted him. He only wished he could take Laura. He was thinking of the trip while he talked over the points of the case which were now established, and he realized with a sense of shock that he had accepted the identification of the murdered man without the slightest excitement. Folly was the chief cause of that. Foster was fascinated by the man's behavior. Folly was a *poseur*, but he was brilliant and—essential to being a good detective—patient. It seemed almost as if he wanted a respite.

During a late tea at the canteen, the telephone rang. It was Lancing, whose voice held a mingling of excitement and disappointment. He had been at Spindles in the hope of getting an interview with Folly and had noticed Julius Stafford leaving by the side door; there had been something furtive about Stafford, Lancing said, and he had followed hotfoot. The man had gone upstream for a few hundred yards, to the bridge nearest Bray, and then hurried along the towpath. He had crossed the bridge at Riversmeet and caught a local bus that ran to a neighboring town. Lancing had not wanted to be seen following him and had borrowed a bicycle from Symes at the café. The bus stopped frequently and there had been a chance of catching it, or of getting to its terminus soon after it. In fact Lancing had arrived ten minutes behind the bus. The driver and conductor had noticed that Stafford went to the railway station.

"And that's where I lost him completely," said Lancing. "I'm speaking from the station now. There hasn't been a train out for nearly an hour, so he couldn't have traveled by train, and presumably he's in the town somewhere. Can I do anything while I'm here, Foster?"

"I'll telephone the local police, I think," said Foster. "You might as well get back."

"All right," said Lancing. "I say, can you fix an interview with Folly for me? He looks a tartar—what is he like?"

"He's terrible," said Foster. "He does nothing but eat. He probably regards newspapermen as the bane of his life, but he'll be at home with me until a quarter to eight, I think, and if you care to look in I'll give you an introduction." He was grinning at Folly, who was in the throes of devouring a large cream bun.

"Good man," said Lancing. "Thanks."

"Strange as it may seem," declared Folly, still wrestling with his bun as Foster replaced the receiver, "I do not regard newspapermen as the bane of my life. I find them useful, intelligent people. What does your particular reporter imagine he is, though? A policeman?"

"Lancing's very good," said Foster. "He knows where Stafford went." He laughed at Folly's expression, put through a call to the neighboring town's police, and then put out a general call—not to detain Julius Stafford but to report if he was seen. That done, he sat back in his chair and looked at Folly, whose eyes were nearly closed.

"I bet Stafford doesn't show up for several days," said Folly, opening his eyes suddenly. "We might get Hibbett before then, but I don't really think it's likely. *Must* I come out with you and see this newspaperman?" he demanded. "I am looking forward to a quiet evening at the White Horse interrupted only by your Chief Constable—I suppose he will be gracious enough to meet me."

Foster smiled. "He wants you to dine with him at eight— didn't I tell you? And before that we're going to my house."

"If you insist," said Folly with a long-suffering sigh. "One thing I beg of you. Leave it until the children have been put to bed. I know that I am a subject of humor," he continued, "but strange children may look elsewhere for their amusements."

"How did you know that I had a family?" said Foster.

"Children please you," said Folly. "I noticed you smiling at one at Spindles." He laughed. "Of course, Foster, I'll be delighted to meet your wife."

So it happened that Superintendent Folly, who was a bachelor, and Foster watched the three children at their evening meal, and before long Folly was telling them a story about a big, bad man in a boat. When Laura came downstairs after tucking them in bed she said:

"They won't go to sleep for hours after that."

"Do 'em good," said Folly. "I don't like machine-made children. I don't like anything that's machine-made. Funny the Abbotts haven't any children, isn't it?"

Foster laughed. "They've only been married two years."

"I've a curious impression that they're a childless couple," said Folly. "I—now, Mrs. Foster, what have I done to deserve a look like that?"

"I'm beginning to think you *are* uncanny," declared Laura. "Yesterday afternoon when I was talking to Mrs. Abbott she told me that she was afraid that she wouldn't be able to have a family. It troubled her, I know; they both want one. It's the result of an old operation, I gathered."

"Curious," said Folly. "Was it the first time you'd met her?"

"Yes. She had no idea who I was. I think I caught her at a moment when she was feeling rather wistful and low—she was watching the children. She has a way with them—that was the impression I got."

"A very good impression," said Folly. "Curious fact that she should unburden herself to a stranger. Only people who can't confide in friends usually do that, except the incurably garrulous, and Mrs. Abbott isn't one of those. Evidence that she was feeling some kind of strain even then—prepared to take her hair down in front of a complete stranger. Curious indeed," declared Folly. "Mark my words, young Foster, there'll be an explosion at Spindles one day. Even if they get away with this business and we pin it on Hibbett—which I'm inclined to think is most likely—there'll be trouble. Last people in the world who should try to live together. Oh, well, we'll see."

"So you think it was Hibbett," said Foster.

"I think nothing of the kind. I said I'm inclined to think he's most likely. Possibly he killed the man and skipped out, leaving the body for the Staffords to get rid of. Nasty shock for them, especially if they had quarreled with the man or otherwise had a good reason for wanting him dead. People like the Staffords might well rush into some silly business such as hiding the body instead of calling the police and being frank. They can't help doing the wrong thing. Emotional instability, you see."

"That would let Abbott out," said Foster.

"Nonsense!" roared Folly. He looked at Laura with comical dismay. "Is your husband always as dull as this? It lets no one out. We've still four suspects. Possibilities don't rule anything out!"

Folly had left behind him at Spindles an almost unbearable atmosphere. Tony and Gillian would have stood up to it better had Anne not been beside herself with worry. She had been collected enough when she told Folly that it was quite customary for Julius to go away for a few days at a time, but usually he let her know he was going. Now she was obviously terrified in case anything happened to him. Although she went up to her room and did not come down again, the fact that she was in such a state affected the others. Tony was preoccupied with his own particular anxiety, and Gillian found the situation quite beyond

her: Tony could not bring himself to talk; Anne would not. There
were policemen and villagers in sight all the time, even on the
other side of the river. The garden gave her no peace of mind,
and soon she was back in the house.

Tony had watched her from the porch, and now he stood up
and put an arm about her waist as they went inside.

"Try to take it easier, darling. I know it's difficult, but if we
look at it the reasonable way, we've got to admit that it's most
unlikely that I killed Lovelace in a fit of rage I've completely forgotten. In fact, it's fantastic. I suppose you know," he said slowly,
"that it's fairly certain that he was killed at Chelsea, and that's
why Julius and Anne hurried down here."

"Of course I do," said Gillian. She caught her breath. "Tony,
Julius is my brother. Anne—"

It cleared the air a little when, quiet-voiced, they discussed
seriously the possibility that Julius or Anne had killed Lovelace.
They were so absorbed in their conversation that they did not
hear the car draw up outside, nor the footsteps on the drive as the
car went off. When the knock came at the front door they broke
off, and Tony said wearily:

"Oh, Lord, more policemen and questions."

"I'll go," said Gillian.

She walked sharply to the door; he heard her fumbling with
the catch and the squeak as the door opened. Then she cried,
"Snub!"

"Hallo, my poppet!" came the deep, laughing voice of Snub
Savory. "Here you are then, all at home like a dutiful housewife,
and looking very pretty. Spare a kiss for your best man. Ah, I
was, remember."

Tony limped to the hall, his eyes glowing. "Snub, why the
dickens didn't you let us know?"

"Complaints, complaints, that's all I get from authors," said
Snub. He was a youthful-looking man, rather below medium
height, and very well dressed. His homely face, always good-na-
tured, was wreathed in smiles. His fair, curly hair was thinning.
He put down a suitcase and advanced, clasping his hands together and looking about him. "Not at all bad. The Muse should
be busy here—how's work, you scoundrel? You probably haven't
written a line since you've been here; all you've been doing is

read manuscripts for other people, which is kind but unprofitable."

"Is it any good?" asked Tony.

"The Castle thing? We'll talk about that later." Snub looked from one to the other and frowned slightly. "Have I come in the middle of a lovers' tiff?" he demanded.

"No," said Tony. "We're having a spot of bother, but it'll work out. You've got to be the best listener in the country for the next few hours."

"After you've made me a cup of tea, I hope," said Snub.

It was a great relief to see him and talk to him. His levelheaded common sense was always soothing, and Tony had found that he was rarely at a loss, no matter how difficult the situation. It was characteristic of the man that he did not seem surprised or horrified, but discussed the situation quietly and practically. By the time supper was ready both Gillian and Tony felt very much happier, and that in spite of Anne's calling out in a muffled voice that she did not want any supper, only to be left alone.

Snub stayed until Wednesday morning.

The days passed surprisingly quickly and with no interruptions. Castle, while he was waiting for the local bus to Milton to get a prescription for his wife, told them that Foster had gone to London with Superintendent Folly. Mrs. Castle was now conscious and in some pain but remarkably cheerful, although she had not yet been told that the pain might be nothing more than the return of life to her legs. Twice Abbot and Savory called at the vicarage, each time finding that Castle was in the village; Snub's opinion of his book was the same as Tony's, and it was ironic that the opportunity to see Castle about it did not come while he was there. Castle had forgotten everything else in the new hope about his wife.

Anne had been more herself on Monday and apologized for not having greeted Snub, but remained pale-faced and jumpy. There was no news, either of Julius or Hibbett.

Tony was standing at the bookstall at the station after Snub's train had gone, when another train came in. He glanced up, for no particular reason, and saw Julius passing through the barrier.

· 18 ·

JULIUS RETURNS

"WHY, HALLO, Tony!" Julius came striding toward the bookstall and slapped Tony heartily on the back. "Nice to see you. How are tricks?"

"Where the devil have you been?" demanded Tony. A week earlier his tone of voice would have been enough to start a row, but now Julius only grinned and said darkly:

"Thereby hangs a tale! Let's have a cab, shall we?" He beckoned a taxi, which came up to the station entrance. "Hop in, old chap," he added. "Ah! it's warm, isn't it?"

Tony just looked at him.

Julius seemed fitter; his complexion was good and his eyes were clear. Tony had imagined that on these periodic disappearances he drank heavily, but there was nothing to indicate that he had been doing so, and there was a jauntiness about him which seemed genuine. He smiled broadly as the taxi started off.

"You look like a ghost," he said. "What you want, old chap, is a few days off on your own. Go up on the East Coast or somewhere like that, and blow the cobwebs out of your head."

"Is that what you've been doing?" asked Tony.

"More or less," declared Julius. "I don't mind admitting that after ten days at Spindles when I just couldn't write a bar I nearly went off my head. Oh, it wasn't the place; I should have known better than to try and work, but I've a contract, you know. I've borrowed a couple of hundred on account of my next little jingle, and that's nearly gone. Still, I shouldn't have tried. I just wasted my time. So I did what I always do—went off and communed with my spirit and a lot of strangers."

Tony said, "I suppose it didn't occur to you that the police might look askance?"

"I don't care a rap for what the police think," said Julius, and he sounded as if he meant it. "Don't let them get you down, old chap. That fellow Folly has been here, hasn't he? I read something about it. Just you let me deal with him. I'll make him realize that being a Superintendent in the C.I.D. doesn't give him authority to lord it over everyone who—"

"Aren't you taking it a bit too calmly?" asked Tony.

"No!" Julius laughed exuberantly. "*I've* got nothing to worry about, and I don't suppose you have. I can't imagine *you* committing a murder! You want to stop worrying about it, old chap. Take my advice and get away for a bit—see what a difference it's made in me. I don't mind telling you that I feel as if I can go upstairs and really start work. I've got it in my mind now—I couldn't get back soon enough, as a matter of fact. How do you like this?"

He started to hum, then sing, waving his hands as if he were holding a baton. Tony sat back, watching and listening, as if in some queer, hypnotic way Julius created the illusion that he was listening to a light orchestra. Tony did not recognize the air, but it had a lilting loveliness, and the taxi driver looked over his shoulder with an appreciative smile. Julius had his eyes closed and was thoroughly absorbed; it was clear that he was rehearsing something which had been in his mind for some time, for he hardly faltered.

He finished as the taxi passed through the village.

"Well, what about that?" he demanded.

"Very good," said Tony quietly.

"That's jolly decent of you, old chap," said Julius. "I will say you're not mealy mouthed about my music, like most people. How is Anne?" He looked slightly sheepish.

"Worried out of her life," said Tony.

"Poor kid. She shouldn't be, though—she knows I haven't been away for some time. Still, I can handle Anne. How's Gillian, by the way? No, don't trouble to answer, I shall soon be able to find out for myself. I suppose," he added as the taxi pulled up, "you've had a quieter time now that the police have left—the newspapers said that 'they were pursuing their inquiries in London.'"

"That only applies to Folly and Foster," said Tony. "The others are still here."

"Lot of time-wasting nincompoops," sneered Julius. "I suppose it will take them a month to realize that if that corpse was dumped into the river from our boat, someone else took the boat and tried to get us in bad. Well, here we are." He got out of the cab and put his hand in his pocket. He drew out a few coins. "Oh, confound it, I'm out of change," he said. "Pay the cabby for me, will you?"

"So he's broke," thought Tony as he obliged. Julius was striding up the drive, calling something that Tony could not catch.

When Tony reached the hall Anne was coming down the stairs and Gillian was approaching from the kitchen. Gillian was frowning, obviously not intending to give her brother a warm welcome. It was difficult to assess Anne's thoughts. She walked slowly, and she was dressed in black, which she seemed to prefer these days. Her face was white, and she looked very thin; there was something almost tragic in her expression. Her complexion was transparent, and her eyes had an unnatural glow.

"Hallo, old girl!" cried Julius. "It's done the trick! I've got exactly what I wanted!" He stepped forward, and as Anne reached the last few steps, lifted her by the waist and held her high. Even then, her expression did not change. "Come on!" he adjured her when he set her down. "Don't be angry with your favorite brother, pet. I tell you it's worked again."

Anne said, "Why did you go then of all times?"

"Pooh, if you're thinking about the police and their interfering insolence, I'm not going to allow myself to be dictated to by them," said Julius. "And I'll soon tell them so and send them off with a flea in their ear if they come worrying us again. Cheer up, pet! I tell you that I've got something the world is waiting for." He took off his hat and flung it toward Gillian, who was standing and staring severely at him, and then went tearing up the stairs.

Anne watched him and then followed. At the landing she looked down. She was smiling faintly, and Tony got the impression that a great load had been lifted from her shoulders. For some reason he thought of her fiancé. She had received a long letter from him at breakfast, but she had merely glanced at it. She was just not interested in Teddy Barr.

She disappeared, but before Tony and Gillian had spoken, Julius began to play the air which he had been humming. It was fascinating. They stood looking upward, holding hands. The whole house rang with the music, and there was no doubt that

it had a touch of genius; it would capture the public imagination
like nothing Julius had done before. It was as if in the few days
of his absence he had matured and grown in stature and understanding.

"I know one thing," said Tony slowly, "he can't have much on
his conscience."

It had been an exciting, exhausting, and in some ways incredible few days for Inspector Mark Foster. Folly had enthralled the Chief Constable when he and Foster had dined with
him, and Harrington had not hesitated to give Foster permission to go to London, putting Garth in control of local investigations, with Buckingham to help him. On the journey to
London Foster had wondered how Garth would take it, but from
the moment he had stepped out of the train at Waterloo all anx-
ieties of that nature dropped away from him.

Everyone seemed to know Folly, from taxi drivers to news
vendors.

They went straight to his office, and in fifteen hectic minutes
Folly made sure that all the necessary enquiries had gone out, up
and down the country, for Hibbett and Julius. He had an office
which he shared with his Chief Inspector, who was out, and
there were several easy chairs. He settled Foster in one and then
proceeded to tell him the story of Scotland Yard, as he put it. He
seemed to have no further interest in the case in hand but was
intent on describing exactly how the Yard system worked. From
time to time other men entered, were introduced, asked Folly a
question or two about some other case, and then went out. Folly
gave his answers without hesitating and with full assurance. It
was an experience that Foster would not have missed for a fortune. Folly was obviously popular with the men as well as with
his equals.

After lunch Folly took him on a tour of the offices. Fingerprints, records, and photographic departments were visited, and
everywhere Folly received immediate attention. Some of the men
were amused by him, most of them were eager, all were defer-
ential. The man's reputation was certainly not confined to the
outside world. The vast apparatus of the largest crime-fighting

organization in the world was spread out before Foster's fascinated eyes. Finally, Folly took him to the Black Museum. He
led the way down into the cellar of the Yard and conducted him
round the exhibits of a thousand cases, most of them murders.
The walls were festooned with hemp ropes; glass cases held pis-
tols, knives, tubes of poison, cracksmen's tools, and a thousand-
and-one grisly items. Folly's memory was inexhaustible and he
reeled off story after story. The exhibits dated back more than fifty
or sixty years, and Folly seemed as familiar with those of the
eighties as he was with those of his own era. One curious thing
emerged; not once did he explain his own part in any of the cases
brought to a successful conclusion.

When at last they had finished he led the way upstairs. "I can
drink a gallon of tea after that," he said. "Between you and me,
Foster, I talk too much. It's a fact. Don't tell anyone I've admitted it, or my life wouldn't be worth living." He bustled into
his office and rang for a messenger. "Tea, please," he said. He
grinned at Foster. "It doesn't amount to much after all you've
seen downstairs, does it?"

"It isn't even my murder," said Foster.

"Oh, yes, it is," said Folly. "Don't you start being humble. I've
got to see the Assistant Commissioner now, but I'll probably send
for you when I've broken the news that I've brought a country
bumpkin to have a look round." He grinned. "Meanwhile you can
go through this stuff—the full record of the Lovelace case. He
was a spare-time author's agent as well as a music publisher. Did
a lot of funny stuff, such as selling other people's work and forget-
ting to pass on the proceeds. We couldn't prosecute—no one had
the guts to make a formal charge. It was about that, by the way,
that Abbott's quarrel with him started. He swindled Abbott out
of a fairly large amount, I think, but there's no proof of it—
just rumor. Anyhow, read all about it." He tapped some folders
that were on his desk.

Foster picked up the folders. "Was Lovelace really a music
publisher?"

"Oh, yes, he published a lot of stuff—he was Julius Stafford's
first publisher. Stafford, as far as I could find out, was one of the
few men he didn't swindle at one time or another. Curious and

interesting fact, you'll notice, but it does *not* give Stafford a motive for murdering him. In point of fact, it's a good reason why
he shouldn't have done so."

"But you said that Stafford was one of four suspects," said
Foster.

"Now, come, man! I said that he was one of four people who
could have killed him. That's not saying that he *did* kill him.
On the other hand," he added, easing his huge bulk through the
doorway, "it's not saying that he didn't."

Folly was out of the office for more than an hour, and
during that time Foster became acquainted with all the features
of the case. The build-up, written in the economical prose of
Yard reports, was fascinating. There were even biographical
notes going back to their youth on all the main characters concerned.

He was then taken up to meet the Assistant Commissioner, a
mild-mannered man with an apologetic air, and later, at Folly's
insistence, spent the evening at a theater and the night at Folly's
bachelor flat. Folly indulged himself in every way; it was a
dream place, with luxury and comfort the first consideration. The
supreme feature was the magnificent bathroom, with a huge bath
specially built to accommodate him.

"Cleanliness," said Folly with the air of a man about to deliver
himself of a profound statement, "is next to godliness. Like it?"

"It's wonderful!"

"Talking of godliness, are you?"

"Am I what?"

"Godly. Not an impertinent question," said Folly. "I'd like to
know. I've told you before, the first essential in police work is
understanding people. I don't pay much attention to Trevelyan
and his fancy name for it—people and their thoughts, habits,
prejudices, and work. Get to know your man is the first principle
of police work, even with little rats like Hibbett. Well, are you?"

"Not excessively so," said Foster cautiously. "I mean, I don't go
to church regularly. My wife—"

"Curious fact that many men think that their wives can stand
proxy for them in church," said Folly. "Not a thing I've ever been
able to understand—it's one of the little mysteries of life. Take
the religious lives of the people in this case, now. Hibbett—ab-

solutely nil. Julius Stafford—he worships at the twin altars of music and himself, but he does not, as far as I can discover, acknowledge his Maker. That rules out any question of a high-minded crime on his part. Anne Stafford—indifferent for the most part, and High Church when she thinks of it. Nothing personal in her religion, except insofar as it affects her brother, whom she worships. She would be prepared, I feel sure, to commit murder to save him from hurt or to preserve him and his work for posterity. High-minded possibilities in Anne Stafford. The Abbotts. Low Church, with a bent toward nonconformity, particularly as far as Abbott is concerned. Genuine Christian convictions in both cases. It affects their lives—considerate to others, helpful where they can be—look at the way Abbott gets on with that man Castle, for instance. And his interest in village affairs. I rule Gillian Abbott out as a possible murderer, *absolutely*." went on Folly firmly. "I put Abbott high on the list of suspects, because he might have committed murder during one of his fits of rage. I've already cast some doubt on their genuineness. The fact remains that they *might* be genuine, in which case his religious convictions would have no influence on his actions when he was in the grip of such a rage. Trevelyan tells me this is quite possible," he added. "He also tells me that it is quite possible for Abbott to do something in such a mood and afterward be completely unaware of what he did. But I very much hope that this isn't what happened—that's the kind of case which is extremely difficult to handle. We'd have to face opposition witnesses in the medical category, and when experts fall out it always confuses a jury's mind. Or should it be minds?"

"I don't know," said Foster. "Have you any firm opinions about who killed Lovelace?"

"No. Preferences, which you might call prejudices. It often turns out that the most likely murderer is the last one who will do it. See textbooks. I think Hibbett is as likely as any of them, as I told you. He's not above murder, but the question is whether he could screw up enough courage to do it. Alternatively, of course, he might have flown into a rage, and what people do when they completely lose their temper is incredible. The way Lovelace was hacked about points to someone who really went berserk. You yourself pointed out that if he were sliced up to conceal his identity there would have been no need to cut his shoulders and neck. Lovelace, I think, was sitting in a chair—remember the deeper wounds were high, and they grew more shallow farther down, suggesting downward strokes with a knife, when someone just went wild and slashed him mercilessly. Another curious thing you haven't mentioned—the weapon."

"It might have been a carving knife," said Foster.

"Yes. It would be more important if the body had been fresh for us; as it is we're never likely to be able to fit the weapon to the wounds. Well, we'd better sleep on it."

Foster spent the next morning at the flat, going through the files and trying to weigh up everything to be learned from them as well as all that Folly had said. He could not see any further through the mass of evidence and was disappointed when Folly telephoned to tell him that nothing had been seen of Julius Stafford or Hibbett. He lunched alone, for Folly had to attend a conference, and then walked to the Yard.

He heard Folly's voice, booming as if with some excitement.

"*Where?* Are you sure? . . . What time? . . . Don't you dare lose him until I get there!" The receiver was banged down, and a bell rang somewhere nearby. Foster turned into the office as a messenger came hurrying from a room opposite. "Just in time!" roared Folly. "Nearly left you behind. Messenger, my car, my usual driver, petrol for a hundred and fifty miles at least, better make it two hundred. Hibbett," he flung at Foster. "Village in Sussex, not so very far from Milton. Curious fact emerges: the village is on the same railway line served by the station from which Julius Stafford probably traveled. Often wondered why he went there to catch a train, not to Milton. We may stay the night. Don't talk for a minute—I've got to clear one or two little things up."

He spoke into the telephone to several different people, a few words here, a few sentences there, giving Foster the impression of being in charge of a dozen different cases. The clearness of his mind was a revelation, and as Foster walked with him along the corridor he felt humble in the presence of a master.

A Wolseley was waiting outside with a driver in plain clothes.

"Hallo, Yule." Folly smiled at the driver. "This is Chief Inspector Foster of the Milshire Police. We're going to Appleby, a village seven miles this side of Brighton. The Horse and Hounds public house. Do you know it?"

"Yes, sir," said Yule.

"When was Hibbett seen at Appleby?" asked Foster.

"That is what we are about to find out," Folly said gently. "Note the curious fact that emerges. He's a townsman, a Cockney. He hates the country. Yet he visits Bray and now Appleby. Not for love of the green grass or the twittering of the birds, you can be sure of that."

They sped through London and the suburbs, then took the Brighton road. Folly was deep in thought, and Foster was wondering whether the forthcoming interview with Hibbett would bring them to the end of the case. He admitted hoping that it would; he did not want to harass Tony Abbott any further if it could be avoided.

· 19 ·

HIBBETT CORNERED

APPLEBY WAS a straggling village built on a hill with a view of Brighton, its majestic neighbor. The main street was wide and had terraces of shops on either side. A few thatched cottages and old buildings were almost hidden by the ugliness of red and yellow brick and cement-faced houses. Folly frowned when he saw it and muttered something under his breath.

Yule turned a corner and pulled into the yard of an old hostelry. It was larger than Foster had expected and much older than most of the buildings in the village, and it had undeniable charm.

"That looks like the local watchdog," said Folly, seeing a tall, ungainly, red-faced man standing near the entrance. Folly's guess was correct. The man looked round expectantly as the car pulled up alongside him. Folly opened the door.

"Superintendent Folly," he said grandly. "Where is Hibbett?"

"In room seven, sir. Inspector Wright is in room eleven, sir. He expects you, sir, he——"

"Ah, yes," said Folly. "Thank you." He led the way inside, pushing through the swinging doors.

It was immediately obvious that Inspector Wright was not a man who would understand Folly. He was a smaller edition of Garth, with little humor and a great sense of his own importance. He was long-winded, too, as he told Folly that Hibbett had been traced thanks to the keenness of one of his men and that a careful check had been kept on his movements.

"Has he left the pub since you located him?" asked Folly.

"No, not once. Hibbett, alias Welch, alias Webster, the name by which he has registered here," said Wright solemnly, "arrived at 7:30 P.M. on Sunday. We have managed to ascertain that he did not leave the hotel until 10:15 P.M. on Monday, when he went to the hamlet of Geeves, two and a quarter miles south of Appleby, where he visited Geeves Cottage. The owner of this cottage is an old man who has lived in the district for many years and has an extremely odd reputation."

"Odd?" barked Folly.

"That is so. He is eccentric. One might almost say he is a hermit," declared Wright. "Nothing is known against him, although during the war there were times when he was suspected of signaling to German aircraft. The suspicions were aroused because he was extremely critical of the war and called himself a pacifist."

"Hmm," said Folly.

"I have not had time to get a full report ready for you about Professor Gimbert——"

"Professor?" interjected Folly.

"That's what he calls himself—professor of music."

"Well, well!" said Folly. "Remarkable how music crops up in this business, isn't it, Foster? An eccentric professor of music. Gimbert, Gimbert, the name is familiar— *Foster!* Have you seen it lately?"

"It does sound familiar," admitted Foster. "I—"

"Man, man, you read the dossier after I did," said Folly, his eyes glowing. "Think! Julius Stafford studied music in Prague and Vienna and London. His London maestro was Professor—"

"Gimbert!" exclaimed Foster.

"Well, we are making discoveries," said Folly. "Professor Gimbert. Inspector, you've some very brilliant men down here. I wonder if you would be good enough to find out if a man answering the description of Julius Stafford has been to Geeves recently, or at any time, for that matter. Stafford is the man who——"

"I have the description here," said Wright. "It is about the same case, is it not?"

"Yes," said Folly.

"No report that he's been seen in this neighborhood has come in so far," said Wright. "But I will make special inquiries."

"Look here, this is really urgent," said Folly. "I don't think we ought to leave it to a local constable—we want someone with a really acute mind. I wonder if you'd mind going to Geeves immediately, using my car, and making the inquiries in person."

Inspector Wright stood up immediately and said that he quite appreciated the situation and would gladly go to Geeves himself. Would he have the pleasure of meeting the Superintendent there later?

"If you haven't telephoned a message to me here, I'll come out as soon as I've had a few words with Hibbett," said Folly. He waited until Wright was hurrying away, then he grinned at Foster. "That's got rid of him; now we can tackle Hibbett on our own."

The passages of the Horse and Hounds were narrow and gloomy. On a landing a little way from room eleven was a dull electric light, which was faintly reflected by the brass numbers of the nearby doors. There were heavy oak beams in the walls and ceilings, and the floorboards creaked as Folly walked onto the landing and peered at the numbers. Somewhere in the hotel a radio was on, and the strident notes of a saxophone came along the passage. Passing traffic was audible, and the footsteps of people in the street could also be heard through an open window on the landing.

"Room seven," whispered Folly. "Be careful, he may know that he is being watched. He might be desperate."

He did not tap on the door but turned the handle cautiously and then tried to open it; it was locked. He muttered an imprecation and stood back, clenched his fist, and hammered on the door with a vigor which made it shake.

There was no answer.

"If Wright's let him go—" began Folly.

"Hush!" Foster stood with his ear close to the door. "I can hear him moving."

"Good!" Folly thundered on the door again. "Hibbett! Welch! Webster!" The names echoed up and down the passage. "Open this door immediately!"

The door opened almost on his words.

Foster was taken completely by surprise, in spite of Folly's warning, and even Folly seemed unprepared for what followed. The door was pulled open sharply, and Hibbett appeared, holding a thick stick above his head. He struck savagely at Folly, catching him on the shoulder, and then flung himself at Foster. His toe cap cracked on Foster's shin. Foster gasped with pain and staggered against Folly, who was off-balance, and the two men thudded against the wall. Foster made a despairing effort to grab Hibbett's sleeve, but Hibbett wrenched himself away and flew along the passage.

"Hurry!" roared Folly.

Foster turned, but when he put his right foot to the ground there was a stab of pain along his leg and he nearly fell. He saw Hibbett disappear at the end of the stairs. He tried again, but it was impossible to do more than limp forward. He heard Folly's heavy breathing, and when he reached the next doorway, Folly snapped, "Let me pass!"

Foster moved into the doorway. Folly squeezed past him, and then Foster watched a truly impressive sight—the Superintendent was running. The whole floor shook, but Folly went with commendable speed and hurried down the stairs with the nimbleness of a man half his weight. Foster limped to the head of the stairs in time to see Folly disappearing through the front door. Several people were staring at him in amazement. Doors were opening on the same floor, and curious eyes were turned toward Foster. Filled with mortification, he limped down the stairs. His leg was more painful with every step, and he thought that it was bleeding.

When he reached the hall a man hurried from the manager's office, full of importance, and began to ask questions. Wearily, Foster said, "Wait a few minutes, please."

He felt sick and angry with pain. He sat down on a chair in the lobby and pulled up his trouser leg. A woman gasped, for his leg was bleeding freely. He dabbed at it with a handkerchief and saw an ugly wound the shape of a steel toe cap. The sight of it even silenced the manager, who sent a maid for a first-aid dressing. The little lobby was crowded, everyone giving advice on how to treat the wound. Foster was feeling better now that he was sitting down, and his head was clearer.

The shouting outside had diminished; he could picture Folly and the red-faced man running wildly in pursuit.

Then someone opened the door and gasped, "Look!"

There was a rush for the door, and Foster was left well behind, but he limped into the little reception office and stared out the tiny window into the courtyard.

Folly was crouching, massive and alert, a few yards in front of Hibbett, who was just visible. The red-faced man and three others formed a half-circle about the little man, who was standing against the wall with the stick raised. Folly went forward a pace; the others did the same. Hibbett shouted something incoherently and brandished the stick. The half-circle of wary men closed in slowly and remorselessly, and the wildness in Hibbett's eyes increased.

Suddenly he went at Folly like a goat, head downward and aiming at his stomach. The other men closed on him quickly, but Folly was bowled over and went down, his legs raised high into the air. Hibbett had kept his balance and dodged to one side. He tripped up one man and struck another savagely over the head with the stick. Then he raced toward the entrance but was still several yards from it when three policemen appeared, their truncheons raised.

Foster had to admire the man's tactics.

Hibbett doubled back on his tracks, going within a foot of the helpless Folly, who was trying to pick himself up; the scene would have been indescribably comic in any other circumstances. The red-faced man lunged forward and received a blow on the forehead. He fell back.

"He's coming here!" screamed a woman.

Foster swung round, nearly fell again, but forced himself to push his way through the crowd toward the stairs. Hibbett burst through the doorway, still swinging the stick, wildness in his eyes. His lips were open and he was gasping for breath. He was not finished yet, however. He raced toward the stairs, striking out with his stick to try to keep Foster away. Several men in the crowd came forward, but they were reluctant to get too near; it was a token attempt to assist rather than a serious endeavor.

Foster swept his arm round; the stick caught him a powerful crack just below the elbow, but the impact loosened it from Hibbett's grasp. It fell. Foster flung himself at the man, who was trying to get down the passage. For a moment it looked as if he would succeed, but Foster managed to grab his coattails. Hibbett, exhausted, dropped to the floor, taking in great gulps of air and no longer showing fight. The men who had been so wary of advancing now came forward boldly.

"Go back, please," said Foster.

His leg was extremely painful, but he meant to consolidate his own capture of the man.

As he stood over Hibbett, the door was pushed open and Folly appeared. He was disheveled and dusty, his hair was rumpled, his eyes were burning.

"Did you lose him?" he demanded of the crowd in general. Then he pushed his way forward and saw Hibbett and Foster. "Excellent!" he said. "So, Mr. Hibbett-Welch-Webster, you are so frightened of the police that you will commit assault in an effort to get away. *You!*" He swung round suddenly as the red-faced man and a uniformed policeman entered the hall. "Take him upstairs to his room."

The onlookers, who had been staring open-mouthed at the scene before them, now fell back, and the red-faced man came forward quickly, jerked Hibbett to his feet by his collar, and then hustled him up the stairs. The uniformed policeman followed close behind.

"Come along, Foster," said Folly. "I—what on earth is this?"

A maid appeared, carrying a bowl of water, a towel, and a small box marked with a red cross. Foster explained briefly, and Folly said, "Give them to me, my girl."

He took them from her, beckoned Foster to follow him, and went upstairs to Hibbett's room. Hibbett was sitting back in an easy chair with the red-faced man standing over him.

"Stand up!" roared Folly. Then, to the red-faced man: "You, sir. Are you proficient in first aid?"

"Why—why, yes, sir."

"Then be good enough to bathe Inspector Foster's leg. Take Hibbett's chair, Foster, you need it far more than he does—*at the moment*," he added grimly.

Hibbett backed to the fireplace. His furtive face was set in fear, and his eyes were wide open and terrified. Now and again he drew in his breath sharply. His trousers were torn, his collar and tie were halfway round his neck, and his hands were bleeding at the knuckles. He did not move his gaze from Folly. The red-faced man tried to give full attention to his task but kept glancing up as if he too found it difficult to look away.

"Albert Hibbett, alias Albert Welch, alias Albert Webster, I hereby charge you with the willful murder of Jeremiah Lovelace, at 18a Bliss Street, Chelsea, and I warn you that anything you may say may be used in evidence. Well, sir?" thundered Folly. "What have you to say?"

Hibbett gasped, "I—I never, it wasn't me, it wasn't me!"

"Nonsense!" Folly boomed.

"He was dead when I got there," gasped Hibbett. "Abbott killed 'im, mister. There was blood on 'is face and 'ands an' on 'is clothes. Abbott killed 'im!"

· 20 ·

HIBBETT'S EVIDENCE

"I SEE," said Folly heavily. "You wish to save your own neck. Naturally, you would rather see another man hanged. You will not succeed. Your lies will not serve you."

"I tell yer it's true," gasped Hibbett. His eyes were staring, and he took a step forward, his hands outstretched. "Lovelace was dead when I got to the flat—that's Gawd's truth. I went ter see Lovelace, I knew 'e was there." Hibbett gulped. "'E owed me a hundred quid, and I wanted to git it aht've 'im. I went upstairs. The door was open, I never broke in. I got inside an' Abbott was standin' there wiv a knife in 'is 'ands—all over blood 'e was. An' Lovelace, *Gawd!*" Hibbett shuddered. "You should 'ave seen 'im. I got aht quick, I knoo you ruddy narks would try and pin it onter me. I got aht quick!"

Folly said, "And you would have me believe that you went into the flat with no intention other than to get your debt repaid—a debt of money—and saw Mr. Abbott standing with a knife in his hands and covered in blood. *Most* interesting, Hibbett. But it is a lie!" Folly thundered. "You were seen to enter and leave."

"I wasn't in the flat all the time," gasped Hibbett. "I was too scared. I was leggin' it aht when I 'eard someone else coming up the stairs. I dodged into the bog and 'id for a bit, that's what I did. That's why I was in the 'ouse so long."

"Abbott was seen to leave the house, and he had no blood on his clothes," said Folly. "He might have changed had it been his own flat, but it was not. He could have washed the blood off his hands and face but not off his clothes. Come, Hibbett. You are lying. Admit it."

"I tell yer I'm not!" cried Hibbett. "It's Gawd's truth. I knoo the narks would try to pin it on me—" He began to tremble from head to foot.

The red-faced man had given up all pretense of trying to bathe

Foster's leg, but when Folly glanced round at him he dipped the sponge into the water quickly and dabbed it on the wound so vigorously that Foster winced. The pain in his leg was trifling with the issues now at stake, however. He found it hard to disbelieve the man, and yet it was obvious that Hibbett did not expect to be believed. Foster wondered what Folly's reaction would be, and whether he would attempt to bully his prisoner into making a confession—but Folly spoke quietly and seemed to have some sympathy for the man, almost as if he too were inclined to believe him. He asked question after question, each one to the point. He put the same query in several different ways, and he tried trick questions, all uttered in the quiet, reasoning voice which Foster agreed was the best method of interrogation just now. He failed to shake Hibbett's story. It was elaborated at some length, but the essentials were the same. He said that Abbott had looked like a madman—just as he had when he had attacked him at Spindles. He himself had been frightened, partly because of the knife in Abbott's hand. He had slunk out of the room and hidden until he heard Abbott go downstairs. He did not remember what Abbott had been dressed in; he only remembered that there had been blood all over the floor, over Abbott's face and waistcoat, and over his hands. He told the same story so often, and with such little variation, that despite his sickening sense of dismay, Foster found it increasingly convincing.

Folly tried another tack; why had Hibbett gone to see Abbott at Spindles?

Hibbett made no bones about admitting that he had gone to tell Abbott that he had seen the whole thing and to extort blackmail. He seemed relieved to have to make the admission, as if he realized it would strengthen his story. He did not then know whether Abbott had recognized him or even noticed him at Chelsea; but afterwards, he was quite certain that he had, and believed this was the reason for the attack on him at Spindles. It was true, he admitted, that he had been hiding in the wardrobe and Mrs. Abbott had seen him, but it wasn't true that he had grappled with her; he had run to the door, and then Abbott had rushed in and attacked him.

"Why were you hiding in the wardrobe?" asked Folly.

Hibbett answered readily: he wanted to hear the conversation between the Abbotts when they were getting ready for bed. It would probably tell him whether Abbott did know what he had come for; the more he went on, the more Hibbett emphasized his intention of blackmailing Abbott. Blackmail seemed to him a trivial crime.

"Now tell me why you went to see Lovelace," said Folly.

There was no hesitation about that, either; Lovelace had known him seven years before and had visited him just after his return to England. He had some jewels with him, and he wanted money for them. He knew that Hibbett was a man who could sell "hot stuff"; Hibbett imagined that the jewels had been stolen and took the two stones Lovelace gave him to a well-known East End jeweler. He got five hundred pounds for them, and Lovelace had promised him a commission of a hundred pounds. When he first saw Lovelace after selling the gems, Lovelace was in a frantic hurry, snatched the money, and hurried off. Hibbett thought that he was being bilked. He went to see Lovelace at his Bloomsbury lodging house, and seeing the police waiting outside, watched from a safe distance. When Lovelace arrived, he too saw the waiting police, and hurried off again. He went to another rooming house and, two days afterward, went to Bliss Street. There Hibbett, thinking the Chelsea house less likely to be watched by the police, made his effort to get his commission on the sale.

"I know one fing," Hibbett said. "Lovelace 'ad that cash on 'im, I know 'e 'ad."

"How can you know such a thing?" demanded Folly. "You have probably told me a hotchpotch of lies. Why add an unnecessary one?"

"It's the truth, I say. 'E 'ad the cash, 'e was leanin' forward in 'is chair, an' 'is coat was open. 'E 'ad 'is wallet 'arf aht've 'is pocket, an' I could see the cash. Most of it was there, that's a fact. I *saw* it, I tell yer."

"Hmm," said Folly. "Had you ever seen Abbott before?"

"A long time ago. I knew 'im by sight, Mister Folly, sir."

"If you must give me a name, call me Superintendent," said Folly with unexpected asperity. "When did you see Abbott before?"

"Years ago, Mis—years ago. 'E 'ad a row wiv Lovelace, an' Lovelace give me the job o' watchin' 'im, in case 'e 'ad anuvver go at 'im. 'E never, though. Soon arterwards Lovelace 'opped it. I never see 'im again until the day 'e brought me the sparklers."

"And what was the name of the buyer of stolen jewels whom you patronized?" asked Folly heavily.

"Listen, Super, I can't squeal——"

"There is no crime under the sun too mean or too beastly for you," said Folly bitingly. "Your life may depend on the evidence of this purveyor of stolen gems whom you profess to be so anxious to protect. His name, Hibbett!"

Hibbett murmured: "Old Sam—Old Sam Frazer."

"Well, well," said Folly in a cooing voice; obviously the statement delighted him. "Old Sam Frazer—he will be *very* pleased to give evidence on your behalf, I am sure. He has succeeded in escaping the attention of the police for as many years as I can remember. Excellent, Hibbett! I am almost disposed to feel grateful toward you. You have not forgotten, I trust, that you are under charge and that what you have said can be used in evidence."

"I never croaked him," Hibbett said. "I don't care wot you get me for, except murder. I never killed 'im."

"I hope not," said Folly. "For the sake of your miserable neck, I hope not." He looked at the red-faced man, who was not standing idly by; he had put a pad of gauze over the wound and stuck it down with adhesive tape. "What is your name and rank?"

"Sergeant Winn, sir."

"Thank you, Sergeant. Take this man downstairs. Have him removed under strong escort to Brighton Police Station. From there I shall probably have him transferred to Milton." He reached the door, seemed about to open it, and then swung round swiftly. "A moment! Hibbett, listen to me. Why did you visit Professor Gimbert?"

"I—" Hibbett gulped. "He—"

"Hurry, man! I have not all day to waste!"

"He's a friend of Lovelace's."

"I *see*," said Folly with impressive scorn. "You visited Professor Gimbert because he was a friend of Lovelace. I suppose you came to bring the sad tidings of his death? Do not treat me like a fool, sir! Why did you visit Gimbert?"

"I've told you!"

Folly spent ten minutes trying to make Hibbett admit that he

was lying, but he failed. He grew soft-voiced toward the end, but
no matter how sarcastic he became, he could not shift Hibbett
from his statement: he had come to see Gimbert simply to tell him
that Lovelace was dead.

"I think you are a fool," said Folly at last. "The truth will be discovered, Hibbett, you will be found guilty of Lovelace's murder,
and your lies will make it worse for you." He glared at the
man, and then snapped, "Was Lovelace fully dressed when you
saw him dead with Abbott standing over him?"

"Why—why, yes."

"You are sure?"

"O' course I'm sure. I told yer abaht 'is wallet."

"So you did," murmured Folly. "What kind of clothes was he
wearing?"

"Just—just clothes."

"Come, man! Try to use what little intelligence you possess.
Were they light or dark? Did he wear an overcoat? Were they of
good or poor quality? You appear to have registered every detail
of the scene on your mind, you must have seen the clothes."

He did not get a really satisfactory answer. As far as Hibbett
recalled, Lovelace had been wearing a gray suit and no overcoat, but he said that he could give no further details. Folly gave
it up and turned away abruptly. "All right, Sergeant Winn," he
said. "Take the man away."

Foster stood up and tried his leg; it was very sore, and he would
not be able to walk far. Questions filled his mind, but Folly looked
absorbed in his own thoughts, and there was no telling what harm
an interruption might cause at that juncture. The waiting grew oppressive. Foster's thoughts turned to the Abbotts. It was no use
pretending, there had been a ring of truth in all that Hibbett had
said.

"I must telephone!" exclaimed Folly explosively. "Wait here!"

After a long interval, he returned.

"I have sent someone to interview Frazer and to try to get the
numbers of the notes with which he paid for the diamonds. If he
confirms the story, then we shall have no option but to arrest
Abbott. I frightened Hibbett with the charge, of course, but after
his exertions he was ready to talk freely. I have never wished so

fervently to disbelieve a man, but scepticism in the present circumstances is against my better judgment. We will stay here, I
think, until I get information from the Yard. It isn't a bad pub,
as pubs go. Don't get up," he added as Foster moved. "Here, rest
your leg on this chair. I *knew* there was something the matter.
I've had no tea. Can you reach the bell push behind you? Thanks.
I do not think we shall get much from this room." He opened
cases, putting them on the bed and taking each article out sepa-
rately and shaking it to make sure that nothing was concealed.
"Motive!" he exploded suddenly. "Motive, Foster. We haven't got
a good one."

"Against Abbott?"

"Naturally."

"The money," said Foster tentatively.

"Don't be a fool. A few hundred pounds would not tempt Abbott. It would tempt few people enough to make them commit
murder. In any case, even if Abbott killed him, it was not for the
sake of what he could steal."

"You seem very sure of that," said Foster.

"I feel sure. I am liable to err, of course, but it is not in character. Even—" He stopped speaking and gave more attention to the
search, but Foster took him up quickly.

"You were going to say that Abbott wouldn't do murder for
a few hundred pounds. Lovelace hadn't paid Hibbett, remember
—*or* for any of the other jewels which he had on him. Hibbett was
sure he had more jewels."

"Yes. We knew he had. It is an obtrusive element. I am anxious
not to give it exaggerated importance. Some murders are committed for profit, but the majority are crimes of passion. We will
only know the whole truth when we know the motive—but I
need not tell *you* that."

They were both depressed because they had testimony of a
kind which might damn Abbott; both of them realized that the
counsel for the defense could pour scorn on Hibbett's veracity
and he would be a poor witness, but when Abbott was charged,
other things and other witnesses would probably emerge.

A maid brought in a poor tea with stale bread and but-
ter and some bright yellow cakes at which Folly stared in dis-

gust. He was halfway through the meal when he said abruptly:

"We should detain Abbott forthwith. We should telephone your headquarters and arrange it. The question is whether in the absence of a known motive, we are justified in waiting a little longer. If we set the robbery motive aside, and I intend to do so as far as Abbott is concerned, then we have to fall back on something which I dislike intensely. That is, murder during a paroxysm of ungovernable rage—all we can offer as a motive for the moment. It is not good enough. My opinion is that when we know the true motive, we shall know the murderer, not before. Only maniacs murder without motive."

"The house is being watched," Foster reminded him. "Abbott isn't likely to get away."

"We thought the same of Stafford," Folly reminded him. "Your men will be more careful, of course, but a determined man can usually find means of getting away. I am not worried that Abbott will try to escape, however. If he did this thing, he will know that flight will heighten suspicion. No. I am worried in case he should do further violence. Remember that he tried to kill Hibbett, and the most likely motive for that was because he knew Hibbett had seen him at Chelsea."

"His clothes——"

"Hush!" said Folly. "He could have carried a clean coat under his arm if he went prepared to kill. He could have borrowed one of Stafford's and replaced it at Spindles. We haven't searched his wardrobe, have we? We should have; we want Lovelace's clothes, too." He popped a piece of cake into his mouth and took a gulp of tea. "We can't afford to take the risk, Foster. We must detain Abbott, I fear. We can then make a thorough search of Spindles. We can go there tonight. I'll phone."

"I suppose you're right," said Foster.

"You know I am right. We will wait for information about Old Sam Frazer, after I have telephoned Colonel Harrington, then go out and interview this unpopular professor and see Wright again."

He went downstairs and remained there for some time, and when he returned he was brisk and confident. As he had reached the manager's office a call had come from Scotland Yard, confirm-

ing Old Sam Frazer's purchase of two small diamonds from Hibbett; Frazer did not know the numbers of the notes and denied
knowing that the gems had been stolen, said Folly, and added
with a grin: "But we'll have the old so-and-so this time. If we get
nothing else out of it, that'll be reward enough." He laughed.
"Well, let's go out and see the professor."

"Have you arranged about Abbott's arrest?"

"Not yet," said Folly with a puckish grin. "Your amiable Chief
Constable is out playing golf and I can hardly go over his head,
can I? I asked the fellow who answered me to make sure that the
house was watched very closely. You'll want some help to get
downstairs, I expect. Come along."

The arm with which he supported Foster as they went was
firm, not flabby. Foster noticed it absently, as he reflected on
the unexpected humanity of this huge man and the way he
snatched at an excuse to postpone Abbott's arrest. Folly was com-
plaining that in order to get rid of Wright he had sacrificed his
car and would now have to get into a taxi. They were waiting for
one in the lobby, peered at from all doors and windows, when
Foster said:

"It's a queer thing that we're both so reluctant to detain Abbott.
I thought I'd succeeded in cutting out sentiment, but——"

"*Sentiment*," breathed Folly.

"Why, yes." Foster stared at him.

"My dear, good fellow." said Folly. "Oh, my dear chap. *Sentiment*. On duty, I have permitted no sentiment for seventeen
years. Sentiment? Come, Foster, grow up—it is not for such a
trivial reason that I am reluctant to detain Abbott. I hoped you
would see better than that—I really did. I am disappointed in
you." He looked aggrieved. "Let me explain. We have no motive,
or none that will satisfy a jury. It is eleven years since I made an
arrest without getting a conviction. Eleven years! No, Foster, not
sentiment: *policy*. Ah, this would appear to be the taxi."

The journey to Geeves was a silent one. Foster now hardly
knew what to make of the Yard man, and he had an uncomfortable feeling that he had fallen low in Folly's estimation.

The village consisted of half a dozen small cottages, a large
house standing on a hill, bleak and forbidding, and a little

church. Outside a cottage which stood by itself, a hundred yards or so away from the others, was Folly's Wolseley. Yule was standing by it, and when Folly and Foster got out of their car he looked at Folly and shrugged his shoulders.

"How much progress has Inspector Wright made, Yule, do you know?"

"Not much, sir," said Yule. "He came out to get something from the car just now, and he looked hot and bothered."

"What could he get from my car?" demanded Folly.

"He'd left his case in it, sir."

"He'd left his case!" echoed Folly. "He'd left— Foster, I ask you to be of service to me. If I appear to be on the point of losing my temper, cause a distraction. I am quite sure that I shall need support in dealing with Inspector Wright."

He made his majestic way along a weedy gravel path. They drew within a few yards of the front door, which was ajar, when Folly stopped.

"Hush, my friend!"

Foster was glad to put his weight on one leg. He heard Wright's voice. He grimaced at the hectoring tone and Folly frowned.

"Did you or did you *not* see this man Stafford?" demanded Wright. "I warn you, Professor, you must be frank with the police."

Suddenly Wright's words were cut short by the sudden playing of a piano; and as the music poured out from the cottage, the whole place seemed transformed. For a man who declared he could not tell an A-flat from an F-sharp, Folly was remarkably impressed, and he was still smiling when he touched Foster's arm and led the way to the front door.

· 21 ·

THE PROFESSOR

THE FRONT ROOM of Geeves Cottage was in indescribable confusion. It was littered with oddments of clothing, furniture, crockery, and piles of newspapers and magazines. In the middle of it all, incredibly, stood a beautiful, highly polished grand piano. At the keys sat a little old man with a long grey beard, dressed in a skirted coat, much too large for him, flannel trousers, and carpet slippers.

He must have seen the door open but did not stop playing. Now the music was soft and persuasive, with a haunting quality, a touch of mastery which made Foster forget the state of the room and look toward the player. Professor Gimbert appeared to be smiling. His eyes were narrowed, and his head held high.

By his side, looking flustered, red, and angry, was Inspector Wright, staring at Folly in dismay. Folly approached the piano and stood where the old man could not fail to see him, gazing at the long fingers which caressed the keys. The hands were veined and spotted with brown, but the movement of the fingers, the gentleness of their touch, proved that they were still supple.

At last the old man stopped. He looked vaguely before him for a few seconds, then sighed and opened his eyes wide. Now there was no doubt that he was smiling.

"It is consoling to meet a man of understanding," he said. "You are very welcome, sir, whoever you are." He had a soft, rather quavering voice, and looked at least eighty years old.

"It is exhilarating, Professor, to hear such playing," said Folly in a voice full of respect. "Remarkable! I am deeply sorry that I had to interrupt you. Forgive me, please. I am Superintendent Folly of New Scotland Yard. My companion is Inspector Foster of the Milshire Police."

"Well, well," murmured Gimbert. "Three eminent policemen

in my humble cottage. I am proud to have you here, Superintendent."

"That's a different story from what you told me," said Wright
in a strangled voice. "You said——"

"That I disliked your manner, my dear Inspector—and I still
do," said Gimbert. "That does not alter the fact that you *are* an
eminent policeman. Does it, Superintendent?" Gimbert's voice
was so gentle that it was hardly possible to believe that irony was
intended.

"Indeed it doesn't," said Folly, as if he were still under the influence of the music. Foster, trying to recall where he had heard
it before, believed it to be one of Stafford's lesser-known pieces.
"I dislike worrying you, Professor. Inspector Wright has told you
why we have to, I think."

"He was enquiring about an old pupil of mine," said the professor. One of the most promising pupils to pass through my
hands. Julius Stafford." The long, pale fingers hovered gently,
lovingly over the keys. "Do you think that he has committed some
crime, Superintendent?"

"He might be able to help us to solve one," said Folly.

"I see. That is a different matter, although you probably hope
to make me answer the questions by pretending that there is no
danger for Julius Stafford. Superintendent, I am an old man. I
have lived for nothing but music. The things of the world do not
interest me. Crime? What *is* crime? There are different opinions. In my view, the major crime is the debasement of music. My
life is music, Superintendent. If a man has it in his being, then
whatever else he does, whatever life he leads, counts as less than
nothing, as far as I am concerned. Believe me, I am serious."

"I've no doubt of that," said Folly. "Has Stafford been to see
you recently?"

"On Monday morning."

"How long did he stay?"

"Until an hour before Inspector Wright called," said Gimbert
gently.

"An hour!" exclaimed Wright. "We'll get him!"

"So he *is* suspected of some crime," murmured Gimbert.

"We want his evidence," said Folly. "He is accused of nothing.
That is the sober truth. Why did he come to see you?" He shot at

Wright, who was fidgeting and trying to attract his attention, a withering glance that brought a smile to the old man's lips.

"He wanted mental refreshment," said Gimbert. "It is not surprising, Superintendent. He gets little sympathy and less understanding from his friends and relatives. His mind is a delicate creative organism, and there are times when its smooth working is interrupted by the people about him, people who, no matter how good their intentions, misunderstand him and make his life miserable. So he came to me for refreshment, as he has often come before. I am afraid of what will happen to him when I am dead," added Gimbert gently. "He is utterly dependent on me—*utterly* dependent. There is some satisfaction, Superintendent, but more worry, in knowing that a man is lost without one. Nevertheless, it gives me great joy to see him, and I wish he would come more frequently. What crime do you lay at his door, please? Do not name some trifling thing. I am sufficiently well acquainted with the affairs of the world to know that only a crime of exceptional gravity would cause you three gentlemen to congregate in the village of Geeves. Is it the murder of Lovelace?"

"How did you——" began Wright.

"A moment, Professor." Folly turned to the local Inspector, his face pale, his eyes flashing angrily.

Foster kicked his shin. Folly opened and closed his mouth. He coughed, and then said in a remarkably thin voice:

"Inspector Wright, if Mr. Stafford were here a little more than an hour ago——"

"We ought to be combing the district for him!"

"You are perfectly right," said Folly. "I must confess that the professor's music—I might almost say magic—has unbalanced me. We should be searching for Stafford now, or at least, one of us should, and Inspector Foster is incapacitated. In any case, this is your district, Inspector, and I hesitate to do anything without your participation. Do you feel that you can——"

Wright was already near the door, and he broke in abruptly, "May I use your car again?"

"Gladly, gladly. But wait. There is a taxi outside, the one in which we came. Perhaps you will use——"

Wright opened the door and half-ran along the weedy path, calling to the taxi driver.

Folly uttered an exclamation: "He's forgotten his brief case, the fool! Ah, thank you, Professor, thank you a thousand times." He took the briefcase from the old man's hand and ran along the path, bellowing in a voice loud enough to sound above the taxi's engine. Yule came hurrying toward him, took the case, and carried it to Wright.

"The Superintendent is a remarkable man," murmured Gimbert.

"How remarkable we don't yet know," said Foster.

He felt no inclination to ask questions before Folly returned, breathing hard and beaming.

"Now, Professor, you were asking me whether Stafford was wanted for the murder of Lovelace. I will be frank with you. He is wanted for questioning in connection with the murder of Lovelace. Of course, that man's name has not yet been mentioned in the newspapers. I, however, see nothing remarkable in your knowledge of it. Hibbett, alias Welch, alias Webster, told you."

Gimbert said, "I know him as Welch. Yes, he told me. He also told me a remarkable story, Superintendent. He said that he knew who murdered Lovelace. He had a preposterous suggestion to make. He told me that Julius Stafford would come under suspicion, but that his own evidence would surely prove Julius' innocence. He even went so far as to ask for a certain sum of money, for which he promised to give himself up to the police and tell his story."

"Did he receive the money?" asked Folly.

"He did not," said Gimbert. "Even if I had as much as he wanted, I would not give it to the rogue. Of course, had I thought it possible that you would seriously suspect Julius, or that he was in real danger, I might have listened more readily to the man. However, such a possibility is nonexistent."

"Tell me, Professor," said Folly. "Why are you so confident that Julius Stafford will not be suspected?"

Gimbert gazed at him, his faded eyes quite gay, and began to play. "Lovelace and Julius were very close friends. At one time, before Lovelace went abroad, they were almost inseparable. Then, suddenly, Lovelace went to South America. Why he did this I do not know. But I do know that Julius was greatly distressed—so distressed, in fact, that beyond telling me that Lovelace had left England, he said nothing. And from that time on he could hardly bear to hear Lovelace's name mentioned. That, in my opinion, points to a very great grief, Superintendent. And a man who is so deeply grieved when his friend leaves him does not kill that man when he returns. I did not know that Lovelace was back in this country until Julius told me that he had been to see him. He also told me that he was afraid something had happened to the man. He was in very low spirits. I cheered him up as best I could, of course, and I was glad when my influence succeeded in making him turn to his work. In a matter of hours there was a transformation."

"I see," said Folly. "Did Stafford say when Lovelace came to see him?"

"No, Superintendent." Gimbert stopped playing and turned round on the stool. "That is really all I can tell you—except one thing. A week ago I received a parcel. You will, perhaps, wonder why I prefer to live the life of a hermit down here, instead of taking what you might think is my rightful place in the world to which I belong. The answer is that I grew weary of the commercialism which has eaten like a growing cancer into the minds of men who should love music. What do the *rewards* matter if the conscience is free, and a man has the knowledge that he is giving all that is in him to his art? *Nothing*, Superintendent. What *does* matter is that the world receives all that he has to offer. *How* he offers it is immaterial, so long as the world does, in fact, receive it. Julius agrees with me. But I am afraid," continued Gimbert apologetically, "that I am revealing my feelings too much, Superintendent. I was talking about a parcel. It was a very large one, but alas, it was only a parcel of old clothes."

"Clothes!" exclaimed Foster.

"Yes. Come with me," said Gimbert.

He swung himself from the stool and led the way to the kitchen. It was a tiny room, even dirtier and more chaotic than the first. Outside, on a shelf in a dusty glasshouse, was a large brown paper parcel. Gimbert pulled it open, and it revealed a grey suit, a collar and tie, a pair of shoes and socks, a shirt, vest, and trunks. Foster checked these things carefully, lifting one garment at a time. The trousers, coat, and waistcoat were neatly folded.

"I was grateful at first," said the professor, "and then I examined the shirt. You see the stains?"

They were on the front of the shirt, and the waistcoat and trousers, dark brown in color, and the material was stiff and dry. There was the faintly unpleasant smell of dried blood. Gimbert watched Folly touch each article, and there was a faint smile in his eyes, but Foster, watching the man covertly, thought he looked a little wary, as if afraid that his story of how he had come by the clothes would be doubted.

Folly examined the paper wrapping, which had been badly torn. The address was missing—it must have been thrown away, said Gimbert apologetically. No, he hadn't recognized the hand-writing—the address had been printed, he remembered.

As his words died away, there was silence. Folly spread the clothes out along the bench and then picked up the coat. He took a wallet from the inside breast pocket and unexpectedly handed it to Foster, without speaking. Foster opened it and shook the contents out on to the brown paper; there was a thick wad of one-pound notes, held together by a rubber band, and several loose ten-shilling notes. Folly was going through the pockets quickly and placed his finds beside the money. A handkerchief, folded neatly; a newspaper cutting; a whole sheet torn from a newspaper; a penknife; a cheap cigarette case with half a dozen cigarettes; a box of matches, and a lighter. That finished the coat. From the waistcoat Folly drew out a heavy watch, a pocket comb, and some bookmatches. He glanced at Foster before he picked up the trousers. Silver and copper, a Yale key, and two trouser-buttons came from the side pockets; only the hip and fob pockets remained. It was clear that Folly hoped to make a find; something in the way in which he worked fascinated Foster and seemed to hypnotize Gimbert.

Folly took another matchbox from the fob pocket. Foster's excitement increased as Folly pushed the box open and gently took out some cotton wool and unfolded it. Something sparkled, and the next moment four scintillating diamonds, each larger than a pea, lay on the palm of Folly's hand.

After a long, tense silence, Gimbert spoke in a high-pitched, wondering voice. "Good gracious me!"

"You were sent a very handsome present, after all," said Folly. "I will not ask you whether there was a letter enclosed or an address. There was nothing, of course. Also, the profit motive has gone. Professor Gimbert, do you know a man called Anthony John Abbott?"

"You mean Julius' brother-in-law?" asked Gimbert. "I have never met him, Superintendent, but he has written to me once or twice. Why?"

· 22 ·

ARREST

FOLLY COUNTERED with another question: Why had Tony Abbott written to him? Gimbert, who seemed to understand that a great deal depended on his answer, turned and led the way back into the room. He opened a drawer in a table by the window. It was crammed with letters, most of them still in their envelopes; several fell to the floor. Foster picked them up. Gimbert ran through the letters, until he came upon a large, square envelope, addressed in a firm masculine hand.

"See for yourself," he said.

Folly took the letter out, and Gimbert began to rummage through the rest. Foster stood beside Folly, peering at the post-mark—July of the previous year. They read the letter together; it was simply a request for Gimbert to read through a manuscript which had music as a theme. Gimbert found the second letter, dated August. It was shorter and said simply that he had received Gimbert's postcard and was sorry that the professor could not do the work requested.

"Is that all?" asked Folly.

"Yes, Superintendent. I can only imagine that he had heard, presumably through Julius, that I was in great need, and being a generous man, he thought that I might welcome the few guineas which such a task would earn. So few people understand that I *prefer* to live like this, you see. I have enough money for all my simple needs."

"I see," said Folly. "Have you heard from Abbott since then?"

"No, never."

"You are sure he has never visited you?"

"I am quite sure," said Gimbert.

"Thank you very much, Professor, for your courtesy and frankness," said Folly. "I will take the parcel with me, of course. Ready, Foster?"

"Yes," said Foster, and turned toward the door.

"A moment!" said Folly unexpectedly. He turned to the professor. "I was enthralled by the tune which you played as I came in. It would be gracious of you to play it again. Am I asking too much?"

"I will gladly do so," said Gimbert. "The day may come when you will hear it too often, I am afraid—it is one of those things which will become a great favorite throughout the country. It has a great deal to commend it, and its popular appeal will be greater than anything Julius has ever done before."

"So Stafford composed it!" said Folly, surprised.

Gimbert began to play, slowly at first, and then with increased tempo, until once again Foster was under the spell of the music. Before it was finished, however, Folly's hands were rubbing the seams of his trousers, an indication that he felt impatient. He had wanted to get something which Gimbert had failed to give him, and now he had to hear the piece out although he wanted to be on his way.

The last note was still echoing through the room when Folly opened the door.

"*Thank* you, Professor. Delightful. What a great loss to our concert platforms! Good-bye for the present."

He went hurrying along the path, carrying the parcel, and Foster limped after him. As they moved off Folly waved to Gimbert, then dropped back in his seat.

Foster said, "I thought you couldn't tell one note of music from another."

"I can't," said Folly almost abruptly. "Hush!"

Foster sat back, trying to make the man out. If he were tone-deaf as he pretended, he had acted most convincingly at the cottage. It was probable, of course, that he had wanted to disarm the old man and had chosen the obvious course, but Foster could not help thinking that there was something else on his mind.

They were in the outskirts of Appleby before Folly spoke.

"We are making progress of a kind," he said. "We have further evidence against Abbott, although we still have no motive. The fact that he knew the address means that he could have parceled up those clothes and sent them to Gimbert if he wished to implicate his brother-in-law. Perhaps that gives us a motive."

Foster stared at him in bewilderment. Folly stopped the car and went on unsmilingly: "We know of no reason why Abbott should wish to get rid of Lovelace. There might be a reason why he should wish to get rid of his brother-in-law. If he could succeed in making a case against Stafford and get him a life sentence, that would be getting rid of him."

"Nonsense!" snapped Foster.

"Nothing of the kind! You are making the sentimental approach—that Abbott is not a man to do such a thing. I tell you, Foster, that there are deep emotions hidden beneath this ugly business. Abbott is capable of a high-minded crime—there is no doubt of that. He might well think there was a good reason for being rid of Stafford."

"I simply don't believe it," said Foster flatly.

"Indeed? I submit it as a considered possibility," said Folly huffily. "However, let us turn to the facts. Hibbett is cleared of suspicion of the actual murder. He might conceivably be an accessory, but he did not kill Lovelace and was not alone with the man immediately after his death."

"Otherwise the wallet would have been empty and the diamonds gone."

"Good. We must admit then that if he is freed of suspicion of the actual murder, there is a greater likelihood that his story is true—his evidence against Abbott, I mean. There is further indication that he spoke the truth. With his knowledge, he saw a way of extorting money from Stafford, or from Gimbert on Stafford's behalf. Being an employee of Lovelace's, he knew of the remarkable relationship between master and pupil. He has the twisted kind of mind that is both parasitical and cunningly tenacious. He is shrewd enough to know that if he admitted that he tried to use the murder of Lovelace as a lever with which to obtain money, he would be making himself an accessory after the fact, possibly damning himself as the actual killer. So he pretended that he simply went to tell Gimbert that Lovelace was dead. The case against Abbott strengthens. Would you like to telephone the man and warn him that he will be shortly under arrest?"

"Don't be a fool," said Foster.

"You are such a lover of sentiment that I thought you would like the opportunity," said Folly sarcastically. "I do not think that we shall find Stafford tonight, but I think that he might return to Spindles tomorrow. I also think that it will be better to arrest Abbott when Stafford is at hand. Have you any objection?"

"No," said Foster.

"Thank you. It means, of course, that we give Abbott another opportunity to run away, but I cannot convince myself that he will take it. As I said before, I think he might conceivably commit another murder in the hope of saving himself. The risk is not negligible, but I think we can allow it to remain for another twelve hours. Shall we go to Milton tomorrow or tonight?"

"I'm quite prepared to leave it to you," said Foster.

"Thank you." Folly smiled suddenly. "I'm sorry, Foster, I shouldn't have snapped at you. You may be quite right in thinking that the suggested motive against Abbott is fantastic. However, *nothing* in my experience is too fantastic when such people are involved. Remember that Abbott is a writer, a quieter type altogether than Stafford, but a writer. Some of his kind think they live as a divine right. Abbott may be one of those. Remember, also, that we know that he and Stafford have quarreled and are often on bad terms. Remember that this is an involved, ingenious business and that Abbott writes stories which are involved and ingenious. He might possibly be making capital out of his writing experience."

"Confound it, he doesn't only write crime stories," protested Foster.

"Study his work," said Folly. "I have done so. Everything he writes, be it murder mystery or straightforward novel, has the stamp of a complicated, ingenious brain. Oh no, my friend, make no mistake, he has the mind to conceive something on these lines, have no doubt of that. Also remember that we are dealing only in possibilities. Let's look at the newspaper cuttings."

He took them out. One was about a recital of Stafford's early work; another, much smaller, was from a provincial paper. Folly widened his eyes.

"Lovelace was interested in *Anne* Stafford," he said. "This is about her engagement to Mr. Edward Barr, younger son of Colonel and Mrs. Edward Barr, of High Lodge, Warwickshire. Now why should Lovelace be so interested in Anne's affairs?"

"I give up," said Foster.

"For the moment only, I hope. Well, let us see whether by any chance Wright *has* found Stafford."

All that Inspector Wright could tell them was that Stafford had caught a train to London from Brighton at about the time when they had all reached Geeves. Wright was obviously feeling bitter and angry, and Folly looked sour when he got away from the man, but cheered up on the way back to London. He was sure that if Stafford went as far as Victoria he would be seen by men watching the station.

He was right; at Scotland Yard there was a report that Stafford had reached Victoria and gone to a hotel in Buckingham Palace Gate. Folly decided to be satisfied with that, but before he took Foster to his flat he telephoned Milton and, winking broadly at Foster, spoke to Garth and asked him to take especial care that night to make sure that no one left Spindles.

"Now we can relax," he said as he replaced the receiver. "By George, I'm hungry. Come along, let's see what we can find."

In spite of their annoyance with Julius, it was difficult for the Abbotts to be ill-tempered that Wednesday afternoon. It was a fine day, with just enough wind to prevent it from being too hot. Anne had completely recovered and looked younger and gayer. Julius was happily humming his tune over and over again, occasionally going upstairs and playing it over, but satisfied now that, in a burst of wild energy, he had completed the score. Somehow the change affected Gillian and Tony, and the presence of the police did not disturb them as much as it had done.

Toward the middle of the afternoon Tony was working in the garden, turning over the soil with more zeal than knowledge in a happy dream of next year's roses, when he saw Castle and Anderson arrive in the doctor's car. Soon afterward Anderson left. Before long, Castle appeared at the gap in the hedge, and Tony's heart rose when he saw his expression.

"Good news?" he asked.

"So good I can hardly believe it's true," said Castle, stepping through the gap. "Mildred is in very little pain now, and she can stand without assistance. It is a miracle, Abbott, and I shall never cease thanking God for the fate that brought you here."

"Oh, I had nothing to do——"

"And I shall never stop trying to help you in the unhappy circumstances which surround you," said Castle quietly. "It's a most difficult situation even for me," he added with a grave smile. "If Agnes had not burst out as she did, I doubt whether Mildred would have come downstairs and precipitated the crisis which for her has had such happy results. On the other hand——"

It was Tony's turn to interrupt. "I don't think the story about the boat would have made any difference; please don't let it worry you. We're trying to forget about it," he added with forced cheerfulness. "It won't be surprising if the police go away and we see nothing of them again. It's almost certain that they are busy on the case in London. Let's talk about something much more cheerful—your manuscript, for instance."

"I'm afraid I set too much store by that and your very generous remarks," said Castle. "Don't hesitate to tell me the worst. I can stand it."

"I don't think there is any worst," said Tony. "My agent agrees with me that after a little pruning it will find a publisher without any difficulty and might be a reasonable success."

"Seriously?" Castle gasped. "But of course you would not joke about such a matter." There was a glow of deep pleasure in his eyes. "I can rely on a hundred and fifty pounds, you say?"

"Quite definitely," said Tony.

"Then as soon as Mildred is able to walk more freely, I can send her away for a month or two," said Castle. "It could not have been more opportune. You know, Abbott, if it had not been

for you, I doubt whether I would have plucked up the courage to
show it to anyone. It's hard to believe, even now, that it might
appear as a book, actually printed and published. I wonder if I
have been a little too harsh in some of the things I have said about
ritual, and—"

Tony smiled. "I think that's where it needs the pruning. Let me
get it. Snub left his notes with the manuscript, and it's on my
desk."

They went to his study together and then strolled back to the
vicarage. Castle was obviously eager to read the suggestions that
Snub had made, and Tony left him, made more cheerful by the
man's obvious pleasure and the joy he was feeling. The whole situation had shown a marked turn for the better. If Julius and Anne
retained their new cheerfulness life would be much easier, and
the only thing remaining was to see the last of the police. Tony
felt remarkably calm and composed, and it seemed impossible
now that he could ever have been subject to those tempestuous
outbursts of rage. It was nonsense to think that he might have
killed Lovelace without remembering it. Apparently the man had
been cut up badly, and there had been no blood on any of his
clothes. The absence of the chief policemen encouraged the be-
lief that they had found a different trail, probably starting from
the man Hibbett.

He sat back in his study chair and looked out the window. Gillian was coming from the village with a shopping basket over her
arm. She waved a greeting.

Some time later as, hand in hand, they wandered round the
garden, they heard footsteps on the drive, and then a man's
voice calling: "Fire, fire, fire!" Other watching men hurried along
the drive and from the fences, and Gillian ran ahead. As she
turned the corner of the house she saw a cloud of smoke coming
from the study.

Tony saw her climb through the window ahead of the first policeman. When he reached it Gillian had stamped out most of
the fire, and the room was full of smoke, but there were no flames.
P. C. Grimes bent down and picked up a smoldering object, one
end of which was untouched.

"What's that?" asked Tony.

"That's a fire lighter, a kind very popular around here," said Grimes, looking at him steadily. "Now who would want to set fire to your room, sir?"

"Don't be an ass," said Tony. "It must have been an accident. Probably I dropped a cigarette end or left one burning."

"And it fell on the fire lighter, which was also there by accident," said Grimes. "I don't think there's much accident about it, sir. This was done deliberately."

Gillian said, "It might have burned the house down."

"Not with so many men watching," said Grimes, a little smugly. "I'll take this with me, *if* you please."

He went off, followed by the others, leaving Gillian and Tony standing in the middle of the room. Without speaking they began to remove the charred rugs. Suddenly there was a quiet knock on the back door; Gillian heard it and said at once, "I think that's Archy."

She hurried out, and Tony watched her with a set expression on his face. In spite of all that had happened, and the urgency of the investigations which centered around Spindles, she could drop everything and rush to see what young Archy Kelly wanted. More than once Tony had seen an expression in her eyes which reminded him of the time, only twelve months ago, when she had told him that she was pregnant. It was hard to recapture the thrill now. After four months she had been taken seriously ill and rushed to the hospital for an operation, which had ended the pregnancy and her hopes of ever bearing children.

They rarely talked about it, but each knew what the other felt.

Now she greeted Archy with a lilt in her voice. She brought him to the study, where he stood gravely as she told Tony that his mother had gone into Milton for the afternoon and had told him to ask permission to play in the garden.

"Of course," said Tony.

What Archy really wanted was a large colored atlas, which he had been given to look at several times. He went off with it, and Gillian walked round the house with him. When he had gone to sit on the grass beneath the tree, she glanced in at Tony's window.

"Grand little chap," said Tony.

"Yes, he—"

Tony said gently, "I've an idea of what's in your mind, sweet. I heard you telling Mrs. Kelly that we would like to adopt a child. I don't think you ought to build your hopes too high, you know. She'll go back to London sooner or later and almost certainly want to take young Archibald with her." His smile rallied her, and somehow the conversation had a soothing effect, making them temporarily forget the fire and all that had gone before.

"What we can do is make sure he has—" began Tony. He broke off. One moment he had been smiling and looked more content than for some days; the next the color drained from his face and the smile disappeared. A car engine sounded at the end of the drive as it changed gear. Gillian swung round. A large car was approaching, and she could see the massive figure of Folly, with Foster beside him.

She hurried into the house, calling out to Archy to go back to his mother in good time. The child called an answer. The car pulled up outside the front door, and Foster got out with some difficulty, limping noticeably. Folly followed him after a struggle. He looked portentous and forbidding. Foster's expression was enigmatic, but he looked as if he had something on his mind.

"Good afternoon, Mr. Abbott," Folly said heavily. "I wish to have a few words with you and your friends. Be good enough to ask all of them to come down here."

Tony made no reply, but shrugged his shoulders and called out to Gillian. Then he shouted for Anne and Julius, who appeared at the head of the stairs. When he saw the police Julius' face darkened.

Just at that moment, Grimes came up to report about the fire. Folly nodded, and the information seemed to make him thoughtful. In a clear, slightly overloud voice, he said, "Presumably there was something in the study which someone wishes to destroy. However, we need not worry about that now. The study can be searched when we have gone—Sharp will be able to do that, won't he?"

"Of course," said Foster.

"Good."

All this time Julius had been slowly approaching. Now he stood in front of Folly, eyed him coldly up and down, and then said in a tone of deliberate insult, "So, the minion of the law is back!

I've been waiting for this opportunity. When are you going to remove your men from my garden?"

"When I consider it safe," Folly said, as sharply. "I want neither obstruction nor insolence, sir."

"Who the devil do you think you are?" bellowed Julius.

"Julius, don't—" began Gillian.

"Let him bellow and let him abuse me," said Folly scornfully. "It will make no difference." He turned his baleful eyes on Julius. "What I think I am, sir, is an officer of the law, here in the course of his duty, which is to arrest a man for a cold-blooded and brutal crime. Have you anything more to say?"

"You must be mad!" gasped Julius.

"If anyone is mad, it is not I," said Folly. "This way, if you please." He led the way to the study, and the others followed him, Foster bringing up the rear. He looked from one to another. Julius red and angry and a little uneasy; Gillian flushed, charming, and pretty, wearing a pair of gardening gloves, and with some dust on her nose; Tony pale but quite composed and giving the impression that he feared the coming interview; Anne calmer than any of them and looking a little exalted—she was a curious person, Foster thought. Gimbert probably did not know how she worked and slaved for her brother.

"Well, get on with it," growled Julius.

"You do well to remind me that I must make haste," said Folly. "You are aware, I think, that Jeremiah Lovelace, known to all of you, met his death at the hands of a callous and brutal murderer. He was murdered in your flat at Chelsea, Stafford!" Folly's voice grew suddenly loud, and he pointed a quivering finger at Julius. "His body was brought here and then dropped into the river. Well, sir!" His voice echoed about the room. "Why did you drop the body into the river?"

Julius said, "It's a lie. I didn't—"

"So you deny it," breathed Folly. "Very well. The body *was* removed from this house. It was—" He broke off and turned to Tony with one of those unpredictable changes which made him so dangerous. "Anthony John Abbott, it is my duty to arrest you for the willful murder of Jeremiah Lovelace. Anything you say may be used in evidence. Tell me, why did you kill him?"

· 23 ·

SOME OF THE TRUTH

"If I KILLED him," Tony said, very quietly, "I remember nothing about it, Superintendent."

"Remarkable," murmured Folly. "Are you calling yourself a homicidal maniac?"

"It's madness! He couldn't have!" cried Gillian. She stood with her hands clenched and raised, her cheeks drained of color.

"I greatly regret causing you pain, Mrs. Abbott," said Folly in a surprisingly gentle voice. "I do not wish you or anyone to imagine that I enjoy this task. However, murder has been committed, and I have evidence that it was committed by your husband. I can remind you that there is such a thing as a defense in English criminal law. Killing can be justified if the provocation was strong enough—if, for instance, it was a matter of self-defense. Was it, Mr. Abbott?"

"I know nothing at all about it," said Tony. "I did not bring the body here, I did not know that there was a body. I did not take it out in a boat or dump it, and I am sure that my wife did not."

Folly stared at him levelly. "I see. In that case, Mr. Stafford, what can *you* tell me?"

"It's a farrago of nonsense!"

"I do not come here to make such a charge as this without reason," said Folly, irritably. "I have *all* the evidence required that Lovelace was killed at your flat on the afternoon of May 11 and that the body was removed hurriedly and that the floorboards at your flat were washed, but it was forgotten that blood gets into crevices and cracks."

Folly seemed to be paying all his attention to Julius now. Gillian was sitting down, as if her legs would no longer carry her, and Tony was standing quite still. Julius was flushed, angry, and a little uneasy, and Anne was clenching and unclenching her hands.

"Well, Mr. Stafford. The truth, please. You arranged for the removal from Chelsea. You arrived here first. You had the best opportunity to dispose of the body. You are in great danger of being arrested as an accessory after the fact. The whole truth might save you. I offer no guarantees, but I repeat—the whole truth might save you."

"It's a lot of damned nonsense!" snapped Julius, his voice slightly unsteady.

"I see. You harp on nonsense. Mrs. Abbott!" He swung round so sharply that Gillian jumped. "You arrived here at about half-past ten on the night of May 12. Is that true?"

"Yes, yes, of course it's true."

"Your husband was with you?"

"He was."

"No one was here when you arrived?"

"No. It was about an hour before Julius and Anne came. They had gone out for a drink."

"They had not. They were not seen at The Angler, and they had no means of transport to go farther. In my opinion, they were disposing of the body. Mrs. Abbott, loyalty to your husband is praiseworthy. But it may endanger the lives of your brother and sister. Is it not a fact that you knew your husband had murdered Lovelace and at his urgent request you persuaded your brother and sister to remove the body?"

"No," said Gillian. "That is not true."

She stood up, looking calmer. She saw the danger with all its ugly implications, and she knew that she must keep her head if she was to help Tony at all. She dared not look at him.

"On the day before your arrival, did you visit Chelsea?" asked Folly.

"No."

"Did your husband—"

Tony spoke quietly, with a gesture. "Yes, I went to the flat the previous afternoon."

"So you remember that," sneered Folly. "I am glad to know it. Did *you* ask the Staffords to—"

"I saw Anne but asked her nothing," said Tony.

"A fine story! Miss Stafford—" Folly swung round again. "Against your better judgment, you were persuaded to remove the body from the flat and scrub the floorboards. The truth, please."

Then part of the truth came out.

Anne broke down completely. She spoke in a tense, barely audible voice, and as she talked Foster took shorthand notes of her statement. The room seemed hushed; there were long intervals between her sentences, and she was looking at Tony all the time.

She had gone out, she said, a little while after Julius had left the flat. She knew Lovelace was there—he had been to see them and admitted that he was hiding from the police. She and Julius had known Lovelace several years before, and had agreed to help him for old times' sake. She had gone out to get extra provisions, and had been gone nearly an hour. On her return, Lovelace was sitting in the small dining room not only dead, but terribly mutilated. She had not known what to do. She knew that Tony had been there, for he came again and asked her about the moving; on his first visit, he said, he had found no one there and had gone away immediately. Yes, Tony had a key to the flat. She did not know whether anyone else had been there. She knew that Tony did not like Lovelace but did not know why. After he had gone, she had waited in an agony of suspense for her brother's return. He had come in nearly drunk. She knew that she might be suspected of Lovelace's murder——

Then, for the first time, Folly interrupted her. "Why should you be suspected, Miss Stafford?"

She said, "I didn't like the man. He—" She broke off and looked at Julius. "He was a bad influence on my brother."

"So you thought we would suspect you of murdering a man who was a bad influence on your brother," Folly said heavily. "Remarkable."

"Stop bullying her," cried Julius.

"You, sir, do not appear to realize that if your sister had a motive for killing Lovelace, you probably *shared* that motive."

"It isn't true," said Anne in a flat voice. "Julius liked Lovelace. Only I knew that he was always a bad influence. He—"

"My dear Miss Stafford, Lovelace had been out of the country for some years! Be plausible if you can't be truthful."

"I'm telling you the truth," said Anne. "I don't know who killed Lovelace. *I* didn't, and Julius was out all the afternoon. I don't believe Tony did, and he certainly didn't ask me to move the body. I was frightened, Julius was drunk. I persuaded him to help me—"

She continued, giving each detail of their actions. She even told of Julius' idea of putting the pretended contents of Tony's suitcase in the garden, to make the story of a third party more plausible. Quietly, inexorably, the story built itself up, until all the truth was known about all events from the moment she and Julius had left the Chelsea flat. At last she looked at Julius as if she was asking him to forgive her. No one spoke, and she went on in a tone almost of desperation: "I began it; I persuaded Julius to help me. He knew—" She broke off again and Julius said:

"Oh, pet, pet!"

Folly moved to a chair and sat down heavily. "Thank you very much, Miss Stafford," he said. "I am grateful for your frankness. It is much the wisest course. Won't you please round it off by telling me *why* you had a motive for killing Lovelace. The present story just won't do, you know. I can assure you of one thing; no one will be punished for a crime he or she did not commit. I have already made it plain that I have evidence, reliable evidence, to justify the arrest of your brother-in-law. However, I will be frank with you—a third party *might* have committed this murder. We shall not necessarily consider the case finished with this one arrest. Much remains to be discovered; your reason for wishing to see Lovelace dead is one thing. Please, Miss Stafford." His voice was gentle and pleading. "Why was Lovelace interested in your engagement to Mr. Barr?"

"I—" began Anne.

"Pet!" cried Julius in an anguished voice.

"It's no use," said Anne, "it will all come out eventually. I had a very good reason for wanting Jeremiah Lovelace dead. He—he was my husband."

It was Julius who took up the story, admitting that what his sister said was true. He—they both—had once been very friendly with Lovelace, during which time Anne had eloped with him.

No one except Julius, not even Tony or Gillian, had known anything of the marriage, for almost before there was time to tell
anybody Lovelace had proved to be an utter rogue, and Anne
had left him. Since then he had disappeared, and they understood
he had gone to South America. Hearing nothing from him for
nearly seven years, Anne had presumed him dead and was now
engaged. The shock of seeing him again had been very great.

All that any jury could require in the way of a motive was
there.

"Only it applies to the wrong person," Folly said, an hour later.

He and Foster were in an office at the police station, and Sergeant Buckingham was sitting in a corner, his eager eyes on Folly.

"The wrong person," Folly repeated. "She had every reason
in the world for wishing to kill Lovelace. She had the opportunity.
With such a motive she would not be influenced by his money or
the diamonds. She knew Gimbert's address and could have
packed up the clothes and sent them to him."

"That's a curious thing," said Foster. "I can't understand why
they took the trouble to strip the body. You didn't ask them that,
either. There were several questions you could have asked."

"Always keep something up your sleeve," Folly said, with an
absent smile. "Always, if possible, know the answer to a question before you put it to your man. It gives you confidence, you
know. We'll keep the matter of the clothes to ourselves for a little
while. Well, what do you think of things generally?"

"That perhaps we were premature in arresting Abbott," said
Foster.

"You forget one most important thing," said Folly. "Anne Stafford did not feel that she could stand by and allow Tony to be accused and the case against him strengthened by our version of the
disposal of the body. Had we not arrested Abbott we would not
have heard her story. It's really very bad," he added with a scowl.
"We should have found out that Lovelace was married. That goes
to show that you can't be too thorough. Now if we could shake
Hibbett's story, if we could—" He paused and then sat up
sharply. "I think we can!" he cried. "I'm sure we can! Foster, a
fig for your sentiment. You didn't take to Julius Stafford nor did
I. Yet here was a man prepared to help his sister when there was a
lot of risk involved. A man who kept silent when a word from him

would have started us on the right trail. A man who is largely dependent on her, I grant you, so there might have been a selfish motive. However, if he would do so much to save her, would he not go even further? *He* was at Geeves. *Hibbett* was at Geeves. We have not yet proved a meeting, but one could easily have taken place. Gimbert told Julius of Hibbett's visit and suggestion. Supposing it was not Abbott but *Anne* whom Hibbett had seen holding the knife. And supposing Julius, realizing that Hibbett had seen her, bribed him to say it was *Abbott* whom he saw. Abbott's known propensity to violence would substantiate this. Possible?"

"I suppose so," said Foster.

"Julius Stafford isn't a chap likely to be moved for the sake of someone else," said Buckingham. "As you advise, sir, the people come first—what kind of people and how their minds work." He paused as if he expected to bring a storm upon his head, but as Folly kept silent he went on. "Stafford would want to save his sister all right, but he wouldn't go to all that trouble just for that. No, sir! He might have done it if he wanted to frame Abbott. We know they're bad friends, and we don't know what else there is behind it. He used Abbott's suitcase for the bricks, Abbott's trunk for the body. He pretended that he suspected that Abbott had used the boat——"

"Careful, Buckingham. You're doing well, don't spoil it. He's admitted using the boat himself."

"I know he has," said Buckingham, "but only because he had to. I'm putting up a case suggesting he wanted to frame Abbott although he knew his sister had killed Lovelace."

"Even I have seen that possibility," admitted Folly. "Go on. What other pointers are there to such an ingenious frame-up?"

"Sending the clothes to Gimbert could be one," said Buckingham. "The fact that the body was stripped is a puzzle, isn't it? All right, then—Stafford knew that Abbott had Gimbert's address. He'd guess we'd find out. So he sent them to the old man. It wasn't likely that we'd think he or his sister had done that—it'd look too obvious."

"Not bad," said Folly. "Not bad at all."

"Well," said Buckingham spiritedly. "I think it's as good as any theory we've had yet, anyhow!"

"Perhaps it is. Well, what else is there? That fire—it *might* have been an accident. Then the clothes. Foster, how long will your fingerprints people be with the wrapping paper on that parcel?"

"Go and see," said Foster to Buckingham, who went out at once. There was silence until Foster admitted that the case seemed to get more involved as they went on. He was still sceptical of the wisdom of arresting Abbott and made that very clear.

Folly grunted but made no comment. He said, instead, "I wish we'd stayed and searched Spindles ourselves, you know. Sharp's a sound man, but—"

Foster said, "We left four men there. What do you hope they'll find?"

"If Abbott killed him, something happened to the clothes he was wearing," said Foster. "If Anne Stafford did, something happened to her clothes—we've agreed that there must have been a lot of blood. I—" He broke off, for the telephone rang. He lifted the receiver. "Yes," he said. "Yes . . . what's that, Sharp?" His voice rose. "Where? . . . Behind the books in his study? . . . Yes, bring it out at once."

He replaced the receiver and looked into Folly's eager eyes.

"A blood-stained coat, shirt, and tie were stuffed behind the books in Abbott's study," he said. "Yes, Abbott's—they've found his name tabs on them."

"Well, bless my Aunt Sophia!" exclaimed Folly. "As obvious as that. Now we know why he tried to set fire to the room." He heard the door open and turned his head quickly. "Ah, Buckingham. Results?"

"That wrapping paper, sir," said Buckingham, and paused.

"Well? Go on, man, go on!"

"It's covered with Abbott's fingerprints," said Buckingham.

"Well," Folly said, after a long pause. "Now perhaps you two gentlemen will admit that the arrest of Abbott was fully justified and perhaps delayed too long. He might have destroyed those clothes."

"If Abbott was clever enough to have planned this crime, he'd have got rid of the clothes before this," snapped Foster.

"Nonsense, man. What are you, counsel for the defense? If Abbott committed it he wasn't clever. It's only clever if someone else did it and is trying to frame him. If we could only find a motive against Abbott," he cried. "I'm almost inclined to fall back on his ungovernable rage. He killed him, then realized with horror what he'd done. Then he lost his head. I wonder what he will say when he sees those clothes?"

It was half an hour before Sharp arrived with the coat, shirt, and tie. Folly heaved himself to his feet and took them, beckoned Foster, and strode toward the room where Abbott was being detained.

Tony was standing by the window, smoking. Folly strode up to him, waving the clothes in his face.

"Well, Abbott. Your clothes. Bloodstained. Behind your bookcase. *Your* clothes, I tell you—the clothes you were wearing on the day you killed Lovelace. Stop pretending, man. *Why* did you kill him? Can't you see that the motive is your only hope? If it were good enough, you might shorten your sentence considerably."

Tony took the coat, looked at it, and then returned Folly's gaze steadily. "Yes, they're mine," he said, "and I was wearing them that day. I hadn't missed them. You know, Folly, I've never denied killing Lovelace. I've only said that I didn't remember anything about it. Until this moment I was terribly afraid I attacked him as I did Hibbett. Now, thank God, I know that I didn't. I know for certain that I did not discover bloodstains on my clothes and did not hide them away. I'm very glad you found them, Superintendent. The question I suggest you apply to yourself now is, Who put them there?"

· 24 ·

SUPERINTENDENT FOLLY IS AGITATED

"Yes, I agree with you," said Folly, half an hour afterward. "He reminded us that Hibbett broke into the house and might have gone to the wardrobe before he was caught and hidden the clothes downstairs, after daubing blood on them. We can certainly have another go at Hibbett on the strength of what we know."

Foster nodded to the telephone. "You'll bring him down to-night, won't you?"

"Yes," said Folly. He stood up and stared at Foster. "You know, Foster, something is missing. The big trouble in this case is that too much has come too quickly. From the moment you discovered where the body was dropped into the river, we have made continual progress, and our setbacks have been remarkably few. Now, tumbling over each other, come the items of evidence against Abbott—all except that elusive motive."

"On the evidence that we got at Spindles," said Foster, "you should have detained Anne Stafford. She had opportunity and motive and is certainly an accessory."

"Yes, yes, I know. We needn't be in a hurry to detain her though. Abbott was enough for our immediate purpose."

"Enough for—" began Foster.

"Oh, my dear fellow, *please* use your mind. There were four people at Spindles, all of whom might be involved. There was also Hibbett, as an outsider, and my early favorite. The fact that the jewels and money remained in the clothes rules him out except as an accessory. The man's rapacity is too well known for us to consider anything else. While the other four remained together they could conspire and confer to their heart's delight and possibly outwit us. Now their ranks are open. The first result was the truth about the removal of the body; the second, the reason why they were too frightened to tell the truth when they were in London. Oh, have no doubt about it, that's what happened. They were afraid that her unfortunate marriage would be discovered; and even if it wasn't, that the scandal of the murder would deter her fiancé. He's a rich young man whose parents already oppose the marriage. However, we didn't get *all* the truth. When Anne Stafford broke down I watched Abbott, watched him closely, and I expected a confession. I freely admit it. I thought that he would see the danger in which his sister-in-law had placed herself and, knowing the truth, that he would save her. That is the way his mind would work. More than anything else, Foster, I am troubled by his attitude when she implicated herself so completely. He is not a man to allow anyone else to suffer for his sins."

"He isn't the man who killed Lovelace," said Foster firmly.

"All right, all right, that doesn't matter. It would only matter if he were about to be convicted. We must assume that one of the four is guilty. I thought an arrest would force a confession. It provided, instead, a most unsatisfactory anticlimax. Don't keep reminding me that I may have made a howler, *please*."

"I only want you to admit it," said Foster, relieved.

"Only a fool would refuse to do so. Hmm. We want to see Hibbett again, and—I *think* we'll send for that steward at the National Club who told us that Stafford had been there all the afternoon. Yes! If he was lying he will have time to repent on the journey." Folly put through a call to Scotland Yard, and while he was waiting for the call to come through, he went on: "I'm not happy about the case. Every now and again I get worried by the possibility that there will be another crime. *Something* remains beneath the surface. It may be the real motive. Ah!" he broke off as the telephone rang and gave instructions to his own office. Hibbett and the steward were to be brought down as quickly as possible.

"Well, what now?" asked Foster.

"Food," said Folly. "You never seem to think of it. I *can't* work on an empty stomach."

"You've never tried," laughed Foster.

A meal was sent in from the White Horse, and during the course of it Harrington arrived and Folly took the opportunity of going over every inch of the case and closely examining all doubtful points. The final crumb devoured, Folly suddenly snapped his fingers.

"Fool!" he cried, taking out a notebook and turning over the pages quickly. "Savory, Savory, private telephone number—ah!" He put in a call to Savory's home, and while waiting, said, "The man knows Abbott as well as anyone. It will be interesting to find out if he knows Hibbett. Curious fact, you know—Abbott hasn't asked for legal aid. Most people demand it immediately. I—" He broke off at a tap at the door.

"Come in," called Harrington, and a constable entered and looked at Harrington.

"A Mr. Savory called, sir, and asked to see you or Chief Inspector Foster."

"Aha!" exclaimed Folly. He canceled the call to London and was standing by the telephone when Snub came in.

The agent looked agitated; his curly hair was disheveled, and there were smuts on his face.

Harrington was standing up. "Good evening, Mr. Savory."

Snub said, "Good evening. Since when has it become the fashion to make arrests on serious charges without giving the accused an opportunity to send for legal aid?"

"Nonsense!" boomed Folly. "No aid asked for. The opportunity remains. Have you brought legal aid for your client, sir?"

"I have arranged for legal aid for my friend," said Snub abruptly. "I wish to see him, at once, and alone."

"I am afraid—" began Harrington.

"I beg you, Colonel, to permit it," said Folly elaborately.

"Any man who seriously thinks Tony Abbott capable of murder ought to be in a lunatic asylum," said Savory.

"You are offensive, sir!"

"Or else he is a fool," said Savory. "What motive have you got?"

"That, sir——"

The telephone rang, and Folly seemed glad of the opportunity to turn away. "Hallo," he boomed. "This is— *What!* We will come at once." He banged down the receiver and swung round. "Anne Stafford has confessed to the murder," he said. "Come, gentlemen, to Spindles! Mr. Savory, your interview with Abbott is postponed. You may come with us if you wish."

As dusk fell over the countryside a mist rose from the river and crept sluggishly toward Spindles, blotting out the ground and the hedges and gradually rising above the trees, concealing all movement and muffling all sound. Its effect was felt inside

Spindles; it seemed to worsen the plight of the three people under police surveillance. Sergeant Buckingham and two plainclothesmen watched from the hall and landing. Anne sat in the great odd-shaped drawing room staring into the empty fireplace, her hands clasped about her arms as if she were cold. An awful, oppressive silence hung in the room. Julius was sitting in an armchair but did not look at ease. Gillian was torn between a great relief at the importance of the confession to Tony and a horror at the thought that Anne might be convicted. That Lovelace had been murdered did not bother her; of them all, she alone had never known the man.

Outside, policemen were on duty. It was impossible to see more than five or six yards, and not always as far as that. With the darkness the mist became thicker. All sound had ceased. Spindles was like a house of death.

There was a faint glow of light from the vicarage study, and inside the room there was absolute disorder. Castle was on his knees, peering beneath his desk, breathing heavily, and with an expression of dismay. He stood up, pushed his hands distractedly through his hair, and muttered, "It can't have been stolen. That's impossible!" His precious manuscript had been on his desk when Mildred had called him, and he had hurried upstairs to sit with her while the police were in Spindles. Together they had watched Tony Abbott being taken away and seen Gillian standing on the porch with a hopeless expression on her face. Castle had gone to offer comfort but had quickly seen that there was no desire to talk to him in the house where the shadow of Blackshaw's corpse hanging from the tree seemed all pervading.

So Castle had come back. When he went to look at the manuscript and Snub's suggestions, they had not been on his desk. He turned the room upside down and questioned Maude twice and Agnes once, fruitlessly. Suddenly he heard Agnes's footsteps in the passage, and the door opened abruptly

"Well," she said, "have you found it?"

"No. Agnes, are you *sure* you haven't been tidying up in here?"

"Tidying up!" she exclaimed. "It would take me a week! But I *can* tell you where to find that book of yours."

"Where?" snapped Castle.

"At Spindles," she hissed. "That home of thieves and murderers. To think that *my* house has ever known such evil folk."

"That's enough!" cried Castle.

When she flounced off with an ugly look in her eyes he repented the outburst, but when he went to find her to apologize, she had gone out. All Maude could say, wringing her red hands, was that she had looked like a creature possessed of the Devil and had gone into the misty darkness without hat or coat, muttering to herself. Castle realized it was hopeless to try to find her and returned to make another futile search of the study, growing more agitated and alarmed. It was such a senseless thing to steal, and to suspect anyone from Spindles was ridiculous.

Yet—there *was* evil in that house.

A mile out of Milton, Superintendent Folly had stopped the car by a telephone kiosk and hurried to it, returning ten minutes later with a seraphic smile on his face.

"I really am sorry, Colonel. Forgetful of me. I've sent for Abbott. You don't mind, I trust?"

"I don't have to mind," said Harrington good-naturedly.

"You're very good. I think it will be wise to have them all together. I have also sent for Professor Gimbert. He will not like traveling, I feel sure, but the more I think about him the less happy I am about his story. Stafford went to see him, followed by Hibbett. He might have told the truth; on the other hand he might have held back something of importance. Normally, I do not like gathering all suspects and witnesses together. However, with your permission, my dear Colonel, I will do it."

"Granted," said Harrington, straight-faced.

They were approaching Riversmeet when the mist closed in on them, and Yule slowed down to five miles an hour. It took three-quarters of an hour to cover the two miles from Riversmeet to Spindles, where Yule pulled up and said decisively:

"I don't think I ought to try turning into the drive, sir."

"Confound it, there is a long walk," said Folly.

"That's better than knocking the car about, sir," said Yule firmly.

Grimes loomed out of the mist when they approached the gate but had little to report. There had been some voices in the vicarage, where something appeared to be missing, but not a sound had come from the inside of Spindles. Grimes explained carefully where the men were stationed, and then they left him. The front door opened, and the bright hall light shone on Buckingham's fair head.

"Where are they?" said Folly. His voice was loud. "All right, there's no hurry, I'll see them a little later. Don't let anyone leave the room." He and Harrington started up the stairs, and Foster followed slowly, grimacing. He caught them up in the bathroom, where Folly was examining various toilet articles.

"I could tell them something about bathrooms," he grunted. He picked up a tube of toothpaste and squeezed a little onto a new toothbrush. Then, solemnly, he brushed his teeth; in a few seconds the froth from the paste was over his lips and a little was on the tip of his nose. "Good!" he said, and rinsed out his mouth and beamed. He dried off the brush and put it in his pocket. "Now let's have a look at the studio," he said.

The studio had been tidied up, but all the music scores had been preserved, some of them crumpled but straightened out. "I wish I knew more about this stuff," said Folly. "It looks as if this is the work Stafford started on—what's it like, Foster?"

Foster took several sheets and scanned them, humming to himself. Folly began to frown. "Either you're terrible or it's tripe," he said.

"It isn't very good," said Foster, "but there's nothing surprising in that. It's been discarded."

"*Hmm!* No report that anything of interest was found up here, is there? No. All right, now for the study." He led the way downstairs and turned into the narrow passage which led to the study. Being set off from the rest of the house, it was not visible from any of the vantage points from which the police were now watching, and was under observation only by a fairly frequent patrol.

Halfway along the passage, Folly sniffed, and Foster thought that he smelled burning. Folly suddenly broke into a run, reached the door, and opened it. It jammed for a moment, then a billow of smoke made them cough and gasp.

"*Another!*" cried Folly. "Not Abbott this time!" He dashed into the room, where flames were flickering near the window. Harrington called for Buckingham, while Folly switched on the light and started to stamp on the smoldering carpet. He began to choke, and soon Foster was doubled up in a paroxysm. Buckingham rushed into the drawing room and discovered that there was no fire extinguisher. He called for men and they brought buckets of water. Gillian and Julius came running; only Anne remained in the drawing room. The smoke was thick, and billowed and curled in the draft from the open door—but gradually the men subdued the fire, leaving the carpet saturated, the furniture ruined, and the woodwork and walls scorched badly. Smuts floated everywhere, and the room was filled with the acrid smell of burning.

On the floor were dozens of pieces of loose paper, charred yellow and brown; the writing on some sheets was no longer legible. Folly stood in the middle of the room, smuts and wisps of smoke floating about his head, reading a sheet of paper covered with a neat handwriting.

"Anyone recognize this?" he asked.

"It's probably some of Abbott's work," said Foster.

"It concerns church organization. Was your husband interested so deeply, Mrs. Abbott, that he——"

Gillian was staring at the paper and spoke as if she had not heard the question. "That's the *Vicar's* manuscript! But Tony gave it back to him!"

"Bring the Vicar here," snapped Folly, and looked at Buckingham with a terrifying scowl. "How was this fire started when the house is supposed to be watched so closely? It is disgraceful! I —what's that?"

He broke off, for from outside there came a high-pitched, almost maniacal scream. It stopped, then started again, and all but Folly and Foster stood rooted to the spot.

· 25 ·

THE FIRES EXPLAINED

CASTLE CAME hurrying from the vicarage, roused by the screams. Mildred Castle was at her window, calling out in alarm. The lights from the study window and from Mildred's room cast a faint glow about the garden between the two houses, and in the glow Grimes was seen struggling with a woman who was tearing at him, trying to get away, and giving vent to those awful screams. It was Buckingham who climbed through the window and slapped her face and so succeeded in stopping her.

"And who in the name of goodness is this?" demanded Folly in his mildest voice.

Foster said, "It's Mrs. Blackshaw, Agnes Blackshaw."

"I saw her crouching outside the study window, sir," said Grimes. "I thought I saw a flicker of light and came along to investigate. She was doubled up with laughter, silent laughter. She isn't——"

"That will do, Constable, thank you." Folly stared at the woman and then at Castle, who came through the gap in the hedge. "Bring her into the house," Folly said, and in a few minutes she was in the blackened, scorched room. There was an ugly glitter in her eyes, and she glared at Gillian and shook a fist. Castle was standing by the door, looking helplessly about him, and suddenly he caught sight of a page of his manuscript. He picked it up, stared at it, and went very pale.

Folly stepped forward, took Agnes's arm, and sniffed at her hand. He dropped it and backed away as she struck at him. She was trembling from head to foot and looked like a witch, with her hair disheveled and her clothes ruffled and soiled with black. One sleeve of her long, grey dress was singed.

Folly said mildly, "You have been handling paraffin or fire lighters. Did you start this fire, ma'am?"

"Yes, I did, and I would again!" she screamed. "This is my

house, my house, my house! Now thieves and murderers live in it. It is besmirched with their foul touch, fit only to be burned down, burned, burned, *burned!*"

"Did you start an earlier fire?" asked Folly in the same soft voice.

"Some fool put it out!" she cried. "But it did not matter, I came again." She lowered her voice and looked at Castle with an expression of great cunning. "It gave me a chance to undo more evil. You, Harry, have lent yourself to the devil himself!"

"Agnes—" said Castle, in a broken voice and glanced toward the window. As he did so, Gillian seemed to come to life; she was thinking of Mildred Castle in her room alone, and she turned to the door, looking at Folly. "I must go to the vicarage," she said, and when Folly raised no objection she hurried out. They could hear her calling from the garden and heard her enter the front door of the vicarage. For a while there had been silence, with Agnes glaring at her brother-in-law, who looked suddenly old and broken.

"So your brother-in-law has lent himself to the devil," Folly said, encouraging Agnes to continue.

"Please—" began Castle.

Agnes screamed, "Ever since the murderers came to Spindles he has befriended them—befriended people who have blood on their hands! Oh, I know them for what they are. I know the evil that is in them—and in you, Harry! I took your book! I read the terrible things you have said about the Church, the terrible lies you have written, *so I destroyed it!* I set it alight and here it is— *look, look, look!*" She stabbed her quivering finger in a dozen directions toward pages which were mostly burned, while Castle stepped to her side and rested a hand on her shoulder. She tried to fling it off, but he held her firmly.

Suddenly she began to cry.

Folly admitted that the first weakening of the evidence against Tony had come. He saw how easy it was for Agnes to come through the gap in the hedge to the window of the study, and he examined the overgrown trees and bushes that practically hid the room from sight. He raised no objection to Castle's taking Agnes away, but asked the Vicar to send Gillian back. She came promptly, less troubled now, for she had shared something of her burden with Mildred Castle. Julius, very subdued, had contributed nothing to the conversation, and Anne was still sitting with her hands clasping her arms, staring into the empty fireplace.

A car drew up outside and was followed by a second and a third. Abbott was brought in to the drawing room, and Folly did not stop Gillian from going to him. Then Savory and two plain-clothesmen from Scotland Yard came in with Hibbett. There was also a tall, thin-faced man with a stoop who looked about him bewilderedly. His arrival brought the first look of animation to Julius' face.

"What the devil are you doing here, Bright?"

"The police asked me to come," said the thin man.

"Mr. Bright," said Folly to the room at large, "is a steward at the National Club. We may require his evidence this evening."

Foster, sitting on the arm of a chair with his injured leg stretched out in front of him, expected Folly to start on Hibbett. There was, he knew, the possibility that the Yard man would wait until Gimbert arrived, but that would not be for some hours, and Folly would hardly keep Harrington waiting for so long. There was no knowing to what lengths Folly would go, however. But now he said nothing, looking about him with a baleful stare, as if he hoped that by keeping silent among all the people gathered together he would force someone else to speak.

At last, abruptly, Folly said, "Abbott, come with me please."

Tony joined him, and Folly assured Harrington that he would not keep him waiting long. Breathing heavily, he led the way upstairs. Tony did not speak as they hurried along to the bathroom, but he looked puzzled.

Folly said, "Abbott, I am quite serious. Your life might depend on what happens in the next few minutes. I want you to follow my instructions carefully. You recall the evening when you attacked Hibbett?"

"Yes."

"You told me that you were brushing your teeth when you heard a scream. I want you to brush them now, please."

Tony stared, then shrugged his shoulders and obeyed. The froth was thick about his lips when Folly snapped, "That is enough! Come, please." He gripped Tony's arm, and hustled him down the stairs. Tony was too bewildered to protest. Folly strode into the study, and Tony followed. Harrington gaped and Foster raised his hands helplessly. Folly led Tony across the room to Hibbett, and his voice grew suddenly thunderous:

"Hibbett! Is this how Abbott looked when he attacked you? Was he frothing at the lips in this way?"

"Yes, yes!" Hibbett backed away, as if afraid of another attack, but Tony stood still and Folly raised his voice to an unprecedented pitch.

"Very well, sir! Is this how he looked, with froth on his lips, when you saw him at Chelsea? Answer me! Is it? *Is* it?"

"Yes!" cried Hibbett.

"Thank you," breathed Folly. "Thank you. You are a brazen liar, Hibbett. That is now proved. The froth is a particular brand of toothpaste. I do not believe that Abbott brushed his teeth immediately after attacking Lovelace. You elaborated your story too much. *Hibbett!* You saw someone standing over Lovelace, with the blood streaming from the terrible wounds in his face and neck. You saw the blood dripping from the knife, but you did not see Abbott. *Whom did you see? Whom——*"

"Stop!" screamed Anne. "Stop! He saw *me*. I was standing there, I saw him. He was frightened and ran away. I've told you that I killed Lovelace because I wanted to marry again, because—" She broke off, and her lips were trembling, her hands rubbing against one another in the agony of her confession.

"I see," said Folly, and he looked at her with an expression almost of commiseration. "You know the penalty, Miss Stafford. You know the consequences, and yet you stand by your story—that you killed Lovelace."

"I tell you I did! He maddened me, he—"

"And after killing him you took off his clothes."

"Yes!"

"Where did you send them?"

"I—I sent them to—to a friend of my brother's."

"Name him, please."

"Professor Gimbert."

"Why?"

"I—I believed he would help me. I meant to go and see him, but I didn't get the chance."

"I see. What did you do with your own blood-stained clothes?"

"I burned them—in the fireplace at Chelsea."

"I see. I inspected the ashes but found no trace of burned cloth," said Folly.

"I cleaned it out, and we burned some papers afterward. Ask Julius, he will tell you—we burned some papers. Julius, didn't we? Answer me, Julius."

"Yes," said Julius with an effort. "Yes, we did."

"We make progress," said Folly. He still looked at Anne. "You have told me that you went out for an hour and came back and found the dead body. So that is a lie. You killed him and, when you realized what you had done, with great cunning and heartlessness you tried to make it appear that your brother-in-law, Mr. Abbott, had committed the crime."

"I—yes, I did, but I couldn't keep it up."

"I see. Where did you get the paper in which to wrap the clothes you sent to Professor Gimbert?"

"It was in the flat. Julius had just received a big parcel of music. I tore off the label, and—and—"

"When Mr. Abbott came in and saw you in a different room, you gave him the wrapping paper and made sure that he handled it freely, so that his fingerprints were on it. You then used gloves when you were tying up the parcel. Is that right?"

"Yes!"

"Look here," began Tony.

"Quiet, sir, please! Let us continue, Miss Stafford. You prompted your brother to put the body in Mr. Abbott's trunk, to use his suitcase——"

"They happened to be handy, that's all. They happened to be handy. I—I didn't realize that it would—would help."

"I see. You were not such a scoundrel as you might have been, Miss Stafford. Let us proceed to the next step in the course of your remarkable crime. You took some clothes belonging to Mr. Abbott, stained them with blood, and hid them behind the bookcase in his room. Isn't that right?"

She stared at him and then gasped, "Yes. Oh, God, don't torment me! I've confessed. I couldn't go on with it, Tony, I couldn't let them convict you."

"A point in your favor, certainly," said Folly. "Well, gentlemen, we know now how the crime was committed and how cleverly it was made to appear that Mr. Abbott committed it. Now all that remains to be obtained is the corroborative evidence. *Hibbett!*"

Hibbett raised his hands, glanced desperately at Anne, opened his lips—and then stopped as Julius roared:

"You little swine, if you say a word against her I'll kill you with my own hands! Folly, don't listen to her—she's lying to you! Abbott killed Lovelace—she's trying to save him. *Ever since he married Gillian Anne's been in love with him!* Anne, my pet, don't lie for him any more, tell the truth." He went down on his knees beside her. "Don't sacrifice yourself for him, he's too worthless, he's——"

Tony said, "It's fantastic! If Anne really——"

"Be quiet!" snapped Folly. "Come, Miss Stafford, is it true that you love Anthony Abbott, your sister's husband? Is it true that you have reached the supreme height of devotion and you are prepared to sacrifice your life to save that of the man you love? Come, please! Let us not continue this tragicomedy a moment longer than we must. Is it true that between you and Mr. Abbott there has been deep requited love? If that is so, it would not be hard to understand why he killed Lovelace: *to save you.* He would take the risk for your sake, you for his. A story of great devotion. Let us have the truth now, please."

Gillian was staring at Tony, her hands clenched. It was a strange scene: Anne in the center of the room, Julius kneeling with his arms about her, her face white and her eyes bright with unshed tears.

Savory broke the silence. "I am quite sure your notion is fantastic, Folly. Tony is devoted to Gillian."

"Hold your tongue, sir, or I will have you put out!" cried Folly. "Miss Stafford, I beg you to tell the whole truth. Is it possible that Lovelace attacked Abbott, that he was killed in self-defense? That is not a crime, you know."

Anne raised her head and stared at him with dawning hope in her eyes. "Yes," she said in a strangled voice. "Yes, that's what happened. Lovelace had a gun."

"Now why didn't you tell us that before?" Folly asked gently. "Why didn't you admit everything from the beginning, Miss

Stafford? There would have been no danger." He waited, and then he smiled gently and patted Tony's arm. "You didn't tell us that because it isn't true. None of it is true. Neither your confession nor your evidence against Tony Abbott. You—"

He broke off and swung round, for there was a tap at the door. His eyes were stormy and his hand was clenched and raised when an anxious policeman poked his head round the door and said, "Telephone for Superintendent Folly, please. It's from Brighton."

"Colonel, Foster! I charge you not to allow a word to be uttered while I am absent." Folly strode out, leaving a silent, motionless gathering in the drawing room of Spindles.

· 26 ·

MOTIVE

No ONE SPOKE while he was gone. He left the door ajar, and they could hear his voice raised in monosyllabic questions. Then they heard the sound of the receiver being replaced and his heavy footsteps on the hall floor. Every eye was turned toward him, and, as if conscious of being the center of the stage, he approached the middle of the room slowly and stood in front of Anne and Julius. After a long time he spoke in a soft voice.

"Miss Stafford, you are an accessory after the fact of murder. I am sorry. I shall do all in my power to make your ordeal easy for you. I have never, in all my long experience, come into contact with a woman who is so utterly devoid of self-interest and who is prepared to go to such great lengths of self-sacrifice. I shall not add to your mental torment by asking you to speak again. You have done all that any human being could do to deceive the police, and for a splendid motive. It is a motive that others might feel was misguided, but in your opinion it was sufficient to justify everything you have done. I hoped to bring another witness here tonight. I sent for him. I have just learned that he is dead. I speak of Professor Gimbert, who, unable to stand the strain of being interviewed and facing the full exposure of this long-established train of deceit, died of heart failure soon after I sent a man to fetch him." His voice hardened, and he turned to Julius. "Well, sir—what will you do *now?* Where will you get your inspiration?"

Julius, on his knees, stared up at him. All the color had gone from his cheeks, and he was trembling—there was no doubt that he had received a terrible shock. He licked his lips, tried to speak, and failed.

"Julius Stafford," said Folly in a hard, even voice. "You murdered Jeremiah Lovelace because he knew that you have never in your life composed a piece of music worthy of being played. *Professor Gimbert composed your music for you.*" He swung round, and in the hush that followed pointed a quivering finger toward Hibbett and roared: "You saw Stafford! He bribed you to name Abbott! You, Bright! Stafford paid you well to say that he had been at the club all that afternoon whereas in fact he was away for an hour or more. Stafford! You did all those things to which your sister, to save you, has confessed so freely. Lovelace had returned to England with nothing but the jewels. He needed help, and threatened you with exposure as a fraud, a failure, and a scoundrel, unless you gave him this help. You realized that even if you helped him now, he could use this threat again and again. You would never be safe. And so you decided to kill him. After agreeing to hide him in the Chelsea flat, you went to your club. Bribing Bright to say you were there until seven-thirty, you slipped back to Chelsea and murdered Lovelace—leaving his mutilated body for your sister to find when she returned.

"Knowing that he had once been seen to assault Lovelace, you then began a ruthless and cunningly worked-out campaign to put suspicion on your brother-in-law, Tony Abbott.

"Julius Stafford, it is my duty to arrest you. . . ."

Five minutes later, both Hibbett and Bright were making statements that would convict Julius. It was Hibbett, so he admitted, who had taken away and burnt Julius' blood-stained clothes. . . .

Some of the police had returned to Milton, taking Julius and Anne with them, but Foster had elected to stay behind. So far

Folly had not preferred a charge against Anne, although one would be inevitable. Gillian had divulged that Julius was, in fact, only half-brother to the two sisters, their father having been married twice and the girls being daughters of his second wife. "Anne would never let it be mentioned," she said. "Not even Tony knew. She so wanted to be a real sister to Julius. Poor, poor Anne." Her eyes filled with tears.

Foster laid a comforting hand on her shoulder, fished in his pocket for a handkerchief, and gave it to her. "I shouldn't worry too much," he said gently, "in my opinion she'll get off pretty lightly. And Folly thinks the same, and he's never wrong."

"He was about Tony," Gillian declared.

"I'm not at all sure about that," said Foster. "I think he believed that an arrest would start much heart searching. That toothpaste experiment was a touch of genius—I wondered if he were off his head at first."

"Had you suspected the truth about Julius?" asked Savory.

"Not for a moment," admitted Foster. "Folly showed much interest in the sheets of half-written music at Gimbert's cottage, and I remember wondering why he asked Gimbert to play him a piece and then got impatient before it was finished. Now I know that he had some idea of the truth then and hoped to trap Gimbert into something that might be construed as an admission. He failed—he gets impatient quickly when anything doesn't go as he wants it. I wouldn't like to have to work with him for long, but it's been an experience I wouldn't have missed for the world."

Gillian said, "I still find it hard to believe that Julius was such a complete fraud."

"You needn't," Savory said decisively. "I'd never dreamed of it, but I know he turned out some atrocious stuff as well as some that was very good—Gimbert's was the good. I wonder if we shall ever know why Gimbert let his work be credited to another man?"

"Probably not," said Tony slowly. "Well, we do know why Julius went off without telling anyone where he was going, and why Anne was so worked up and worried. And you really think they won't be too hard on her, Foster?"

"I doubt it," said Foster. "She will be found guilty of being an accessory after the fact, of course, but it doesn't necessarily mean a heavy sentence. She must have had a pretty shrewd suspicion that it was, in fact, Julius who had killed Lovelace—although from what I can gather she never let him know what she suspected."

"No wonder she wasn't herself!" exclaimed Gillian. "Inspector, how can we help her?"

"Get legal advice—"

"I hired Pendelton for you, Tony," said Savory, "so he can take over."

"Good!" said Tony. He frowned thoughtfully, but there was a faint smile at his lips. "Well, Folly is certainly a remarkable man. The way he led her into 'admitting' that she knew exactly how I had been framed deceived me completely—I thought she had done it. The fact that Julius did it doesn't surprise me," he added, "and yet— Will Pendelton take Julius' defense too?"

"It will hardly be a defense," said Foster.

"Perhaps not, but—well, I think we ought to do the best we can for him."

"What an astonishing fellow you are," said Savory. "If the man had had his way you'd have had a life sentence."

"Never mind that," said Tony. "I'll see Pendelton when he gets here—he might be able to plead insanity. Confound it, no sane man could plan a thing like that. But I wonder why he actually killed Lovelace instead of turning him over to the police."

Foster said, "Lovelace wasn't a very nice specimen, as you know, and back in England he saw two excellent ways of making an easy living by blackmail. The first way was by threatening to betray Julius to the world. Julius was very vain, of course, and terrified of being shown up. The second was by threatening to divulge that Anne had been, and still was, his legal wife."

"Yes. The only thing—" began Tony.

He broke off as the door opened and Buckingham appeared, looking puzzled. He beckoned Foster, who limped toward him. Buckingham's whisper reached the ears of the others.

"There's a car just arrived from Brighton," said Buckingham. "I can't understand it—an Inspector named Wright is in it, with *Gimbert*."

Foster gasped, "What? I—"

He stared along the hall and could just see Professor Gimbert coming in behind the self-important Wright. Foster hurried along as best he could, while Gillian, Tony, and Savory stared at each other. Savory broke the silence.

"The damned scoundrel! He lied about Gimbert's death to break Julius. I wonder if we can hear what's said?"

They went to the door and heard Foster speaking as levelly as possible while struggling with his surprise. They could just see Gimbert standing and looking at Foster with a gentle smile as Foster explained that Folly had gone into Milton; then there was a shout from outside, and Folly burst into the hall. He was puffing heavily and held his hand up for silence. Tony and the others went forward, intent on catching every word.

Gimbert spoke next. "Well, Superintendent, now you have uprooted me, perhaps you will explain why."

"Yes," said Folly, and he took a deep breath. "Gladly, Professor. I wanted your evidence to convict Julius Stafford of the murder of Lovelace. You were to supply the motive. You were to admit that Stafford's name is given to your compositions. However, your evidence will be superfluous. Stafford has admitted it. He has not, however, said *why* you connived at this fraud. You are under no obligation to talk. Nothing you say can affect the issue. However, you can satisfy my curiosity, Professor."

"So he *did* murder Lovelace." Gimbert sounded very old, very tired. "He swore to me that he hadn't. I am sorry, Superintendent, I never dreamed—" He paused. "Why did I let him publish my compositions as his? It just happened. At first I helped Julius to correct his own work. Gradually I fell into the habit of writing everything for him, or nearly everything—the foolish fellow would insist on publishing *some* of his own work. There is no crime in what I did, I hope—not even by your strict standards, Superintendent. You have found out, I suppose, that Lovelace knew and proposed to blackmail Julius?"

"Yes," said Folly.

"And also that Welch, or Hibbett, as I believe you call him, was Lovelace's messenger. I told you the truth about Hibbett, Superintendent. In fact, I told you the whole truth—except that I pretended that I did not know who sent me Lovelace's clothes."

"Ah! Who did?" asked Folly

"Julius," said Gimbert. "He asked me to leave them untouched until the police arrived. I wonder why?"

"He hoped it would help to forge the chain of evidence against his brother-in-law," said Folly. "That was why he stripped the body. It was not a sudden idea, trying to pin the murder on to you, Abbott. However, I am convinced that his sister knew nothing about it. I understand, now, that he even pretended that he really suspected her and would have let her get a life sentence. The man is a devil. Oh, a small thing. The blood on your clothes was rabbit's blood, Abbott—perhaps that would have saved you. Professor, I am sorry this happened—but thank you for coming —oh, Inspector Wright, I have booked rooms in Milton for you and Professor Gimbert. You will find them extremely comfortable, I'm sure." He ushered them out and turned to the others.

"It is well ended, Foster. Forgive my little trick about Gimbert's 'death.' When I was in the telephone booth I was arranging to be telephoned as if from Brighton—I wanted Stafford to think the call was from there. Abbott, forgive me. The evidence was strong. One must act on evidence even if one is not always convinced. Foster was a stanch champion of your innocence— you should be grateful. If you take my advice, you will consult a specialist about your dangerous temper. Mrs. Abbott, I will do all I can to ease the ordeal through which your sister must go. Believe me, please. Oh, one thing. Do you wish to make a charge against Agnes Blackshaw?"

"No," said Tony promptly

"You are very forgiving. Her first effort at fire raising nearly got you convicted. Oh, one thing I have been wanting to ask: Was Castle's manuscript good? It is such a shame if it was, and I am hoping that it was bad and therefore best destroyed."

"Unfortunately—" began Tony.

"Destroyed?" Snub Savory asked sharply.

Tony told him what had happened, and Snub chuckled and rubbed his hands.

"I knew I was wise," he said. "No one ever takes a copy of a handwritten manuscript, so I had it typed. I've three copies in the office, and copies of my notes, too. We'd better tell the old chap, hadn't we?"

Some time later, while Julius was awaiting trial with his sister —on whose behalf a Mr. Edward Barr was working furiously— a letter reached the Reverend Harry Castle, and within minutes of opening it he was rushing through the gap in the hedge, calling Tony's name. Tony looked out the window of the redecorated study. Mildred Castle was standing by the window of her room, well on the way to recovery, smiling happily. Castle waved the letter, and Tony recognized the familiar Savory letter heading.

"He's sold it to the first firm he offered it to," cried Castle. "A hundred and seventy-five pounds advance on royalties, Tony. Oh, my dear chap, I can't thank you enough, I really can't! It's miraculous." He turned and shouted: "Isn't it, Mildred? Miraculous!"

"Yes!" called Mildred.

"You wrote it, you know," said Tony, as Gillian hurried from the house to congratulate the Vicar. Then she went to see Mildred, and the Vicar and Tony stood talking. Tony had been wondering whether to leave Spindles, but he had decided to stay, although it was rather too large for him and Gillian. The cricket club was in existence again—that very afternoon there was a match with the Milton "A" eleven—and now the conversation turned toward it.

Agnes Blackshaw, upon Dr. Anderson's recommendation, had been allowed to go into a private home, where she was receiving psychiatric treatment.

Suddenly, Archy Kelly turned through the drive gates, alone, carrying a letter gravely in front of him.

"Grand little chap, that," said Castle. "You've made a difference to him, too. Mrs. Kelly is going back to London, I hear."

"No!" exclaimed Tony. He thought of how much Gillian had come to care for the child and how her affection was so great because there was no hope at all of children of their own. He forced himself to smile as Archy came up. "Good morning, Archy."

"Good morning," said Archy solemnly. "Please, Mr. Abbott, my mummy has gone away, and she asked me to give you this."

"This," to Tony's surprise, was a typewritten letter in an envelope addressed to Mrs. Kelly. Tony opened it, and as he read his eyes began to shine.

Dear Madam,

With reference to our interview, I can inform you that to the best of my knowledge, after making full inquiries, Mr. and Mrs. Abbott would make excellent foster-parents for your grandchild. The fact that his mother is dead and the father unknown does, of course, mean that the responsibility rests with you, as the only known surviving relative. I suggest . . .

There was much more; it was obvious that Mrs. Kelly had seen a golden opportunity of finding a home for Archy and had made sure that there would be no legal obstacles. Written at the foot of the letter, in an untidy hand, were the words: "I do hope you can take him, Mrs. Abbott. His mother was not married, she got killed in a accident . . ."

"Gill!" cried Tony, almost incoherently. "Gill! Archy, come with—" He stopped, lifted Archy, and limped eagerly toward the vicarage, the letter fluttering in his hand.